PRAISE FOR
Zen Attitude

Anthony and Edgar Award Nominee

"A gifted storyteller who delivers strong characters, a tight plot, and an inside view of Japan and its culture."
—*USA Today*

"Massey manages to combine a very entertaining mystery with lessons in Japanese culture."
—*Publishers Weekly*

"Massey continues her perceptive take on contemporary Japan in a clever mystery with a credible plot. . . . With *Zen Attitude*, Massey clearly shows her rare talent."
—*Ft. Lauderdale Sun-Sentinel*

Jim Burger

About the Author

SUJATA MASSEY was a reporter for the *Baltimore Evening Sun* and spent several years in Japan teaching English and studying Japanese. She is the author of *The Salaryman's Wife, Zen Attitude, The Flower Master, The Floating Girl, The Bride's Kimono, The Samurai's Daughter, The Pearl Diver,* and *The Typhoon Lover*. Her books have garnered numerous awards, and critics have called her stories captivating, her writing clear-eyed and unique, and her characters complex, appealing, and wryly humorous.

ZEN ATTITUDE

Sujata Massey

Harper

An Imprint of HarperCollins*Publishers*

This is a work of fiction. The characters, incidents, and dialogues are products of the author's imagination and are not to be construed as real. Any resemblance to actual events or persons, living or dead, is entirely coincidental.

FIRST HARPER PAPERBACK PUBLISHED 2005.

Library of Congress Cataloging-in-Publication Data

Massey, Sujata.
    Zen attitude / Sujata Massey.
        p. cm.
    ISBN-10: 0-06-089921-2
    ISBN-13: 978-0-06-089921-9
        1. Shimura, Rei (Fictitious character)—Fiction. 2. Women detectives—Japan—Fiction. 3. Antique dealers—Fiction. 4. Japanese Americans—Fiction. 5. Tokyo (Japan)—Fiction. I. Title.

PS3563.A79965Z34 2005
813'.54—dc22   2005052839

05 06 07 08 09 RRD 10 9 8 7 6 5 4 3 2 1

A Special Note

Kamakura is a lovely Japanese city with many Zen temples, some of which bear similarities to the temple described in this book. My Horin-ji is fictional, as are many other Kamakura sites. While Kamakura is famous for its festivals, the Tanabata Festival is not celebrated within its city limits but in Hiratsuka, a nearby town that is definitely worth a stop in early July. For historical and geographical details, I must credit *Trails of Two Cities: A Walker's Guide to Yokohama, Kamakura and Vicinity*, which was written by John Carroll and published by Kodansha International in 1994.

Many friends who have helped since the beginning of my adventures in fiction contributed to *Zen Attitude*. I am especially indebted to John Adair, owner of Kurofune Antiques in Roppongi; Shinji Kawasaki, of Kyoto Screen; and Tetsuro Kono, of the Tokyo National Museum. Kamakura residents Shizuko Asakura, Junko Katano, and Eiko Mori provided wonderful access to their town and Tokei-ji Temple. Two alumni of the Tokyo University Aikido Club, Koichi Hyogo and National Police Superintendent Naoto Yamagishi, continue to steer me through Japanese police procedure. I also thank Rusty Kanakogi, the former U.S. judo champion and Olympic coach; Christopher Belton, the novelist and translator; the monks of Dai Bosatsu Zendo, a Zen monastery in New York

State; and J. D. Considine, pop music critic for the *Baltimore Sun*. As always, any mistakes should be attributed to me and not to the above people.

I welcome comments from readers who are interested in mysteries and Japanese culture. To send me a note or learn more about the Rei Shimura series, visit my Internet home page at:

http://www.interbridge.com/sujata.

Sujata Massey
Baltimore, Maryland
1998

Cast of Characters

Rei Shimura: Japanese-American freelance antiques buyer.

Nao Sakai: Owner of an antiques concession within the Hita Fine Arts tourist shop.

Jun Kuroi: Flashy car salesman working at a dealership in Hita.

The Glendinning brothers: Hugh spends long days working as an international lawyer for Sendai Limited. **Angus**, his black-sheep brother, is a world traveler.

Yasushi Ishida: Aged antiques dealer who serves as Rei's mentor.

The Mihori Family: Owners of Horin-ji, a famous Zen temple in the historic city of Kamakura. **Abbot Mihori** oversees the property, while his wife, **Nana**, collects antiques and works to preserve land in Kamakura. Their only daughter, **Akemi,** is a former judo champion at loose ends. Cousin **Kazuhito** was formally adopted into the family in order to become the next abbot.

Mohsen Zavar: Iranian immigrant who came to Tokyo for a better life.

Nomu Ideta: An aged, bedridden antiques collector who lives in Tokyo's high-class Denen-Chofu neighborhood. His sister, **Haru Ideta,** devotes herself to caring for him.

Lieutenant Hata: Roppongi police detective.

Yoko Maeda: Owner of Maeda Antiques, a small shop struggling to stay open in Kamakura.

Wajin: A mysterious monk who works in the garden at Horin-ji.

Junichi Ota: Hugh's long-suffering personal lawyer.

Mrs. Kita: Rei's customer with a healthy appetite for antiques and gossip.

Plus a collection of monks, salarymen, illegal immigrants, and ladies of leisure, all searching Japan for spiritual or material riches.

ZEN
ATTITUDE

⚏

1

From the beginning, I suspected that Nana Mihori's *tansu* would cost too much.

The Japanese antiques market is brutal. There are hardly any good pieces left anywhere, so even if you have the cash, the chances of finding a dream piece are slender. Going into the assignment, I expected trouble. Still, I never expected that a chest of drawers could cost me almost everything I owned.

The first thing I lost was a vacation. Hugh Glendinning, the man I moved in with on Valentine's Day, had stopped pleading and waving tickets around and simply flown off to Thailand by himself. I was left with nothing but work: chiefly, the pursuit of an antique wooden chest I was becoming convinced existed only in my client's imagination. During the last two weeks, I'd driven from my home base in Tokyo north to Nīgata and then west to Kyoto. On the way, I'd suffered a flash flood and enough mosquito bites to keep a small anopheles colony drunk for a while. The rainy season had ended and I was into July heat, all without finding the *tansu*.

I was obsessing over my various failures while caught in a massive traffic jam on the Tomei Expressway. Adding to my irritation was the fact that everyone in the surrounding cars seemed to be triumphantly setting off on their holidays. Fathers manned the steering wheels while mothers passed snacks to children battling with inflated plastic water wings. I was contemplating grabbing a pair of wings and floating off to Phuket when the cellular telephone rang.

"Rei Shimura Antiques," I answered while fumbling with the receiver. I had recently read that car-phone users were as dangerous as drunken drivers, and given my lack of coordination, I believed it.

"Rei-san, where are you exactly?" Nana Mihori's patient voice crackled across the line. We'd talked every one of the last thirteen days, including the day before, when I'd called her from outside Nara to say I was going home. I'd seen many chests that almost met her requirements, but she wanted a special *tansu* she'd seen in a book. All my clients wanted something they'd seen in a book.

"I'm pretty close to the Izu Peninsula. I think." I squinted at a road sign far ahead of me, thinking how unfortunate it was that I was still nowhere near knowing the standard base of 1,500 to 2,000 *kanji*, or pictographic characters, needed to be a literate adult. I'd grown up in San Francisco with an American mother and a father from Japan. Speaking was easy for me, and usually all I needed for my job as a freelance antiques buyer.

"It is convenient that you are still outside Tokyo. I've learned about a very nice store in Hita that carries high-quality antiques from all over the country. My friend Mrs. Kita found a handsome clothing chest there last week."

"Isn't Hita near Hakone?" The hot-springs region she was talking about was far from my route.

"Rei-san, you have been working so hard for me, I want to make sure you get your buyer's commission. But after all your travels, I worry it's an imposition to ask you to stop. . . ."

"Oh, it's no trouble at all. Where's the shop?" I balanced the phone against my shoulder and began digging around for a pen. The truth was, I needed her badly. My business was five months old, and the foreign expatriate clients I'd hoped to attract had turned out to be pretty stingy. My Aunt Norie had recently introduced me to Nana Mihori, the wife of the owner of a famous Zen temple in Kamakura, a picturesque city an hour south of Tokyo. Nana's funds were unlimited, as was her potential for good word of mouth. I couldn't let her down.

Saying good-bye to my customer, I noticed that a boy and girl riding in the Mitsubishi Carisma on my right were imitating me by talking into their soft-drink cans. I mouthed *moshi-moshi,* the standard telephone greeting, at them. The kids giggled and said something back. What was it?

Abunai, I realized belatedly as something big and brutal jolted my car. *Danger!*

I dropped the phone and clung to the steering wheel that had loosened under my fingers. I stomped on the brake and glanced in the rearview mirror. It was filled with the sight of a small commercial truck whose driver was waving me toward the expressway's narrow shoulder.

How I could crash a car in all-but-stopped traffic was beyond me; I was the queen of bad luck. Repairs to the luxurious Toyota Windom would probably be astronomical. And the worst part was that it wasn't even my car; it belonged to Hugh.

Feeling numb, I watched the truck driver emerge wearing a cheerful yellow jumpsuit and matching cap. Under other circumstances, I would have smiled.

I crept out of the Windom, aware of how disreputable I appeared: a vaguely Japanese-looking woman in her late twenties with short hair, shorter shorts, and a shrunken UC Berkeley T-shirt. I hurried toward him in my flip-flop sandals, my Japanese driver's license and Hugh's automobile registration clutched in hand.

The trucker was carrying something too; a small unopened can of Yodel Water. He offered it to me in a bizarre gesture of hospitality. I accepted, glancing at the cheery slogan written in English: ALWAYS MAKES YOU FRESH AND COOL WHEREVER YOU TRY IT! *Not today,* I thought, my T-shirt already beginning to stick to my back.

Together we surveyed the results of our collision. The truck's damage appeared minimal: a bit of the Windom's shiny black paint had rubbed onto his fender. But my left taillight was smashed. The driver picked delicately at the remaining glass chips, wrapped them up in a tissue, and handed them to me.

"*Dōmo sumimasen deshita*." The man's formal apology startled me before I remembered that under Japanese law, the vehicle hitting the other is automatically at fault.

"I'm sorry, too. I was distracted," I babbled.

"It is solely my fault. And look at what I've done to your beautiful car." The man's voice cracked. I realized then that he was probably worried about having gotten into an accident while driving a company vehicle. I was going to reassure him that I wouldn't sue, but he already had his hand in his wallet.

"What about the paint on your truck? Are you sure you won't have trouble at work?"

He looked at his fender and shook his head. "It is ordinary depreciation they will not notice. But I must reimburse you. I will not leave until I do so!"

I had been drifting. He had been nosing into my lane. I supposed we both were at fault. I took the money without looking at it, still feeling guilty. "If you give me your address, I can send you a copy of the bill and any change—"

"Please don't trouble yourself!" He had jumped back into the truck again. Since no names or information had been exchanged, he could rest securely and believe that the matter had ended. I tried to push my unease aside as I sipped the sweet Yodel Water and steered back into traffic.

Two hours later I was in Hita. I had called ahead to the shop Mrs. Mihori had told me about and learned that Hita Fine Arts did have a number of antique *tansu* in stock. The antiques dealer told me he had one *tansu* that probably came from Yahata, a wood-working town on Sado Island I had already fruitlessly searched.

"Where did you acquire the piece?" I asked, resentful of his good fortune.

"From a good source. It's available at the moment, but I'd advise you to hurry. A woman customer came in yesterday and asked me to hold the *tansu* for her. She didn't return, so I have just decided to release it for sale."

Appearing slightly uninterested can lead to discounts, a very good thing. But I had no time or energy to play games. I drove straight into Hita's shopping district, nabbing an illegal spot in front of Hita Fine Arts. I wasn't worried, because I'd know pretty quickly if the *tansu* was worth buying.

I wasn't hopeful. The shop screamed tourist trap, with an exterior that mimicked the red and gold splendor of a Shinto shrine. The first floor was crammed with mass-produced ceramic fishbowls, brightly gilded screens, and tacky acetate wedding *kimono*, all pseudo-Japanese items that were probably made in China.

Nana Mihori had wanted me to come. I reminded myself of this as I made my way to the main desk where a sign boldly proclaimed, WE SPEAK ENGLISH! WE TAKE DOLLAR!

"Nao Sakai works upstairs in furniture," the receptionist said when I asked for the antiques salesman I'd spoken to on the car phone. "That's behind the T-shirt section and next to the stamps."

It didn't sound as if there was much priority given to antiques. Upstairs, though, the section was surprisingly well stocked. I checked out a gorgeous kitchen *tansu* and a few smaller chests that looked as if they'd been crafted in Sendai and Yonezawa.

A slender man with sharp features was sitting cross-legged at a rosewood table, chatting on the phone with someone. He looked at me and said, "If you wish to buy a new T-shirt, they are over by the window."

"I'm Rei Shimura. I telephoned earlier about the *tansu*." I crossed my arms over my wrinkled shirt and stared him down.

Sakai smiled widely, reevaluating me. "Shimura-san? I've, ah, kept the piece for you in the back."

I followed him into a dim stockroom filled with a forest of cardboard boxes. Through the gloom, I saw a dark maroon chest of drawers adorned with ornate, hand-chased iron hinges and lock plates.

Mrs. Mihori had sketched what she wanted, so I pulled out her drawing to make comparisons. She was looking specifically for a *kasane*, a bridal chest in two sections, each with two drawers, that could be stacked on top of each other for a commanding appearance. She wanted the wood to be top-quality paulownia decorated with cranes and turtles, symbols of good luck that often marked furniture built in the Sado Island town of Yahata. The metalwork on this piece was burnished black but not too dark, as it might be if it had been artificially aged. The hand-forged nails with irregular heads also looked right for the mid-nineteenth century.

"You know furniture," Mr. Sakai said flatteringly as I began pulling out the drawers for inspection. They were smoothly joined, and there was also the happy circumstance of no insect holes. In my time spent shopping around Japan, I'd been saddened to find that many *tansu* interiors had been devoured by wood-eating moths. These fresh-smelling cedar drawers were pristine and appeared to have been recently sanded, which made me pause.

"Did you refinish this?"

"Absolutely not! This is a small business, *neh*? I just take consignments and turn them over as fast as I can."

There was no price tag on the chest. As if hearing my unspoken question, Mr. Sakai said, "The old gentleman is having some hard times, so he will part with it for a very reasonable price: one million, five hundred thousand yen."

He was asking a little over twelve thousand dollars, which was fair but worth testing. "Is there any way you could make it a little cheaper? I'm sort of on a budget."

"Hmmm. You come from Tokyo?" He studied me carefully. I hoped my story had not lost credibility because of my high-priced address. "I could include the cost of delivery, I suppose."

"Okay. I just need to make a phone call to my mother." There was no need for him to know I was buying for a client, especially since I was getting him to comp the delivery. He agreed, looking somewhat wary, and I ran out to use the Windom's telephone. A young man with greased-back hair and a lime-colored rayon suit was standing outside, examining my smashed taillight. People in Japan always worried about other people's troubles, so I smiled at him and bowed slightly, indicating that I knew about the damage.

I slid into the Windom, keeping the door open to catch a breeze while I was on the telephone. Miss Tanaka, Nana Mihori's housekeeper, said that her mistress was busy with a delegation of visitors. I hung up, wondering if I should buy without authorization. I didn't think so, since she'd rejected two other *tansu* I'd found on the trip.

I took out Mrs. Mihori's sketch again. It was unlikely I'd ever find such a beautiful Sado piece again. I couldn't lose it. Maybe I could put it on hold. I hurried back into the shop, where I found Mr. Sakai talking to a new customer: a woman in her forties wearing a silk blouse and skirt the color of green tea. She looked exquisite until she turned, revealing a large black mole on her left nostril.

"The problem is that there's a new customer." Mr. Sakai indicated me with his hand.

"But I'm ready to buy and I have the money right here!" The woman waved a handful of yen notes at him, very bad form. I realized that she was probably the customer who had put the *tansu* on hold.

"Excuse me. I'd like to get things settled with the Sado Island *tansu*," I said.

"She's not talking about my *tansu?*" The customer looked coldly at me.

"Actually, it's a difficult situation now," Mr. Sakai apologized.

"I'll buy the *tansu* if you just give me a chance to contact my mother," I said, nervousness growing. "I can give you an answer within a couple of hours."

The woman gasped, and Mr. Sakai looked pained at my insolence. "That is impossible, I'm afraid."

"*Yahari hafu da,*" the woman murmured to Sakai. The phrase meant "because she's a half blood"—implying that my racial makeup allowed for my rudeness.

"There can be no more holding of this *tansu*. Whoever is ready to buy it will receive it." Mr. Sakai cleared his throat and looked at the small crowd that had collected: two salesclerks from the souvenir department and a few shoppers.

Making an executive decision, I whipped out my credit card with the ultra-high limit.

"Because of the consignments, I deal only in cash." He looked at my card as if it was dirty.

A store this big had to accept credit cards, but Mr. Sakai was probably playing tough in order to avoid paying percentages to anyone. Knowing this system, I had brought more than I needed—about 2.2 million yen jammed in several Pocky pretzel boxes in the bottom of my backpack. I shrugged and said, "Fine. I'll pay cash."

"I was here first!" the lady in green snapped.

"One point five million. Was tax already included?" I started counting off ten-thousand-yen notes, wishing I didn't have such a big audience.

"I'll pay more than her! Fifty thousand yen more," the woman said.

She couldn't do that. It wasn't ethical. I gave Mr. Sakai a beseeching look.

"I must work in my client's best interest," he said in a low voice.

"I'll pay one million, five hundred and sixty, then." I was sweating despite the air-conditioning, feeling myself on the edge of a calamity.

"One million, seven hundred thousand yen." The woman gave me a scathing look.

"One million, eight hundred." If this was an auction, I was hanging in.

As Mr. Sakai muttered nervously, the woman raised me again, offering 1.9 million. Would she go higher? I couldn't tell from her face. I was at the end of my money and couldn't afford to risk any more rounds of this sick game.

"I'll give you two million, one hundred thousand." With a steeper jump in price, I might scare her off.

The woman paused as if aware that things had gone too far. But she spoke again.

"Two million and two hundred thousand yen."

At that, I shook my head. I was giving up. I stuffed my cash back in the Pocky boxes and zipped up my backpack with shaking fingers. It was wrong to pay so much over the original price; I knew it in my bones. In any case, I shouldn't do it without Mrs. Mihori's permission.

As I stormed through the fishbowl display on my way out the door, I felt a tug on my backpack. Someone had seen my money and was trying to grab it. Reaching back blindly, I connected with soft flesh.

When I turned, I found I'd knocked over a young saleswoman who had been upstairs.

"Miss!" she panted. "You can still buy the *tansu*, I came to tell you--"

"*Gomen nasai*," I apologized, helping her up. Why hadn't I looked before lashing out? Thank God she hadn't hit her head on one of the massive fishbowls.

"The other customer did not have enough money. Mr. Sakai sent me to say you can have it for two million one hundred thousand, like you offered." The girl's lip quivered, as if she was about to cry.

I felt like crying myself. If this was an auction house, the overzealous woman would have been forced to pay. I thought about that as I climbed the stairs and approached Mr. Sakai's section.

"Two million is actually what I have in my bag this minute. However, I could go to the bank." The woman was digging through her handbag, tossing out yen notes like used tissues.

Mr. Sakai looked past her at me. "Banking hours are over. I apologize for the confusion, Shimura-san."

Now that I knew my competition's finances, I had a bargaining chip. "I'll buy it for two million, total, and that includes free delivery, as we agreed before."

"Final sale, *neh?*" Sakai was already writing the receipt.

"Final sale," I repeated, and the *tansu* was mine.

2

Outside the shop, my exultation was tempered when I saw the same young man who'd been lurking earlier perched on the car's trunk.

"You'll need to get that fixed, *Onēsan*," he drawled, pointing to the taillight. "Your bulb is broken."

I frowned. He was calling me "big sister," a slightly flirtatious form of address. It was par for the course coming from vendors in the vegetable market, but I didn't like it coming from a well-dressed stranger. Although he wasn't entirely strange; he reminded me of someone I couldn't place.

"I'll do it in Tokyo," I said, glancing up at the sky darkening with the onset of evening, and then at the taillight, which was in worse shape than I'd realized. The truck driver's aplogy had been too distracting.

"*Heh*? You can't drive cockeyed all the way to Tokyo. Which neighborhood are you going to?"

"Roppongi." The land of foreigners and gourmet pizza. I had lived somewhere more modest and

authentically Japanese before Hugh Glendinning had
entered my life.

He whistled and ran his hand over his glossy
pompadour. "Fantastic place. I used to hang out in
Yoyogi Park, which isn't too far—"

"With the Elvis dancers?" I relaxed slightly. On
Sundays a giant tribe of young men dressed in
pegged jeans and black leather jackets danced to
recorded 1950s music in the park. Now I knew who
he reminded me of—a Japanese Elvis.

"Tokyo city government shut down the outdoor
dance parties. Now I don't go there anymore." He
pulled a business card out of his wide-lapel jacket.
"I'm Jun Kuroi. I work for the Toyota dealership in
Hita. I stopped when I saw your car and was wondering if it was ours."

"It's not," I said, examining the card.

"Too bad. I would have given you a loan car.
That's part of our service plan."

The card looked genuine—it had the official,
whirly Toyota emblem—so I admitted, "I do need to
get my light fixed. How expensive will that be? I've
never had to take the car for servicing."

"Those Windoms never break down, do they? I
drive one myself." He gestured toward a shiny silver
model with a dealership name over the license plate.
"I think we're talking about four thousand yen. You
can charge it, of course—"

He'd said the magic word given my finances. I
got into the car and followed him along the road to
the dealership, a small glass and chrome showplace
filled with highly polished cars.

"Hita's a great little town," Jun said, bringing me a glass of iced coffee while I waited in the customer lounge. "As long as you're here, you should make use of your time. Why don't you drop in for a soak at the hot-spring baths before you go back to the city? I'd join you if I could, ha-ha."

"I'm really here to work," I said, and explained about the *tansu*.

"Wow, I'm into antiques. Fifties record albums, nothing that Hita Fine Arts would carry. What did you spend there?" he asked, leaning forward from the leather chair across from me.

When I told him, he whistled. "Two million yen's a lot of money! But you obviously know the best. Come to think, you're still in a ninety-six. The new models are almost out, and I could give you a nice bargain on a trade-up."

"No, thanks, it's not even my car," I said. Car salesmen were the same the world over. Only the accents were different.

I was glad for the new taillight, because the sun had gone down by the time I arrived at Roppongi Hills, the monster white skyscraper Hugh Glendinning called home. An opened suitcase told me my lover had returned from Thailand, but he was not in the apartment. The only thing waiting for me was the new *tansu*, bound in protective bubble wrap and cardboard. While I'd listened to Jun Kuroi's ramblings and waited for the car to be repaired, the delivery company had made it to Tokyo. There was a message on the answering machine from the building concierge, who apologized for letting the delivery crew into the apartment without my prior approval. They had not been wearing uniforms; that, and the fact they hadn't asked him to sign a receipt, had made him slightly upset.

The *tansu* had arrived; that was the important thing. I pulled off the wrappings, marveling at it. I wasn't used to buying antiques in such beautiful condition. My strategy was to rescue beat-up, unloved pieces at country auctions and city flea markets. A scrubbing with steel wool and linseed oil was usually all a *tansu* needed, and it was a good excuse for me to buy a lot of them. Since I'd moved in with Hugh six months ago, his sterile bachelor flat had been transformed by my various collections of antique Japanese furniture, wood-block prints, and textiles. Every few months we threw a whopping party for my clients and his business acquaintances, selling most of the pieces so I could shop again.

The Sado Island *tansu* looked splendid. I knew Mrs. Mihori would be pleased. When I'd finally reached her on the telephone, she had reassured me about my decision.

"Thank heavens you didn't let that terrible woman take it," she said. "And from your description, I know it is going to be perfect. Your aunt is right—you are a human miracle."

I hadn't seen my mother and father for three years, so my aunt and uncle in Yokohama had become substitute parents. Not that much was different about the way the two families lived; my psychiatrist father and interior designer mother had an expansive Victorian town house in San Francisco, while my Japanese relatives had a smaller, modern place that was worth three times as much, given that it rested on land in Yokohama. When I moved to Japan, I'd wanted to be financially independent, so I'd refused to live with my relatives and spent three years in a small, slummy apartment. Then Hugh had come along. I was uncomfortable living off his expense account, but I had to admit that at times like this, a marble bathroom was a most welcome place.

I spent twenty minutes luxuriating and scrubbing in the shower, then slipped into my *yukata*, a Japanese cotton robe, and went into the kitchen to finish repairing Hugh's gift, an interesting wood-framed lantern with tattered paper covering its sides. I already knew what I was going to use as replacement paper.

Shortly after I'd finished the repairs, I heard a key turning in the front door and went out to investigate.

"*Tadaima!*" Hugh dropped his squash bag and bellowed his arrival in the Glasgow accent that could not be tamed no matter how much I tutored him. I laughed and went straight into his arms.

"Don't bother welcoming me," he murmured when we broke apart. "Do you realize I've been back for two days, wondering and waiting and completely without a car? I actually had to take the subway to work."

"But that's so good for you," I teased. "I don't understand why you like driving so much—I'd be happy if I never saw the interior of your car again."

"Ah, but the Windom is my sanctuary. The only

way I can travel from A to B without being stared at by Tokyo's millions."

It must be irritating to be stared at, but I suspected Hugh's problem was compounded by the fact that he looked like a young Harrison Ford. After all, I was half white and received scanty attention. Wanting to change the topic, I offered him a glass of wine.

"What about a nice glass of single malt? Have you been away so long you've forgotten all my rituals?"

"It's too warm for Scotch. How was Thailand?" I opened a container of sesame noodles I'd bought at the building's downstairs delicatessen and handed Hugh chopsticks. We dug into the same container, exhibiting the kind of behavior my genteel Japanese relatives would have died over.

"A good working vacation. The new Sendai plant will open on time, I'm sure of that. The Thais are easy to work with and they speak much better English than anyone around here."

"Better than yours, you mean?"

"Certainly! And as for the girls on the beach— they didn't need to speak for me to understand their designs." He winked at me and said, "Hey, you should have come along."

"What did you do with your free time, exactly?" Even though it had ostensibly been a working vacation, I didn't like the thought of all his empty hours.

"Let me show you." He began unbuttoning his oxford shirt to reveal that the ridges and planes of his well-muscled chest and stomach were amazingly red.

"You fell asleep on the beach!"

"Reading my law journals. I also drank too much Singha beer and did a little shopping for you." He pushed away the empty noodle container and handed me a large paper bag.

I drew out a bolt of shimmering raw silk in the same shade of scarlet Japanese artists used for ceremonial lacquer pieces. It would fit in beautifully with the apartment. I kissed him and said, "You remembered my favorite color. Now I can make the most beautiful pillows for the sofa!"

"Pillows? It's for a cocktail dress. Something lean and mean and cut down to *there*."

"I'm not that good at sewing. I can't make a dress."

"Ask a seamstress. If you hurry, you can have it made up for our party."

I'd almost forgotten about the big bash scheduled for the upcoming weekend. The RSVPs were in and the caterer had her orders, but I hadn't done much more to prepare. Suddenly I didn't want a big party; I wanted time alone with him.

"I have something small for you," I said, leading him to his gift in the living room. I had covered the lamp's boxy frame with tissue-thin orange newspaper, so the candle I'd placed in the middle gave off a rosy glow.

Hugh said nothing for a few moments. Then he exploded in wild, honking laughter. "You papered it with my *Financial Times*! My God, Rei, it's the funniest thing I've ever seen!"

"I thought it so appropriate for your office, a perfect blending of East and West. I can get it electrified for you next week."

"Stop. You electrify me already." He started to pull closed the window blinds.

I couldn't believe he had overlooked the new *tansu*. I gestured toward it, and his eyes widened.

"Where did you find it?"

I launched into a tale of my high-stress day, starting with the smashed taillight. He waved off the accident immediately but stayed fixed on the *tansu*.

"It's absolutely stunning. Can we keep it for a while? How much did it cost?" He moved his lamp over to the coffee table and came back to slide his hands appreciatively over the wooden frame.

"I'm glad you like it, but it's going to Mrs. Mihori tomorrow. It was two million, far too rich for our tastes."

"Speak for yourself, love. I like it better than anything else you've ever bought. How much weight do you think it can bear?"

"Maybe a few hundred pounds, since the frame was made from one of the most durable woods around. It's held up since the early nineteenth century."

"Good." He swung me up so that I was sitting on the edge. "The thought of enjoying ourselves on top of all that money is pretty arousing. Don't you think?"

"But Mrs. Mihori owns it," I protested halfheartedly.

"It's yours until she's reimbursed you, paid your travel costs, and the finder's fee." Hugh peeled off my robe and spread it like a sheet over the chest's surface. "Besides, I'm superstitious. Everything that comes to this apartment must be broken in."

He didn't have to say more to convince me. Just six months into the relationship, we were insatiable. Hugh was a spontaneous and inventive lover, driven to passion in places as various as the bath, the Chinese carpet in the dining room, and the Roppongi Hills elevator. Things were too good to last, I thought, lying back and melting like the candle in the lantern.

"Watch my sunburn," he murmured when I reached for him.

"Not everything's burned, is it?" I asked.

"Not quite. Oh, God! Do that again."

I felt as though I were soaring straight toward the ceiling as Hugh pulled my hips to the edge of the chest. "Don't forget," I panted.

"Don't forget that I love you?" he whispered back.

"You know—"

"Come on, let's have a baby. It would be gorgeous."

"Don't be insane!"

"It's just one more barrier between us, the condom," he grumbled, pulling out. "If you're so worried about what we might spawn, start taking the Pill."

"I don't like chemicals." I was losing my sexy mood, too.

"I know, I know, you're a health food freak. I'll go look for something."

He was rummaging around in the bathroom when the telephone rang.

"Just ignore it," I advised, listening to my recorded voice request in English and Japanese that callers leave a message with date and time. After the beep a voice that sounded exactly like Hugh's began speaking. I looked at him, and he yelped.

"It's got to be Angus. God, what a day!" He sprinted into the kitchen to get the phone.

This was interesting enough to make me sit up and listen. Hugh had three sisters and just one brother, Angus, whom he worried about most. The baby of the family—now twenty—had been expelled from several of Britain's best boarding schools before heading off for three years of unstructured travel in Europe and Asia. Hugh mailed letters to *poste restante* addresses around the planet but never received so much as a postcard in return. Angus had probably moved on, I had suggested. Hugh had said nothing, just seemed sad.

Now I heard Hugh speaking excitedly, his brogue getting deeper than I'd ever heard. I got up, pressing my hand against a spot on my right buttock where the *tansu* had chafed me. I put on my robe and went into the kitchen.

"You're welcome for as long as you like, little brother," Hugh was saying, then put a hand over the receiver. "Rei, are you free this Wednesday afternoon? Could you make a quick run to the airport to meet Angus?"

There was no such thing as a quick run to Narita Airport. Door to door, the trip took several hours, depending on the Japanese traffic gods.

"Sure. Ask what he looks like," I whispered,

thinking he might have shaved his head. After all, his last known address was a Buddhist temple in India.

"What he looks like?" Hugh repeated. "A younger version of me, of course."

Unlikely. Hugh Glendinning was the epitome of the clean-cut, corporate lawyer, even sitting naked at the kitchen table. Angus might have Hugh's tall, well-built frame, thick red-blond hair, and green eyes, but I doubted he would bear himself like the crown prince of Tokyo's international legal community.

"Did you hear I'm living with someone?" Hugh was saying to the telephone. Brief silence. "Actually, from America. But she's different . . . she's, um, vegetarian."

Hugh swore he loved the Asian fish-and-vegetable dishes I made for our candlelit dinners. What would I need to do for Angus, start making steaks and chops? I couldn't buy meat. The thought of it made me shudder.

When Hugh hung up, he practically floated to the living room. "I can't believe he's coming. I haven't seen the lad in five years."

I nestled beside him on the leather sofa, trying to be positive. "I'll make up my old futon for him in the study, but do you think he'll mind sharing the bathroom with a woman?"

"He was sleeping in the jungle! To him the flat and all that comes with it will be paradise."

"He's used to the simple life, which is good. But you can't expect him to resemble you in every way."

"You think a red-haired Glendinning won't stand

out in Narita Airport?" Hugh smiled at me. "You're an angel to meet him. I love you. In fact, let me finish showing you how much." He inclined his head toward the *tansu*.

"Not there. I got caught on something." I flashed him the red mark on my buttock.

Hugh ran his finger over the sore spot and said, "That looks nasty. Put your knickers on, and I'll drive you to St. Luke's."

"I had a tetanus shot last January, remember?" There was no way I was going to the hospital with a sex injury—especially when I had an eagle-eyed cousin who oversaw the emergency room.

Hugh snapped on the harsh overhead light we rarely used and went back to the *tansu*. After a minute he said, "This is what punctured you. A nail you'll need to pound back down."

"*Tansu* are joined, not nailed." One of the things Japanese woodworkers excelled at was building smoothly fitted pieces of furniture that could expand in summer's humidity and contract in winter without cracking.

"This one's unique, then. What's the expression the Japanese use about people who don't fit in? The nail that sticks up needs to be hammered down?"

I went over to investigate. "Oh, you're talking about a nail in the metalwork. That's normal."

"Normal, but not nice," Hugh said, tapping it. "It doesn't even match the others."

"What?" I bent closer to look at the nail in question. It was brand-new, silvery steel, not the same aged black iron as the others. How could I have missed it?

"I screwed up." I felt hot and cold all at once.

"Don't be silly." Hugh put an arm around my shoulder.

"I should have noticed this nail. Damn it, I could swear I looked at every inch of the chest. I'm going to have to take it out. Get my *kuginuki*, will you?"

"Say what?" Hugh looked blank.

"The thing I use to pull out nails. Last time I used it, I stuck it in my underwear drawer."

"Most women keep delicate, frilly things in their lingerie drawer. You prefer tools. What should I make of it?" Hugh came back with the short, pipe-shaped tool that was essential for antique-nail removal.

"This will tell me what I want to know," I said, slowly easing out the nail. I then decided to remove the older nails holding the lock plate in order to better investigate things. Fifteen minutes later, the lock plate was off. I stared at what lay underneath. First was a horizontal blackened ring outlining the metal piece I'd removed. Inside the ring, the previously unexposed wood was a paler color. There was a smaller dark ring within that, and an even paler oval of unexposed wood. I shut my eyes, then opened them. I groaned and asked Hugh to tell me what he saw.

"I see a dark, shadowed area—I guess it's the outline of the lock plate. Is that bad, the color transfer?" He sounded anxious.

"Darkening is okay. It occurs because of the reaction of the iron to warmth in the atmosphere—say, a coal fire burning in a nearby brazier."

Hugh picked up the lock plate in his hand. "Okay,

I see where there's a large oval shape outlined in black. But what's this second dark ring in the center?"

"A ghost," I said.

"What do you mean?"

"It's the outline of a different lock plate that was fixed to the *tansu*. There was a smaller lock plate here originally. You know what that means."

"Rei, I hate these antiques quizzes! Get to the point."

"The chest is not from the Edo period," I said, unable to keep the bitterness from my voice. "Only the metalwork is. It was a newer chest that had its metalwork switched so it could be sold for a high price."

"Oh," Hugh said, finally getting it.

There was no point in further conversation. It was as clear as the proverbial protruding nail that I had made a terrible error. Whether it was because of the dark storeroom or my hurried appraisal, I was unsure. The end result was that Mrs. Mihori's *tansu*, no matter how lovely, was resoundingly fake.

3

First I finished the bottle of wine. Then I cried. As I poured out my misery on Hugh's Egyptian cotton bedsheets, Hugh tried in vain to console me. After that he shifted into lawyer mode and started making phone calls. The first was to Hita Fine Arts, which had closed for the evening. The next call was to his office, canceling a meeting for the following day. Finally, I heard him speaking to Yasushi Ishida, the antiques dealer who had been my mentor for the three years I'd lived in Japan. I had no idea what Mr. Ishida was saying back to Hugh, but I felt comforted enough to fall into an exhausted, alcoholic slumber.

I awoke the next morning with a throbbing headache and the realization that my career was over. The only way out was to flee back to the United States, changing my name and building a new life far away from antiques and Japanese people. I moaned this all to Hugh as we got into the double shower for our usual morning scrub.

"Two million yen is less than seventeen thousand U.S. dollars. I lost more in the stock market last year," Hugh said while adjusting the shower to a pressure he considered properly vigorous.

I turned away from the harsh wall of water and spat, "You don't understand! Twenty thousand dollars is all I have for the business. I'm going to have to go into my emergency funds to make up what I've spent."

"If you raid your savings, you won't have any money left to your name. You should let me buy the *tansu*. I really like it."

"It's kind of you to offer, but no." I couldn't let Hugh take the hit for my mistake; remembering the truck driver who had paid for my smashed taillight the day before added to my resolve.

"In any case, we don't have to decide now," Hugh coaxed. "Wait until your friend Mr. Ishida gets here and gives you an appraisal. When we talked on the phone yesterday evening, he said he thought you should try to arrange a return."

"What if they won't take it back? The *tansu* was a final-sale item."

"You could always approach Mrs. Mihori with the honest admission that the chest is not as valuable as you'd first thought, but she might want it at the appraised value. You'd take a slight loss, not a total one."

"No! She's a high-class, knowledgeable person who would never buy a fake. She's—she's—*Japanese!*"

"Just like the fellow who sold you the chest." Hugh calmly started to shave.

I couldn't argue with that, so I sighed noisily and left, slamming the shower door so hard his soap-on-a-rope fell off.

After Hugh left for work, I crept into the living room and examined the chest again, as if something could have changed overnight. The crooked nail gleamed up at me, black and unforgiving. I'd thought briefly that the *tansu* delivered to the apartment might have been a copy of the one I'd inspected in the shop. Under close examination, I became sure it was the genuine, disingenuous item.

When Mr. Ishida arrived at nine o'clock, he announced that before we looked at anything, we would drink tea. "I have brought a bag of the highest-grade *ocha* from Kyoto. It is especially good for the nerves," he said, handing me a package wrapped exquisitely in dark green paper, a color symbolic of a gift from the heart.

One good thing about my seventy-four-year-old friend was his talent with tea. Another was the fact that I was too awed by him to break down the way I had with Hugh. My voice remained level as we sipped the mild green tea together and I replayed my shopping nightmare.

"So this Sakai person never actually said this was an Edo-period *tansu?*" Mr. Ishida's face, cross-hatched with many lines, looked skeptical by nature.

"No, he didn't. And when I noticed the drawers were sanded, he swore he hadn't worked on them himself."

"Interesting." Mr. Ishida stroked his chin.

"Let me show you what I mean." I was itching to get his opinion.

"You hurry too much, and I am slightly tired from my early morning *tai chi* practice. Permit me to enjoy my tea, please."

Twenty minutes later Mr. Ishida said he was ready to view the *tansu*. He surveyed it from all angles, bending his child-sized frame in half as he removed the drawers and then inspected the empty case. Using my *kuginuki*, he removed the rest of the metalwork in half the time it would have taken me. Then he put it back on. In the end, he settled himself comfortably on a cushion on the living room floor and gave me his appraisal.

"As you'd thought, the metalwork is genuine Edo, most certainly from the town of Yahata. The lacquer finish of the wood, and the shape of the shadow left by the earlier lock plates, lead me to think the *tansu* might have been built later in the town of Ogi, which is also on Sado Island."

"Ogi craftsmen didn't build chests until the Meiji period," I said.

"Very good, Shimura-san. And I conclude your chest is from the late Meiji period, maybe ninety years old. It's in good condition for its age, but I must remind you to fumigate it for fear of insects within."

"What should I tell Mrs. Mihori?" I wanted a solution before we talked about such boring things as fumigation.

"Not saying is the flower." At my blank look, he added, "This is an old proverb that means some things are better left unsaid."

"You mean I should just lie about it?"

"Listen! Your customer has expressed gratitude to you already for two weeks of hard work. She would not feel comfortable rejecting the piece now. Therefore, I do not think you should make a declaration of the problem."

"It's my duty to tell her it's not Edo period."

"You said she is a high-class lady? No matter how disparagingly you speak about the *tansu*, she will feel obligated to buy it. Even if you tell her it is a bad piece of furniture, she will insist on taking it. However, she will never display it in her home, and the rumor will circulate that you cheated her."

I put my head in my hands. The picture he was painting was worse than anything I had imagined.

"You must tell her the *tansu* did not arrive. Or perhaps your apartment suffered a terrible burglary!"

I shook my head. "At Roppongi Hills? This is the best apartment building in the neighborhood. No one would believe it."

Mr. Ishida's face brightened. "If you give me a spare key, perhaps I can arrange a burglary for you. There's a very kind *yakuza* boss in my neighborhood I could ask to help. He will take only what we request."

"Please don't, Ishida-san!" I hated the way many Japanese regarded the Mafia as solid citizens. Even if they sponsored community parades and delivered food to earthquake victims, gangsters were still gangsters. I'd learned this the hard way.

"It was only a suggestion," he soothed. "What would you prefer to do?"

"I'll go to Hita and try to return the *tansu*.

Maybe your appraisal will convince Hita Fine Arts to waive the final-sale policy."

"Take some photographs with you, because the cost of transporting the piece back and forth could be enormous."

His advice made sense. I wouldn't pay for transportation of the *tansu* before I knew I was getting my money back. The damned piece of lacquered wood had cost me too much already.

By train it was just an hour to Hita, a much shorter trip than by car. I sat in the first compartment, near the driver's windshield, so I had a panoramic view of mountains and rice fields. Compared to the freeways, the train was not crowded, with enough seats for all the leisure travelers in their bright summer shorts and myself, dressed up in a suit and high heels I thought looked businesslike. I'd even gone to the effort of swapping my customary backpack for a proper beige leather handbag. It contained a little money, the bill of sale, and Mr. Ishida's official appraisal of the chest as worth one million yen. The figure was nothing to scoff at—it could have covered almost one year's rent at my old apartment—but was half what I'd paid Mr. Sakai.

Disembarking in Hita, I regretted my prissy outfit. If anything, the air was steamier than the day before. My panty hose felt as though they were melting on my legs, and I had to wipe my face and neck with a handkerchief before entering Hita Fine Arts.

"*Irasshaimase!*" Two clerks dusting fishbowls sang out the welcome greeting to me. I pasted an artificial smile on my face and swished upstairs.

Mr. Sakai wasn't doing business at the rosewood
table today. That table and all the large antiques I'd
seen the day before were also gone. I poked my head
into the back stockroom and called into the silence.

"May I help you?" The young T-shirt saleswoman
was regarding me with the same fascinated but fearful
expression she'd had when I'd knocked her down the
day before. She probably sensed I was back to cause
more trouble.

"Yes, thank you. I'm looking for Sakai-san."

"He is not here today."

"Is it his day off?" I had been rash not to call
ahead, but I'd been relying on the element of surprise.

"No. He is gone."

"Gone? Where to, the bank or someplace?
Lunch?"

"Please, you cannot stay in the stockroom." The
young woman ushered me out of the stockroom and
kept watch as I walked slowly downstairs to the customer service desk. I asked to speak to the general
manager and had my business card ready when a
harried-looking man in his fifties came out of a back
room.

"Ah! You are very prompt, but we are not ready
for applications yet." The man handed back my card.

"Application?" I repeated.

"You wish to apply for the antiques concession,
don't you? Somehow, word was spread. We've had
two telephone calls already this morning."

"I'm looking for Sakai-san. That's all."

"Really!" His voice skipped an octave. "Well, I

cannot tell you his location, but if you find him, will
you let us know?"

Feeling hesitant, I asked, "Is there some problem?"

"Did you see how his area looked upstairs?" he
exclaimed.

"It was fairly empty of furniture—"

"That's right. After we locked up last night, Sakai
got in somehow and removed all his wares. The
antiques were his own consignments, so he did not
technically steal from us, but still . . ." The manager
scratched at a *miso* soup stain on his tie.

"He caused you a lot of trouble." I finished his
statement to show I was on his side. "I had a similar
experience. Yesterday Sakai-san offered me a price on
a *tansu* but increased it when another customer came
in. I wound up buying the chest for much more than
its appraised value."

"That is too bad." The manager suddenly seemed
less intimate.

"See, I have it all documented." I thrust Mr.
Ishida's appraisal and Mr. Sakai's receipt on the
counter. The manager looked at both papers without
touching them. At last he commented, "This was
marked final sale."

"Please consider these special circumstances and
the fraud involved."

"It is a shame about your unwise purchase, Miss
Shimura. I must stress that Sakai-san's name is on the
receipt, not ours. All we did was rent him space. Now
I must help the next customer in line. . . ."

I had no chance to come up with a good rejoin-
der. I left Hita Fine Arts in such an unseeing,

depressed haze that I bumped smack into a fishmonger carrying two buckets on a bamboo pole balanced over his broad shoulders. Water sloshed over the sidewalk, and the man had to dash after a crab that had escaped. As he grabbed the fiercely clawing creature back from the road's edge I apologized, not knowing whether I should feel worse for the crab, who'd so briefly tasted liberation, the harassed fishmonger, or myself, wet and out two million yen.

I was going to find Mr. Sakai if it killed me. The most obvious way was through directory assistance; surely he had a phone number and address. I headed for a bank of public phone booths plastered with stickers advertising escort clubs, wishing I were rich enough to afford my own pocket phone. *Pocketo*, as these phones were called for short, were cellular receivers that worked like cordless extensions to a home phone, for up to forty miles. Hugh carried one with him, in addition to the regular cell phone installed in the Windom. He had wanted to get me a pocket phone, but, trying to keep my finances separate, I'd said no.

I was scrounging in my handbag for some small coins when a silver Windom pulled up.

"*Onesan!* Need a ride?" Like a knight in shining armor, Japanese Elvis had popped his gelled head out the sunroof so I could see him.

I fluttered my fingers in a good-bye gesture and stayed by the telephone.

"You never went home! Out partying last night, *neh*? Did you go to the bath I told you about?" Jun Kuroi was staying put. A few cars behind him honked.

"Actually, I'm searching for a man," I began.

"I'm here, I'm here!" Jun chortled.

There was a way he could be useful. I hopped into his Windom and asked if he would be kind enough to let me use his car phone.

"Sure! My boss pays for it, so who cares?" Jun handed me the receiver and I dialed the operator. To my dismay, she said Nao Sakai's home telephone had been disconnected. I pressed her but got nothing more.

When I hung up, Jun asked, "That's the antiques guy, right? Kind of skinny, with a girlish style?"

"Vaguely," I said, thinking that with Jun's elaborate hairstyle, he was a fine one to talk.

"I've seen him around town. He's a middle-aged fool! Why do you want him?"

"Sakai ripped me off," I said tightly. "I'm trying to get restitution."

"I told you Hita Fine Arts was expensive! I could have shown you better stores! I know everyone in town!"

"Do you think you could introduce me to some dealers who might know where he lives? His phone's disconnected, and I can't get an address."

"I'm a car salesman. It's my *job* to find people who don't want to be found. I like to sell my clients a new car every other year, so that means I call or visit them every month to maintain a strong relationship. They get sick of me sometimes." Jun twinkled at me. "But I always find them."

That sounded good. As we ran in and out of various antiques stores, it turned out that everyone did know Jun by name. I also learned that he was the son of the Toyota dealership owner, a fact he had kept to himself.

Nao Sakai wasn't in flush circumstances, according to an antiques dealer who had a shop near Jun's fabled mineral bath. Sakai had maintained pretty poor stock until recently. Since he had apparently abandoned his leased space within Hita Fine Arts, it was a good opportunity for others. There would probably be a bidding war to get into that prime second-floor location near the T-shirts and stamps.

That made me laugh bitterly as we left the shop. Jun suggested a hot bath for relaxation's sake, but I dismissed the idea and asked him to take me to the outskirts of Hita for a peek at the dreary, tin-walled house that Jun's antiques dealer friend said Mr. Sakai had rented. No one answered the door, but the elderly housewife living next door told us that a moving company had packed up Sakai's possessions the night before. The movers had taken all the antiques, leaving Sakai's cheap contemporary furniture on the trash heap out back. Mr. Sakai hadn't said where he was going, but his wife had very kindly given her their television as a going-away present.

"This is very mysterious," Jun Kuroi said as we drove away. "Why would he give away his television? And if he was planning some big rip-off, why did he even bother to send the *tansu* to your apartment in Tokyo? He could have taken your money and kept the *tansu* for himself."

"The moving company should be able to tell us

where the furniture was headed," I thought aloud. "I need to find it."

"Old Granny didn't remember the company's name. She was too busy fussing with her new television, probably," Jun said.

I would have to telephone all the moving companies in the area. Feeling overwhelmed, I asked Jun to drop me off at the train station.

"Don't be sad, Rei-san. If I do enough driving around, I'll find the creep," Jun promised as he pulled into the station's taxi stand, oblivious as always to traffic rules.

"He's gone. I know he's not in Hita any longer." I tried to open the passenger door, but it wouldn't budge.

"Sorry! I use the childproof feature on that side," Jun said, hitting a button on his door to free me. "It's another way to keep the client with me a little longer."

I laughed despite myself. "You're incredible."

"That's what all the girls say." Jun winked at me. "I'm good at everything, *Onēsan*. I'll do what I can to hunt down the creep."

"You do that," I said, expecting nothing.

4

It was high time I leveled with Nana Mihori. I rehearsed my explanation during the ride to her house on the temple grounds in North Kamakura. By the time I'd gotten off the train and walked the fifteen minutes to Horin-ji, I was in a state of panic. I couldn't put anything past Nana Mihori. She had introduced herself to me as a housewife who liked antiques, but I knew her other hobby was running the Kamakura Green and Pristine Society, a local preservation group. Last year a nouveau riche developer had tried building condominiums on a vacant lot for sale in the Kamakura hills. Nana Mihori stopped the plan within a week of its proposal, and when the developer had complained to the press about it, she masterminded a smear campaign against him that shut him out of a deal in another town. His wife was dropped from her women's club, his son was denied admission to good high schools—or so the rumor went.

I passed through the temple entrance, barely taking note of its famous *nio,* carved wooden statues of musclemen with angry expressions. The first time I'd seen them I'd lingered to study their fine carving, but today I headed directly to the abbot's residence. The wooded grounds were lovely at this time of year, filled with blooming bushes of dark blue hydrangea that thrived in Horin-ji's perfectly acid soil. My heels sank into this special earth, causing me to tread more slowly as I approached the low stone wall that set the Mihoris' house off from the temple complex.

Nana Mihori had sounded pleased when I'd called from Kita-Kamakura Station asking if I could drop in. *Drop in and drop the bomb,* I thought, crunching my way up the driveway made of river pebbles. A black four-wheel-drive truck was parked in the driveway; I gave it a brief glance because Hugh had been talking about trading the Windom for something more suited to hauling antique furniture. Toyota Mega Cruiser, it was called. Jun Kuroi would have appreciated it. I wondered who drove the car. I couldn't picture Nana Mihori, who was so feminine that no one ever had seen her in a pair of slacks, behind its wheel.

I reached the residence, which looked as though it had always been there, but was actually only five years old. The day after Nana Mihori's tyrannical mother-in-law died, Nana had ordered destruction of the mildew-covered house that had been good enough for the last two generations of Mihoris. Nana found an architect who could re-create an eighteenth-century aristocrat's villa. The end result was magnificent. A blue tiled roof with low eaves covered the sprawling white U-shaped compound. The house's many windows stretched from floor to ceiling, giving grand views of the garden, filled with rare camellia trees. Behind that lay something really interesting: the *dojo*, a judo gymnasium where Nana's daughter Akemi practiced.

Horin-ji's wooden *nio* looked fierce, but the real fighter on the premises was Akemi, who had been a member of the Japanese women's judo team at the Seoul Olympics in 1988. That was the first time judo was featured as an Olympic sport for women, and Akemi had been predicted to win gold in the middleweight women's class. But she had performed abysmally, disappointing the whole nation and even me, rooting for the Japanese team from my television at home in San Francisco.

After Seoul, a curse seemed to linger on Akemi, and she never placed in competition again. Now she was thirty, judged over the hill but still capable of participating in occasional exhibition matches at schools and sports centers around the country. I'd glimpsed her once, cutting through the Mihori home in her black-belted judo uniform, but she had ignored me.

Today the doors to Akemi's *dojo* stood wide open, and I heard thudding sounds punctuated by sharp breathing and the occasional yell. I sidled closer to get a peek.

In the middle of the rubber-matted floor, a woman and man were locked against each other. They were embracing so tightly it almost looked like a lovers' clinch. The man, at least fifty pounds heavier than Akemi, was using his superior weight to push against her. She couldn't be knocked over; with each push she merely moved with him, not relaxing her grip. They minced back and forth like this for a few minutes, their heavy breathing the only sign of how hard they were working.

The fullness of the sweaty air in the room mixed with pollen outside, and suddenly I knew I was going to sneeze. When the explosion came, the man's head jerked toward the door and Akemi dug her hip under his pelvis and threw him. His arm banged the mat as he yelled.

I scooted off and retraced my steps to the Mihoris' front door, where I buzzed the entry button. After a minute Miss Tanaka, the Mihoris' housekeeper, showed me in, helping me remove my shoes in the spacious, granite-paved entryway. As I put on a pair of straw summer slippers I wondered if Miss Tanaka could smell the seawater that had dried on my suit after the collision with the fishmonger. Her face remained unmoving, but I thought her nose twitched.

"Please, you can go on alone." Miss Tanaka waved me onward, confirming my suspicions.

I'd been in the house several times before, so I knew my way through the series of sliding doors and vast, *tatami*-floored rooms filled with exquisite Zen paintings, ancient ceramics, and the other treasures that a priestly Zen family had accumulated over six hundred years. This was only a fraction of what the Mihoris owned; everything else was in storage in the temple. I followed the sound of recorded classical *koto* music until I found the room Mrs. Mihori used as her personal office. She was kneeling at a low table covered with art books.

"I'm disturbing you," I said, offering the greeting used when entering someone else's space.

"Please come in. You must be very warm!" Nana's eyes glided over my wrinkled suit. "Probably you were hoping for air-conditioning. I'm sorry we have such a traditional home."

"Oh, I love tradition! And the breeze from the garden is very refreshing," I said, gesturing to the windows open along two sides of the room. The other wall was defined by an ornately gilded Buddhist shrine holding two formal black-and-white photographs of an elderly man in a business suit and a woman wearing *kimono*, probably Mrs. Mihori's deceased parents.

"Miss Tanaka will bring us a fan to help move the air. You drink *mugi-cha*, don't you?" My hostess poured cool barley tea for me into a dark earthenware cup.

"This is much nicer than the kind I have at home. Where did you find it?" I asked after I'd taken a sip.

"I buy it at the tea shop near Kamakura Station. Surely you've seen it," Miss Tanaka said as she came into the room carrying a small electric fan. I wondered how long she had been standing outside the door listening.

"I think I've seen the shop. Are the other types of tea sold there such good quality?" I asked, redirecting my question in the hopes of pleasing Miss Tanaka.

"Yes, it's all very high quality. I buy all my lady's

tea there, including the special *macha* blend she uses
for tea ceremony."

"I didn't know you performed the tea ceremony," I said to Nana Mihori when we were alone.

"Yes, I've been a member of the local tea society
for decades. Next week, in fact, I'm going to a convention of tea masters that I'm excited about. But tea
is boring for a young woman like you, probably!"
Nana Mihori smoothed a tendril that had escaped
from her sleek chignon.

"Actually, I wish there were a way I could try it
without having to undertake a regular class." Since I
planned to live a long while in Japan, it was time I
learned how to whisk powdered tea leaves and hot
water into the perfect stage of froth and pour it in the
prescribed manner for my guests. At least my aunt
said so.

"Maybe I could give you a private class. After all,
you've done me such a marvelous favor with the
tansu!" Mrs. Mihori smiled, signaling she was ready
to talk about our deal.

"I need to explain about something that came
up," I began.

"Before you say anything, I wish to show you
where I want the *tansu* to be placed. I think you'll be
surprised." Nana rose to her feet, smoothing down
her dull mauve *kimono*.

"The entryway? Your living room?" I guessed
aloud, and Nana shook her head, smiling. I remembered then that foreigners were usually excited to display antique *tansu* in reception rooms, while
Japanese people liked them where they traditionally

belonged: in bedrooms, to hold clothing and blankets.

"This is where the vice abbot—my nephew Kazuhito—sleeps. He already has a great appreciation of antiques." Mrs. Mihori slid open a door to a traditional room floored in *tatami*. There was no bed; I imagined a futon was rolled up in the closet. My eye was struck by the emptiness of it all. There was a grand Sendai *tansu* with a Zen scroll hanging over it, but nothing more.

"Notice the difference in my daughter's room!" Mrs. Mihori opened the next door, and I was overwhelmed by a jumble of possessions and the odd fact that macho Akemi slept on a princessy-looking bed with floral sheets. Her walls were covered by competition ribbons, photographs, and tattered articles, a tribute to her past.

"She really needs to clean out the clutter," Nana Mihori said, waving me in. "I wanted to put the *tansu* in here for her, across from the bed."

"About the *tansu*—there may be a slight delay."

"Are you polishing it? I thought it was in perfect condition." Mrs. Mihori's sculpted eyebrows drew together.

"The condition was *too* perfect. In fact, I've uncovered a problem." There, it was out.

"Don't doubt your judgment, Rei-san!" Nana reassured me. "Your aunt told me about the sale you made last year to a museum. Anyone who can buy museum-quality antiques can certainly buy for a simple housewife like myself."

"I bought while in a big hurry. When I examined

the *tansu* at the apartment, I found a problem with the metalwork. The original lock plates had been replaced with older ones."

"What do you mean?" Nana Mihori sounded more perplexed than angry.

"The chest was built during the Meiji era, not the Edo period. It's old, but worth considerably less than what I paid for it. I'm sorry to disappoint you, but I feel I cannot present it." I bowed my head, not wanting to see her reaction.

At last her voice came. "What will you do with it?"

"I shall return it." Etiquette kept me from telling her that it probably wouldn't work out.

"I see," Nana said after another silence. "Certainly I am disappointed, but I defer to you. After all, I am no antiques expert. Just an enthusiast."

"I'm sorry I let you down. I would really like to keep looking for a piece for you. I wouldn't expect you to take the one I've bought."

"I think we should just let the matter rest for now." Nana turned a smooth face to me, the one I'd seen her use on guests she was meeting for the first time. It was chilling.

"Let what rest?" a rough, low-pitched voice asked.

Akemi Mihori had crept up behind us. She had swapped her *judo-gi* for a black Spandex sports bra and shorts that revealed bulging muscles in her legs and arms.

"Akemi!" Nana Mihori seemed flustered. "I was just showing your room."

"So you're the antiques buyer! Hey, aren't you

American?" Akemi said in English, grabbing my hand in a handshake like iron. I was relieved when it ended. She used the same hand to vigorously wipe her damp brow, raining a few drops of sweat on me.

"Yes. My name is Rei Shimura," I answered, trying to pretend her body fluids hadn't hit me.

"Shimura-san says there's some problem with the *tansu*," Nana Mihori said. I was no longer on a first-name basis with her.

"Really?" Akemi was persisting in English, although Nana and I were speaking Japanese. "Miss Shimura, do you run?"

"No. I'm not very athletic." I had no idea where she was leading.

"You're a swimmer, right? Given that you smell like the sea." Akemi laughed heartily. "Come on, I thought all Americans were sports fanatics!"

"Sorry to disappoint. I've disappointed your family in a lot of ways."

"Don't worry," Nana said in her newly cold voice, and Akemi's gaze bounced from me to her mother as if she'd finally caught on to the tension.

"I must be going. It's getting late," I said.

Despite the discomfort of our situation, I expected Nana would offer me another glass of tea. She also might have asked about my expenses from two weeks of travel. Instead, she made a vague excuse about needing to return some telephone calls and sailed off in the direction of her office. I knew she was furious.

"Just a moment, Miss Shimura. I want to show you my jogging trail on the way out. How can you walk in those?" Akemi snorted at the sight of me struggling back into my tight pumps.

"You wear a *judo-gi* to work out, don't you? These are part of my work uniform."

"I'd think your fine shoes would get dirty, searching all over the country for antiques! That is, if you do it with any kind of spirit—"

"Obviously I have no spirit!" I wished she would retreat to her gym, but she stuck her short, wide feet into Asics running shoes and followed me outside. When we were a few feet from the house, Akemi slapped me on the shoulder.

"Catering to ladies like my mother must be hell."

"I don't understand." I'd never heard anyone in Japan speak so disrespectfully about a parent.

"Don't believe that I wanted that stupid *tansu*. To tell the truth, your failure will delay my dreaded bedroom makeover." Akemi strode down a dirt path leading away from the house and into the woods. I hurried to catch up and started to say something more about what had happened between her mother and me, but she held up a hand like a STOP sign.

"Let's not talk about antiques! I'm sick of them. Tell me, what do you think of this trail? Do you have them in your country?"

Disoriented, I struggled for words. "Americans are more likely to run on smooth-surfaced jogging tracks or the street. This is different."

"Better, hmmm?"

"Well, it's certainly more natural. I bet the local people love it."

"What do you mean, the local people?" There was an odd expression on Akemi's face.

"Well, surely they enjoy running and walking here."

Akemi sucked in her breath. "No one runs on my trail! It was cleared for me so I could run without any bother."

I thought briefly about how the president of the United States had had a jogging track built at the White House that his staff members were free to use. I didn't bring it up, but asked about her trail's length instead.

"It's just two kilometers. I kept it to that length, curving through the woods so it completely avoids the temple buildings."

A little demon in me made me say, "I'd want to run by the temple to see what was going on and hear the monks playing their drums—"

"That's because you're a foreigner and like Japan! I'd rather listen to Simply Red on my Sony Walkman. You should run with me sometime. I'd jog slowly for you," she added as an afterthought.

"You couldn't possibly go slowly enough!"

"Your legs are longer than mine. Lucky. What sports did you play in high school?" Akemi was studying me in a way that made me blush.

"Like I said, I'm rotten at sports. I swim a little, but that's with my head out of water. I can't stand not breathing."

"Running is very good for your aerobic capacity. I can tell you have a problem with endurance, from the way you were gasping when you caught up to me just now. You need to start slowly. Run until you can't stand it, then walk, and start running when you get your breath back. It's simple."

It was a beautiful and peaceful place, this secret trail in Kamakura. No one would see me if I stopped, gasping for air. No one except Akemi Mihori, a former national judo champion.

"It's hard for me to meet people." Akemi stubbed her shoe against the trail. "Japanese women my age have all sold themselves to the highest bidders and are staying home with their babies. The only people I have around are guys like my trainer, the one you saw me working out with this afternoon."

I thought she must be pretty lonely to have opened herself like that to me. Feeling tentative, I asked if she had plans for Saturday night.

"Nothing. Why?" She sounded startled.

"I'm having a party. I sent your mother an invitation, but I doubt she's coming now. You should come—it might be interesting for you." I was going to say, *You might meet someone,* but decided that would be overbearing.

"I'm not much good at parties."

"It won't be your typical Japanese party; there will be tons of foreigners. Have you ever been to a party with foreigners?" Hugh would be charming to her, although she would probably consider him a "high bidder" of the most repulsive sort. At least there would be others.

"But I'm vegetarian! I cannot eat your Western diet."

"I'm vegetarian, too. We have something in common!" Strangely, I was delighted by this.

She gave me a half smile. "Okay, I might attend. As long as you come back later this week to try running with me."

"If your mother sees me—"

"She and Tanaka-san are going into Tokyo to buy supplies for the tea convention. Neither of them will know you were here."

What was I doing, making steps toward a friendship that I really didn't have time for? Given my business troubles, I should be doing nothing but work. I also doubted I'd be in shape to run more than half a lap. But Akemi's eyes were pleading. I nodded and submitted my hand to another crushing handshake.

5

Back at Roppongi Hills, I found Hugh asleep on the sofa with pages of *The Asian Wall Street Journal* strewn over him.

"Where've you been? I canceled my evening meeting to be here with you," he murmured when I gently pulled off the newspaper.

"I can't unload the *tansu*." I stared at the bridal chest, still smack in the center in the living room. "Can we at least get it out of here? I don't want to look at it."

"Let's move it into the study, then. Maybe my brother can use it for his gear." Hugh stood up and stretched.

"Angus!" I had almost forgotten about the impending visitor.

"He'll be at the airport early tomorrow afternoon. Is that still okay? I assumed your *tansu* problems would be over and you'd be able to fetch him," Hugh said as we began moving each section of drawers into the study, a room already crowded with a fax machine, two computers, and the guest futon.

"My problems are far from over." After we restacked the furniture in a place near the window, I sank down on the futon and told him everything: Hita Fine Arts' refusal to take responsibility for the *tansu*, Mr. Sakai's disappearance, and Nana Mihori's humiliating rejection.

"So you ran around all day and showed no gain for it," Hugh said, rubbing the spot between my shoulders that had tensed with worry. "Sounds like my day. Sometimes I wonder why I'm still working in Japan."

"Well, you probably earned lots of money today. All I made was a new friend. Akemi Mihori."

"The sportswoman?"

"Yes, the one who was in the Seoul Olympics. I think she's lonely, because she invited me to go running with her the day after tomorrow, and she might come to our cocktail party."

"Running? As in moving one's feet quickly?" Hugh paused. "Darling, you can't go from complete inactivity to marathons! If you want to take exercise, try my rowing machine."

"I don't believe in indoor workouts," I said, feeling vaguely insulted. "In fact, I'm going to run around the park tomorrow to practice."

"Tomorrow's forecast is up in the nineties. It's not the day to start running, especially for someone who isn't the world's greatest athlete."

"I'm doing it anyway. I have to."

Hugh kissed me. "Think about it tomorrow

morning. In the meantime, you need a relaxing bath followed by a massage. Let me show you what I learned in Thailand."

The massage led into something even better. I relaxed beautifully, but we overslept the next morning and had just twenty minutes for a rushed cup of tea before Hugh drove off to work. I was still determined to run. Not having proper workout clothing, I slipped on one of Hugh's Marks and Spencer undershirts, a pair of shorts, and the stained sneakers I usually wore for furniture-refinishing jobs. I took the subway to Yoyogi Park, a huge, manicured expanse of green with smooth cement paths. After some cursory stretches remembered from a long-ago gym class, I set off, pacing myself against an old man. Within a few minutes, my heart felt as if it might explode. I slowed to a walk, as Akemi had recommended, and my breath came back. I started jogging again, the old man now being a quarter mile ahead.

I'd heard that running could clear your mind, put you in a blissful trance. It didn't happen for me. All I could do was mourn the fact that I hadn't done anything with my body in the last six months outside of sex, which obviously didn't work enough muscle groups to count. The other park exercisers were overtaking me, even a group of mothers walking with their toddlers. I would have died of embarrassment had I not already been dead from the heat.

In the end, I had no idea of my mileage but suspected it was low. I'd run about seven minutes and walked twenty. I repaired to a soft-drink machine, from which I bought a frigid can of Aquarius, an "ionization beverage" supposedly designed for athletes. I didn't know how I would survive a workout with Akemi.

After dragging my tired bones home, I showered and set about organizing the rest of my day. Because a big chunk would be taken up traveling to and from Narita Airport, I had only a couple of hours to locate Mr. Sakai's moving company. The English-language telephone directory didn't cover Hita, so I had to call Information. I was talking with an unhelpful operator when my call waiting beeped. I said good-bye and switched over to the new call.

"It's Jun from Hita Toyota." There was a lot of static; he was probably on his car phone.

"Elvis!" I said without thinking. "How are you?"

"I've found someone very important. Your buyer."

"For the *tansu?*" I was confused.

"Yes, I've found the car buyer you were looking for. We're on the east side of Tokyo. Can you meet us?"

Someone was in the car with him. That was the only explanation for him replacing the word *tansu* with *car*. "Do I know this person?"

"Yes, you do. He's here for a limited time." Jun's voice was heavy with meaning.

"Sakai?" I breathed sharply. "Jun-san, how did you get him into your car?"

"Not now. I'll explain when you get here. I don't know Tokyo well. I've been driving around in circles—"

I thought it over. "You said you were on the east

side? Go to Ueno Park. There will be signs for it everywhere. I can meet you in half an hour there by the main entrance."

"Got it. We'll probably be parked illegally, so come as fast as you can."

While Yoyogi was a modern, sunny place to run, Ueno was shady and historic and had considerable urban flavor. In fact, the steps leading to the park's south entrance had in recent years become a hangout for men from the Middle East in search of "3K" jobs: *kitsui, kitanai,* and *kiken,* meaning hard, dirty, and dangerous jobs no one else wanted. Japanese police had begun throwing these foreigners out of the country, ostensibly for overstaying their visas but really because of a public outcry over foreigner-related crime. Ueno Park was no longer a safe place for black-market laborers to congregate, so I was startled to be approached by a man with dark curly hair.

"Need a telephone card? I'm selling ten cards for two thousand yen! Fully charged, perfect for telephoning overseas."

I paused, remembering my perpetual troubles mustering up change for the pay telephone. Legitimate telephone cards cost one thousand yen each—more than eight dollars for maybe thirty minutes of local phone calls. Black-market phone cards were a better deal, but if I were caught using one, I could be imprisoned or sent back to San Francisco. I shook my head and went into the park, intent on finding Jun.

Where was he? I scanned the families strolling to the zoo and student groups going to the Tokyo

National Museum. I sat down on the bench closest
to the park entrance and waited. After a minute there
was a rustling in some bushes and Jun Kuroi
emerged, his smooth pompadour covered with bits
of stick and leaf.

"You took long enough!" he chided. "The dude
on the steps was bothering me, so I had to change
location."

"You've got Sakai? Really, truly?"

"Yesterday evening I was hanging in the head
office when a telephone call came from another
Toyota dealer. Apparently Sakai went there trying to
get rid of his eighty-six Corona Grand Saloon. They
didn't want to take his car and were checking if we
might be interested. Sure, I said, and got them to put
Sakai directly on the line. I told him if he brought me
the Corona, I could trade it for something else with
no paperwork required. It made no sense, but he's a
greedy fellow. I picked him up at the cheap hotel
where he was staying in Yokohama and told him we'd
need to stop in Tokyo for the new car."

"How clever," I said, although I was starting to
feel nervous. For the past forty-eight hours all I'd
focused on was the need to find Nao Sakai. Aside
from waving Mr. Ishida's appraisal in his face, I hadn't
figured out how I'd convince him to give me my
money back. My worries grew as I followed Jun into
a side street lined with rickety wooden houses that
looked as if they had been built before the war.

"I left him in there with the childproof lock on,"
Jun said, gesturing to his car perched squarely on the
tiny strip of sidewalk, so at least traffic could get by.

"He was getting suspicious about not going straight to the buyer's home. But you'll know how to handle things, *neh?*"

"He's still in there," I said, squinting at the shape of a man in the front passenger seat.

"Of course. I locked the doors."

When I reached the passenger door, I noticed Mr. Sakai was leaning his head against the window. This didn't surprise me, because Japanese people have a talent for sleeping anywhere. Pass any taxi stand, and most of the drivers will be reclining with little masks over their eyes. On the train, commuters slide into seats and their heads bob downward, miraculously rising when their home station is announced.

"He shouldn't be sleeping! Not with something as exciting as the prospect of a new car!" Jun opened the driver's door and leaned across to address his passenger. "Sakai-san! Wake up, please. I have someone to meet you."

Mr. Sakai didn't respond. Jun reached over to touch his shoulder, and he fell sideways like a soft rag doll. He was wearing the same shirt I'd seen him in at Hita Fine Arts, but it was deeply wrinkled. My gaze flicked over his clothing and up to his face, which had an odd bluish pallor. His eyes were open, staring straight ahead with a fixed expression.

"Do you think he's sick?" Jun sounded nervous.

"No." The signs were obvious, and bile rose in my throat. I squeezed my eyes shut, then opened them. Sakai's corpse still lolled in the seat. I reached across Jun for the car phone, then whisked my hand back. I shouldn't touch it.

"W-w-we will do CPR. I learned it in the Boy Scouts," Jun stuttered.

"There's no point, he's—"

"Don't say it!" Jun screamed. "Don't say it!"

"I'll be right back. Don't move him. And don't touch anything." I was already off and running around the corner back to Ueno Station. All I had in my pocket was a thousand-yen note; I'd have to get change or a telephone card in order to call the police.

In my peripheral vision I saw the telephone card hawker talking to another foreign man. I ran up and gasped out my plea for a telephone card.

"What are you, undercover?" his friend, whose face was marked with a jagged scar, practically spat at me.

"No, it's an emergency. A man—a man is sick. . . ." Somehow I could not say *dead*.

"*Ay Khoda!* No, I do not want your money. Just borrow it." The second man shoved a telephone card into my hand, and I sprinted for the green public telephone box. I got there, slid the card in, and dialed 110. The card slid back out. I realized then that 110 was a free call—there was a red button I could press to go directly to fire, police, or ambulance. I made my request, dimly aware that the man who had followed me was shouting something to his friend. By the time I'd gotten off the phone and turned around to give the telephone card back, both men were gone.

6

Jun Kuroi had been a Boy Scout and the manager for his high school judo team. He gave to Unicef and he helped his grandmother with her garden every weekend. He started listing his accomplishments when a police squad car and an ambulance converged on us five minutes later, but the police were more interested in what had happened in the last half hour.

"The car was parked with the air-conditioning off," Jun confessed. "If he became overheated, he did not have me to help him. It was a terrible mistake!"

It had been warm in the car, but even if Mr. Sakai could not unlock the door, he could have called for help. On the other hand, if he had been hit with a massive heart attack, he might not have had the energy.

"You will make your statement at the police station. Just a formality," a patrol officer who looked as if he was barely out of training assured us.

"Actually, I need my car for work," Jun protested

when a city tow truck arrived and began hooking up the Windom.

I looked at him, startled. Had he really intended to drive back to Hakone in a car in which someone had died?

"But we need to examine your car. Police regulations," the officer said gently.

Jun's face fell. He muttered to himself all the way to the North Ueno police station, where we were led into the main waiting area, a sunny room decorated with cartoon posters on the walls and stuffed animals on the desks. It was as cheerful as a kindergarten, and, sitting there, I felt as powerless as a child. I could explain that my pursuit of Nao Sakai and his sudden death were coincidental, but why would anyone believe it? It was like telling a teacher that you really did your homework, but unfortunately the dog ate it.

Jun and I wound up telling our story several times: first in separate rooms, then together. At present, six men representing the North Ueno police, the park's patrol, and the Tokyo Metropolitan Police were conferring in a private office. Jun and I remained in the happy kindergarten waiting room.

"The wife is coming. They radioed she's in the area," the junior constable told us between chews of apple-scented gum.

"You found her?" I was amazed. "I thought the Sakais moved without leaving any forwarding address!"

"A call was made to Sakai's brother in Kawasaki, who knew where she was staying. The police picked her up and drove her in."

His mention of the brother-in-law reminded me of Angus Glendinning. I looked at my watch. I should have picked him up at Narita Airport half an hour ago. He would be alone and helpless.

I wasn't sure that my guard would allow me an unsupervised phone call. In any case, I didn't want him looking at my black-market telephone card. Forcing my face into a shy expression, I begged permission to use the honorable hands-washing room. The guard rolled his eyes at my feminine euphemism but ultimately pointed me in the right direction.

There was a pay telephone in the alcove outside the rest rooms. I slid my telephone card in, dialed, and was sent straight to Hugh's voice mail where I left a message about my location and my sincere apologies for missing Angus.

I returned to the waiting room, where Jun was twisting restlessly in his seat. I wanted to give him the hint about the telephone but obviously couldn't in front of the policeman. There was no point in talking about anything, so I tried to calm myself by watching the station's caged canaries. I stared at the fluffy yellow and green birds, wondering at their presence in a no-pets-allowed zone, until I decided they were probably working members of the police team. Canaries expired from the slightest whiff of poison gas, a major fear in Japan. These canaries were singing now, but in the case of a terrorist attack, they would be the first to die.

I didn't want to think about death. I jerked my attention to the wall and began trying to read a poster on bicycle safety. With my poor *kanji* knowledge, it took me a good half hour to get through it.

The police station's automatic doors slid open, and two cops entered the room with someone between then. A woman, I deduced from the back view of her pageboy hairstyle.

"Sakai-san, I regret the terrible news." The North Ueno chief of police emerged from his office, bowing to the woman. She turned toward him to acknowledge the condolence, and my breathing stopped for a split second. Her face was dominated by a large black mole.

The woman was the customer who had bid against me for the *tansu*. Shock and outrage mixed inside me, but this woman, who I now understood was Mrs. Sakai, didn't notice. Her watering eyes were focused on the police chief.

"Your journey from Kawasaki City must have been very tiring," the chief said in a low voice. "Please come with me to the office. My assistant will bring you a drink."

"Sakai-sama!" Without warning, Jun Kuroi left his chair and knelt before Mrs. Sakai. "I was with your husband. How terribly sorry I am that he became ill while a passenger in my car. I wanted to resuscitate him, but my friend thought it was too late—"

"I need to sit down," Mrs. Sakai murmured, not even looking at him. The policemen closed ranks around her, and she was led off.

"Please don't do that again. You're upsetting the victim's wife!" the junior constable said to Jun. I tuned out, trying to concentrate on this new knowledge I had about Nao Sakai's wife. I had told the police about the conditions under which I'd bought the *tansu*, but I hadn't given a physical description of the other customer, not knowing about the connection. If I brought it up now, it might make them examine Mr. Sakai's death more intensely. It would also convert my status from an unfortunate witness to an accidental death into something more sinister.

I pondered this during the next hour, during which an elementary school class and several neighborhood residents came in to learn about matters such as household registration and bicycle permits. If only life were that mundane for me. I wondered if I would ever consider it mundane again.

A junior high school student departing with the paperwork for her new bicycle was almost knocked over by a new arrival, a long-haired foreigner with his eyes everywhere except the path in front of him. The man was in his early twenties, dressed in tie-dyed shorts and a tank top bearing the motto *Fükengruven*. A illegal jewelry vendor, I guessed from the size of his backpack and the long silver lizard earring that dangled halfway to his shoulder. But no court of cops surrounded him. When he noticed the canaries, he snickered slightly and ambled over.

"Whassup?" The backpacker stuck a finger in a cage, withdrawing it when the canaries backed away. The young man pulled a hand-rolled cigarette out of the waistband of his shorts. He lit the cigarette, turning as he inhaled so I got an excellent view of his dark green eyes. Yes, I was certain now. He was a nightmare version of Hugh—proof of what might happen if my lover chucked his Paul Smith suits and went Rastafarian.

"*Oi, marijuanakai?*" The young, gum-chewing constable jumped to his feet and headed for the stranger.

"No! It's not pot, is it?" I blurted in English.

"It's clove. What's it to you, lass?" He blew a smoke ring at a canary, which squawked at the outrage.

"He is only smoking a clove cigarette," I translated for the police officer.

"And what is that substance?" the policeman demanded a bit shakily.

"A spice that is very popular overseas, commonly used in cakes and curries."

The backpacker sneered, and the young constable said, "This overseas boy could be fined heavily for disregarding our No Smoking sign. And for animal abuse!"

I switched languages and said, "Put it out unless you want to spend the night here."

"Talk about an uptight country." He stubbed out the cigarette on a bar of the cage, knocking ash into the canaries' home.

"You're Angus Glendinning, aren't you?" I asked.

The backpacker gave me a thorough up-and-down, then smirked. "Rei? I would not have guessed. You dinna look like a mistress."

I swallowed hard and said, "You surprise me, too. Where did you learn that odd accent, the movies?" He hadn't sounded so ridiculous in the few seconds I'd heard him on the telephone.

Angus merely laughed. "Shug said to tell you he'll be a few minutes. He's gone to fetch his lawyer."

Shug. That was the Hugh's nickname, which had never made sense to me. If I were on better terms with Angus, maybe I could learn about it. Trying to sound nicer, I said, "I'm sorry I couldn't get into the airport. How did you get into the city so fast?"

"I rang my bro when you didn't show up. He told me to take a taxi to his office. When I got there, he said we had to haul you out. Now he's off to pick up some lawyer. A hell of lot of running around, and all I want to do is crash." Angus settled down on the other side of me, bringing into my line of vision a filthy sneaker and a grimy ankle tattooed with a snake.

If Hugh had called in Mr. Ota, the Tokyo lawyer who had gotten him out of a nasty jam once before, he obviously thought my problems were serious. When Hugh finally came in unsmiling, I felt sure of it.

"I'm sorry," I said as he bent to kiss me. Jun Kuroi gaped. Obviously he had no idea about all the foreigners in my life.

"Don't say anything to them until you've had a few minutes in private with Mr. Ota," Hugh murmured into my hair.

"It was only an accidental death—I mean, it's terrible, but Jun and I are here voluntarily. You really didn't need to come."

"We'll talk about it later. Anyway, my brother arrived safely and we're going to have a wonderful time."

"There is no need to worry," Mr. Ota chimed in, standing just behind Hugh. He was bearing a massive box of sweets, as if he'd come to make a social call. When he presented it to the constable in charge of us, I understood. He was softening people up, making them beholden.

"Shug, if you want to get her out, you need to give the pigs a payoff. That's what I did in India," Angus said.

I didn't get the chance to ask why he'd been in an Indian police station, because Mr. Ota was gesturing for me to accompany him into a small office that had been vacated for our conversation. Hugh had already narrated for him the story of how I'd met Mr. Sakai while buying the *tansu*, so all I needed to fill in were the afternoon's events.

"Don't you want to talk to Jun?" I asked when he was finished.

"Not at this time," Mr. Ota told me. "I'm going to meet the police chief now. He doesn't know it, but our fathers play gate-ball in the same senior citizens' league."

The importance of this became clear when, fifteen minutes later, he emerged from the chief's office with the declaration that I was ready to go home.

"What about Jun?" I didn't want to leave him behind.

"Go ahead. My father's driving here, they told me," Jun said.

Since his car had been impounded, he would definitely need a ride back to Hita. I said a regretful good-bye, betting this was the last time Jun Kuroi ever did a favor for a foreign woman.

The journey home took forever, since we had to stop in the Ebisu neighborhood to drop off Mr. Ota.

Hugh went into his office with him for a few minutes, then came back out and got into the driver's seat. He looked tired, so I offered to drive. He shook his head.

"I'll drop you and Angus off at the lobby with the luggage, then go to the garage and park. Okay?"

"Sure," I answered, although I wasn't relishing the opportunity to be alone with his brother. When I unlocked the apartment door, Angus scrambled ahead, dropping the luggage in front of me.

"I didn't know my brother was doing so well. This place is fab!"

"The apartment is paid for by Sendai, the Japanese company that employs him," I explained.

"*Ah so*," he said in a parody of Japanese speech. He inclined his head in the direction of a group of wood-block prints by Hiroshige. "Those look expensive. They must have come with the place?"

"Actually, those are mine. I'm a dealer."

"Really? I wouldn't have thought he went for that."

"I'm teaching him," I said, picking up Angus's heavy duffel bag. He took the other end, relieving me of half its weight.

"You're teaching him? Shite!"

The Scottish pronunciation of the profanity didn't make it any sweeter to my ears. Through gritted teeth, I said, "He's a fast learner. Let's go into the study—"

"So what exactly are you dealing? I hear Ecstasy's big here."

He thought I was a *drug dealer*. I squeaked, "Not drugs! I'm an antiques dealer!"

"Really? Don't blow a gasket." Angus laughed.

"This is your room," I said, trying to regain my composure. "There's an apartment key on the *tansu*—the bedside chest. I covered it with a protective cloth, but please use a coaster if you put any kind of beverage down on it. I'd rather you didn't smoke in the apartment, because the furniture and art are very delicate. If you must have a cigarette, you can smoke on the balcony." I realized belatedly I was sounding like my mother.

"Got it, mum." He put his hands up in mock surrender.

"About dinner," I began. "I marinated eggplant and also made some soba noodles and a cucumber salad."

"I'm no flower-eater!"

"Hugh will help you order some take-out food, then." I was exasperated. "There are a ton of menus in the kitchen left over from his bachelor days."

Hugh finally arrived, but before I could tell him about dinner, he spoke in a low, hard voice. "You. Me. Bedroom."

"What are you, Tarzan?" I protested against a background of Angus's ribald laughter.

Hugh ushered me in and slammed the door. He had been quiet on the car ride home, and I thought he was tired. He'd been seething.

"How could you let this happen? My God, Rei."

"I just went to the park to take care of my problems. It all went wrong—"

"Mr. Ota told me the police chief says you're very lucky to have escaped."

"From whom?"

"Jun Kuroi, if that's even his real name! Whoever heard of a guy named Jun? And he could be charged with kidnapping or worse."

"If Jun were a dangerous person, the police would hardly let him go home," I pointed out.

"His father's coming to speak to the police, not to take him home. I didn't say anything earlier because I didn't want to upset you."

"Upset me? That's putting it mildly. You tricked me into leaving!"

"The police needed to ask Jun more questions, not you. But what I'd like to know is the depth of your connection to the suspect."

"Do you mean to ask, was I meeting him for an afternoon quickie? No, Hugh. He's just a guy I met in Hita who helped me fix the car's taillight and is doing everything to help me get my money back for the *tansu*."

"That bloody two million yen! How many times have I told you I'll absorb the cost? It's nothing to me!"

Angus began pounding on the door. "Come on out! No time for shagging."

I stalked out of the bedroom, brushing by Angus, who was holding a crystal snifter filled with what smelled like Hugh's favorite eighteen-year-old Scotch whiskey.

"Mmm, that will go well with pizza or whatever you wind up eating," I said to Angus.

"Take-away's a good idea." Hugh was pouring his own glass of Scotch. "Hey, Angus, careful with the stereo. What do you want to play?"

"I've got Nine Inch Nails, Skinny Puppy, and Revolting Cocks." Angus went on fiddling with Hugh's expensive tape deck. "The cassettes I've been carrying around are a couple of years old. It's hard to stay connected when traveling."

"Maybe you should turn on the radio," I suggested. "There's an FM station that plays the latest international stuff."

"I like industrial music, not sickening pop," Angus said.

"Give Angus a chance to play what he wants," said Hugh, surprising me with his sharpness.

"So what do you want to listen to first? Revolting Cocks are kind of dancey, Skinny Puppy is more noise, and everyone knows the Nails—though I'm not sure you'll have heard this remix from the *Lost Highway* soundtrack."

"Anything." Hugh sank onto the sofa, shutting his eyes.

"Nine Inch Nails, then." Angus slid a cassette into Hugh's state-of-the-art tape deck, and as a terrible clashing of guitars began, I went to the window and looked down.

Fourteen stories below me was a dark, humid city where a man had traveled to meet his death. High up in Roppongi Hills, we had air-conditioning and a song called "Perfect Drug." Hugh's apartment was its own world, a country to which I held a short-term visa. A place where I could stay, but never truly belong.

7

Angus's cassette was still going when I got up the next morning. I unplugged the stereo and stomped into the kitchen to eat breakfast, unable to tolerate the grinding metal sounds any longer. Hugh had already gone off to work, leaving a conspicuously marked *Japan Times* on the table. The article said a car dealer and an unemployed foreign woman had discovered the body of Nao Sakai, an antiques dealer from Hita. Autopsy results would be released within a few days.

I sipped tea and thought about my options. I could stay in the apartment, making phone calls to various clients, but that would mean I'd be stuck with Angus. On the other hand, I could return to the police station to see what was happening with Jun.

After dressing in a blue cotton dress I hoped did not scream "unemployed foreign woman," I discovered Angus had awoken and was lounging on the living room sofa watching an Australian soap opera.

"Oh, you're here!" I said, struck by a sense of duty. "Do you have plans today? Need any suggestions?"

"I'm still waking up, but after a while I might go looking for some local bands that play in a park," he said, yawning.

"Yoyogi Park?"

"Yo something."

I recalled what Jun had told me. "The city government has cracked down and banned musical performances there. You can't even play a radio outside anymore."

"Bloody police state," Angus muttered. "Well, they've got to practice their songs somewhere."

"Look, Angus, I'd help you look for some local music spots today if I had the time, but I don't. There's a good record store in the neighborhood. Maybe one of the salesclerks could tell you about some concerts."

"Get off my back. You're making me feel like I'm back at home, my mum and sisters jumping down my throat," he said.

I leaned against the doorway and asked, "Is that why you travel incessantly? Because you don't like your family?"

"They're the ones who don't like me," Angus said fiercely. "I canna do anything right, coming after him. Imagine what it's like to have everyone talking about your brother. They call him the business whiz, the golfing guru—not that he's ever around, you know?"

"But you're very bright. You were accepted into some pretty good boarding schools," I pointed out.

"Booted from all." Angus sounded proud. "For the love of drugs, sex, and rock and roll . . . didn't Shug tell you?"

"Not exactly." The irony was that when Hugh was young, there had been no money for him to attend boarding school. He'd gone to a free grammar school instead, and only made it to Glasgow University because he had a full scholarship. After graduation he went to work at a silk-stocking law practice, sending much of what he earned to fund Angus's education.

"Your brother drives you crazy, yet you came to stay with him." I studied Angus's sulky face.

"I'm here because I'm on a round-the-world ticket. I need a place to bunk."

"So this apartment is basically your hotel?"

"Don't get pissy with me! It's not your home, either."

"True," I said, remembering the strange unhappiness that had flooded me while standing at the window the night before. "Well, I'm off for the day. I've left a subway map in the entryway and some tour books. Have fun."

"Ta, then." Angus turned back to the television. "Neighbors!" He sang the show's theme in a falsetto, a mocking swan song for my departure.

I rode the Hibiya Line thirteen stops to Ueno. *My unlucky number*, I thought while walking slowly past the cheerful bustle of hawkers in the Ameyoko bargain shopping alley selling everything from dried fish to deodorant. I had developed painful shinsplints from running the previous day and was misted with perspiration when I arrived at the police station.

I went straight to the women's rest room to freshen up. I could hear something unpleasant going on in a toilet stall, the painful sound of vomiting. Probably a young, pregnant office worker. I was drying my hands and face when the stall door opened and a middle-aged woman went to the sink to rinse her mouth. I glanced at her bent frame and, as she slowly straightened, made the identification: Mrs. Sakai, the woman with the mole.

She was looking at her sagging face in the mirror, the cheeks mottled by dozens of tiny red pinpricks, capillaries broken by her vomiting. I knew because it always happened to me. Her pageboy hairstyle looked limp and oily, and her lipstick had worn off into a crayoned line around the edges.

I moved closer to the mirror so she saw my face. At first there was no recognition, but then she turned.

"*Aa!*" she exclaimed, sounding horrified.

"You're feeling ill. I'm sorry." Despite what she'd done in Hita Fine Arts, I did feel terrible for her. She'd lost her husband.

"They tried to make me eat. I couldn't keep it down." The haughty air she'd assumed in the shop was completely gone. She wiped her mouth with a limp yellow and pink dotted handkerchief she pulled from her pocket.

I offered her a fresh package of tissues someone had thrust into my hand at the Roppongi subway station that morning, a sales promotion for something or other. She didn't take it. Sensing my time was limited, I spoke. "About Jun Kuroi—he was only trying to help me. It wasn't his fault that your husband died."

"Helping you?" She sounded distracted.

"You were at the shop that day. If it wasn't for you, I would have paid a fair price for the *tansu*."

Her face flushed. "You think because I was his wife, I was not truly interested in the *tansu*! Let me tell you, I really wanted it—I had developed a fondness—"

"Stop it. You and your husband knew the chest was an overpriced fake."

"Fake?" She looked incredulous.

"The metalwork was changed. I didn't notice, and my mistake was your husband's gain."

"How can you talk about gain? He's dead, he has gained nothing!" Mrs. Sakai took a brush out of her handbag and began raking it through her hair. "My husband paid a fair price to the consignor who gave him that piece."

"If that's true, why were you running away from Hita?"

"We were looking for a new place to live," Mrs. Sakai said, brushing harder. "Anyway, my husband sent the *tansu* to your home in Tokyo. You have no reason to complain. Now, I must excuse myself—"

"What condition was the *tansu* in when it came to your shop? Did your husband make any alterations? Is there a shed or workshop where he kept spare pieces of metalwork?"

"Of course not. He was a top salesman, not a carpenter!"

"Where did he get the *tansu?*"

"Why are you bothering me with this now? My husband is dead!" Mrs. Sakai fumbled with her hairbrush, which clattered on the tiled floor.

I retrieved the brush. Handing it to her, I asked, "Do you think your husband's stress over his shady business dealings might have triggered the heart attack or stroke or whatever killed him?"

"I have no idea—"

"The police may want to question me again. So far, I haven't mentioned our prior acquaintance."

She shut her eyes. I was offering her an obvious deal. At last she said, "The consignor's name is Ideta. Ideta-san of Denen-Chofu."

She was talking about an old-money enclave in southwest Tokyo, an excellent area to solicit antiques. My instinct was to believe her, so I asked for Mr. Ideta's first name and address.

"I don't have that. I'm telling you all that I know."

A last name might be enough; it was likely I could find him by asking around the neighborhood.

"Thank you, Sakai-san. I'm sorry to have bothered you in your time of grief."

"You won't say anything, then?"

I would have reassured her, but two policewomen entered the bathroom. Mrs. Sakai walked ahead of me as if we weren't acquainted. I went out a few beats later, heading to the information counter.

"I've brought Mr. Kuroi some lunch. May I see him?" I held up a *bento*-box lunch I'd bought at a nearby Family Mart convenience store.

"It's early for lunch. Are you a relative?" The sergeant looked at me. He hadn't been there the afternoon before and obviously didn't know who I was.

I shook my head. "Just a friend."

"I'm afraid you can't see him, then. He's very busy with the police."

"Okay, I'll wait."

"You cannot see him," the sergeant said more insistently. I made my lip tremble a bit and he relented. "I can deliver the lunch. You may put a note inside."

I beamed at him and started scribbling on the memo pad he gave me. I wrote using the phonetic *hiragana* alphabet, which I figured would clue in Jun to my identity: "I did not mean to leave you. Please ask this man for help and remain brave." I signed the note "Your true friend" and added the name and phone number of Junichi Ota, the lawyer who had helped me at the station the day before.

It would probably be wise to let Hugh's lawyer know that I'd made a referral. I went outside and, still using the telephone card the man in the park had given me, punched in Mr. Ota's phone number.

"Miss Shimura?" Mr. Ota's secretary-daughter answered in a sweet, high-pitched voice. "How funny that you're calling at this moment. My father is in conference with Mr. Glendinning! Do you want me to put you on the speakerphone?"

I wanted to talk to Mr. Ota without Hugh's interference. "I'm at a phone booth and people are waiting," I said. "I'll telephone later."

If Hugh was in conference with Mr. Ota, it might mean my legal situation had become more perilous. On the other hand, he might have beaten me to the punch and was urging his lawyer to help Jun Kuroi. I hoped for the latter, but an ominous, low drumroll throbbed in me like some kind of warning. When I heard cymbals crashing, I realized the music was real.

Across the street, a traditional *chindonya* band was parading. A ragtag group of five musicians with ornate nineteenth-century hairstyles and *kimono* moved slowly while crooning an old-fashioned song. A sign on the drummer's back advertised the grand opening of a karaoke bar. *Chindonya* was a tradition that had almost died out in modern Japan, but this band was a success, judging from the small crowd of elementary-school-age boys trailing it.

How far would I follow Hugh? Would I accept his paying not only for my shopping mistakes but also my legal defense? I didn't like the way I was feeling. I needed to get out of the hot Tokyo sun and do something that would steady my nerves. I headed for the open-air food market in Ameyoko Alley, and then back to Roppongi Hills.

I had almost finished preparing spinach-sesame rolls when I heard Hugh talking to someone in the apartment's entry hall. It was seven-thirty; maybe Hugh had caught up with Angus, who had left no note as to his whereabouts. When I went to the door, I saw Hugh's companion was Mr. Ota. I regretted the shrunken polo shirt and shorts I was wearing, as well as the fact I'd bought only three trout for the main course at dinner. I wondered how I could stretch it for four people as I offered our guest a pair of slippers.

"I'm sorry to disturb your cooking preparations," Mr. Ota began, apologetic as any Japanese person entering another person's household was supposed to be.

"We heard that you called Mr. Ota's office but refused to stay on the line. Where's Angus?" Not pausing to hear my answer, Hugh strode to the huge kitchen *tansu*, where he kept his magnificent Scotch collection. "I'll pour for all of us if you'll dig up some nibbles—do we have any more of the rice crackers?"

Good, he was signaling that Ota wasn't staying for dinner. I pulled a fresh bag of *sembei* down from the kitchen cupboard, delaying a little as I looked for a pretty Imari platter to arrange them on. The bad feeling I had while hearing the *chindonya* band's drumroll had returned.

When I brought in the snacks, Hugh patted the sofa beside him for me to sit down.

"Mr. Ota came at my invitation," he said. "The findings about Mr. Sakai's death are so odd, I thought he'd better be present in order to answer any questions you might have."

"The coroner released the autopsy results," Mr. Ota said briskly. "Mr. Sakai died of trauma to his trachea. It was, how do you say?" He made a crushing gesture with his hands. "To close the throat . . ."

"Strangulation," Hugh finished.

I shut my eyes, bringing back the picture of Sakai's head lolling on the car seat like a marionette with no one controlling the strings. The air-conditioning sud-

denly felt very cold; I felt the hairs on my arms prickling. I said, "It couldn't be Jun."

"You were very lucky," Hugh said.

"Please, Miss Shimura. I tend to agree with Mr.
Glendinning, although the police have not yet
indicted him. They will probably investigate a number of suspicious aliens, the foreign men who were in
the park—"

"That's racist! The man was kind enough to lend
me his telephone card."

"You took a telephone card?" Mr. Ota exclaimed.
"Don't you know that is contraband? Those men
take old cards and remagnetize them so they can be
used indefinitely. People go to prison for such
actions!"

"Great. Just pack my overnight bag, and I'll join
Jun Kuroi!"

"You won't have to." Hugh put an arm around
me. "Mr. Ota spent last night and much of today
clearing you."

"But I'm not under indictment—"

"There's no chance of it happening, because I have
given the notes from my investigation to the police."
Mr. Ota opened a notebook. "First I interviewed an
employee at Ueno Station who remembers you passing
through his wicket after the twelve-sixteen train
arrived. At twelve-twenty you refused a promotional
coupon from a hawker working the crosswalk by Ueno
Park. A jewelry vendor observed you waiting on a
bench, then saw Mr. Kuroi emerge a few minutes later
from the bushes. An elderly housewife looking out her
window saw you approach the illegally parked car five

minutes later. The woman saw your startled reaction after Kuroi opened the car door. Then she reported you ran back toward the park. After you were gone, Mr. Kuroi went into the car and made contact with the body. A big mistake."

"He was trying CPR," I said. "He learned it as a Boy Scout!"

"Who knows? The police are troubled that he moved the body. And the old woman who was watching—the neighborhood busybody, apparently—said that when Mr. Kuroi first drove into the neighborhood and parked the car, he didn't get out quickly. He spent a few minutes inside doing something she couldn't see."

Jun could have killed Sakai sometime during the car trip, parked, and come to get me. But he had no motive. Why didn't Mr. Ota see that?

"If I paid you, would you represent Jun Kuroi?" I asked.

Mr. Ota seemed to shrink in his chair. "I'm afraid I have a particularly high client load. . . ."

"Better to stay out of it," Hugh seconded. "Jun Kuroi's father owns the car dealership, so he can certainly afford a good lawyer."

"But I'm the one who dragged Jun into this. I have enough money left to pay Mr. Ota's retainer. Don't I?" I added when neither of them replied.

"Please, let's not talk about money." Mr. Ota clapped his hands together. "Actually, I must leave. My wife and daughter are expecting me for the evening meal."

After saying good-bye to Mr. Ota, Hugh attempted

to draw me into his arms. "I'm paying for your representation, Rei. Don't worry, it's not going to amount to much more than the cost of an aeroplane ticket to Thailand."

"A bargain!"

"You know I'd pay anything to keep you near me." Hugh's voice dropped to a husky whisper.

"I can't be bought." I pulled away and headed back to the kitchen, where I took the trout out of the fridge and resumed dinner preparations.

"I didn't mean it that way." Hugh followed me into the kitchen, carrying the dirty glasses. "And what if the situation was reversed? If you had an executive salary and I was living on waiter's tips or something, wouldn't you support me?"

"I've always thought people should try to support themselves," I said, imaging Hugh tricked up in a red polo shirt and tight black bell bottoms like the waiters at our favorite Mexican restaurant. "I want to keep living with you, but I feel badly about not paying for the apartment. I just fell into this life, and it's too expensive for me."

"You fell in love with me." Hugh played with my untouched glass of whiskey. "Or so you used to say."

I'd only said it once, during an incredible night when my body was breaking into a million pieces. My words had been unexpected, and Hugh had been overjoyed. Now he was whipping me with what I'd said.

Angus Glendinning chose this awkward moment to breeze in, dropping his backpack in the midst of the dinner preparations.

"What kind of fish is that? Are you going to fry it up with chips?" He tweaked a fishtail.

"It's trout, and it's going to be roasted with salt and ginger. I'll serve rice, no chips this time. If you want to speed things up, you could mince the ginger. Please wash your hands first." I tried to smile.

Angus trooped off, surprising me by not arguing.

"Talk to me, Rei," Hugh continued. "If you don't think your friend Jun killed Sakai, who else could have?"

"Ueno is rough turf, I noticed when we were driving through," Angus called from the powder room. "One of those manky-looking foreigners might have tried to steal the car when the antiques dealer was sleeping in it. The two fought, and Sakai lost."

It would have been nice to talk in private, but that was an impossibility, so when Angus came back, I told them both how I'd met Mrs. Sakai at the police station and learned the name of the *tansu*'s original owner.

"The wife could have done him! Where was she yesterday afternoon?" Angus asked, grating the ginger in rough strokes.

"Mr. Ota heard that she was at her in-laws'," Hugh said. "Rei, if there's a trial, you're going to have to testify about your catfight in the shop with Mrs. Sakai. There's no point in keeping the relationship hidden."

"I want to know when and where the *tansu* was altered. If I can find the original metal lock plates, I can restore the chest and send a note out to my other clients saying I have a genuine Meiji piece for sale." The idea had come to me while I was cooking.

"You're still trying to get your money back. Even after there's been a death!" Hugh sounded disgusted.

"It wouldn't hurt to look into it. Angus, I'm ready for the ginger." I concentrated on strewing the fish with its trimmings.

"If you hit the *tansu*'s original owner with accusations of fraud, he'll throw you out on your bum," Hugh warned. "How do you plan to handle it?"

"The right way. I have good Japanese manners," I snapped. Opening the oven, I was blasted with hot air. *How appropriate,* I thought, but kept it to myself.

8

"Who are you?" The distorted voice squawked through the intercom box on the high wall surrounding the Idetas' house. It was hard to tell if I was speaking to a man or a woman, which made me squirm a little. I knew nothing more than this was the residence of Nomu Ideta, according to the postman I'd asked a few streets over.

"An antiques dealer based in Roppongi," I answered.

"We have plenty of antiques, thank you."

I needed to sound more tempting. "I actually buy antiques on consignment and resell them for very handsome prices. If I could have a minute of your time, I would be happy to tell you more."

The voice did not reply. I was about to turn away when I heard the door creak open. A woman in her sixties with a sensible short haircut streaked with silver surveyed first my face, then my still-impeccable linen dress. I had stood all the way on the train to keep it that way and suffered a too-tight pair of Bally spectator pumps. I bowed deeply, and when I came up she had opened the door a little more.

"Just for a minute."

"*Ojama shimasu,*" I chirped happily, asking her to forgive my disturbance as I stepped over the threshold into the house's cool flagstone entryway. Here I hesitated, wondering if I should make a move to remove my shoes; perhaps she wanted me to remain in the *genkan* like a typical tradesperson. I ducked my head again and offered my card to her.

"You live in Roppongi," she said, nodding as if to reconfirm my worth.

"I have a very strong business there. Foreign diplomats, businesspeople," I said, eyeing the housewife's fancy apron emblazoned with the designer Hanae Mori's name. "Are you Mr. Ideta's wife?"

She shook her head. "No, I am the younger sister who takes care of him. The doctors recommended a nursing home, but in our case, it is not an option." The woman led me through the hall, past a room that looked empty save for a Buddhist ancestor altar containing black-and-white photographs of an old man and woman similar to the ones I'd seen at Nana Mihori's. Then we entered the living room.

Given the limits of space in most Japanese homes, I expected some clutter, but not anything like this. The ten-by-fourteen-foot room was literally packed with the past; hulking old *tansu* chests, tall ceramic vases, gilded screens. Miss Ideta wove through the obstacles to a group of low chairs by a sliding glass door overlooking the garden. "The entire house is crowded like this. Our father was a lifelong collector."

"It's wonderful, though, to leave such good investments for one's family."

Miss Ideta pressed together her thin lips. "It's been small relief. My brother is in very poor health. We had to move all the furniture out of his room to make room for the doctor's machines."

This was the second time she'd mentioned her brother's illness; clearly it was the central focus of her life. I asked, "So you've sold some pieces already?"

She nodded. "We found a wonderful man to help us. The only reason I'm talking to you, really, is we are curious to have a few more things appraised."

"How long were you working with this man?" I asked.

"Let's see, it was three months ago. A woman who sells antiques wrote me a nice letter offering her services, and I suggested to my brother—who has inherited everything, of course—that it would be worth knowing the value of his estate, given that his medical expenses could become even higher than they are now. The woman came to our house and liked many of our things, but she did not offer us the high prices that a second dealer I talked to promised. We decided to give our consignments to him. He took two *tansu*, a set of bowls, some lacquer . . . things we hadn't used for years."

"How did the dealer perform for you?"

"Everything sold at the prices he promised us! The only thing he had some trouble selling was our Edo-period *tansu*."

"He did sell it, though?"

"Of course," she said proudly. "Just this week. A customer had expressed interest but not commitment, so Mr. Sakai telephoned to ask whether we'd offer a slight discount. I told him yes, because he had done so well for us before, and sure enough, the chest sold."

"How much did you get for the *tansu*?" I asked in a businesslike manner.

"Seven hundred thousand yen."

I struggled to keep my face blank. So Sakai had kept 1.3 million yen for himself! In the future, I would not feel guilty about charging my clients a twenty percent finder's fee.

My next step was uncertain. I could continue to let her think I was an impartial dealer, or I could be honest. The latter seemed as though it had the potential to get me further, so I unzipped my handbag and took out an envelope. I said, "In the course of my business, I occasionally buy from stores. I was Mr. Sakai's customer, and he charged me two million for your *tansu*. Here's the receipt."

A range of expressions chased across her face; first incredulity, then dismay, and finally anger.

"We can't do much about it because he died last night. It was in the newspaper," I added, not wanting to be pressed on how close my involvement had been.

"The shop where he was working, Hita Fine Arts—aren't they liable for his actions?" she asked.

"They aren't, according to the general manager. Sakai was leasing the space and had full responsibility for his business dealings."

"I'm glad I didn't give him anything more."

It hit me then that she hadn't asked about the circumstances of Mr. Sakai's death. All she cared about was the fact she'd been cheated. I supposed it would make the rest of our conversation easier.

"I came today to find out some more about the *tansu*. Its history, for example."

She looked at the Polaroid snapshots I'd taken of the top, front, and sides of the chest and shook her head. "It looks like our piece, but I cannot be sure. I'm not the one who knows the furniture. My brother is. Ah, he's calling now."

"*Ocha!*" I'd heard a raspy voice in the distance, but finally its demand for tea was clearly audible.

"The master." She grimaced, making me wonder if she was trying to be ironic; after all, "master" was the polite word for "husband," too. "Will you wait here for a few minutes? I must take my brother his midmorning tea."

I sat while she moved around the kitchen but was out of my seat the moment she went upstairs with her tea tray. The first thing I did was look at all the superb Edo-period wood-block prints in the room. Her father must have started collecting well before World War II, because these prints were too expensive to buy in the current market. The furniture was a mix of older and newer pieces; amid Meiji-era pieces was a tea chest that struck me as 1920s Korean, probably built to Japanese specifications during its occupation of that country.

I ventured into the next room, which, as Miss Ideta had hinted, was crowded with more treasures.

In front of the Buddhist altar I saw family portraits, including a young man in an army uniform, giving credence to my belief the father had traveled to Korea. Next to his military portrait was a pair of parental portraits as dour as the ones at Nana Mihori's. They seemed to frown at me as I snooped around the room. Most interesting to me was an Edo-period calligraphy scroll hung elegantly alone in the *tokonoma* alcove; my eye wandered from its bold but unreadable parade of letters to the left edge, where a small tear had been crudely fixed with a piece of cellophane tape. If the Idetas had carelessly repaired a treasure like this, maybe they would have replaced the metalwork on the Sado Island *tansu*.

Miss Ideta had said her brother Nomu was the one who knew about furniture. I treaded up the dusty staircase and followed the odor of antiseptic and sickness that seemed to curl out of a room at the end of the short hall. Through a half-open door, I saw a tall IV stand with a plastic bag dripping some kind of fluid through a cord that went into the arm of an aged man lying in bed. There was also a hulking steel machine that could easily have supplanted several big *tansu* chests. I could understand the Idetas' space problem.

"What is it?" Miss Ideta sounded annoyed.

"The doorbell rang." Actually, the neighbor's had sounded, giving me a nice, semitruthful excuse.

"Thank you. I didn't hear it." Miss Ideta stood up.

"Who's the girl? She looks like one of our money-grubbing cousins." Mr. Ideta's voice was as sour as his smell, and his watery eyes ran over me critically as I bowed.

"You really are needing your dialysis treatment, *neh?* So disagreeable," Miss Ideta said. "This is Shimura-san. She, ah, just came to visit."

"What is your illness?" I asked when Miss Ideta had gone downstairs. I probably had less than a minute with the brother before she would be back.

"Diabetes. What kind of a nurse are you that you don't recognize dialysis equipment?" Mr. Ideta growled.

"I'm not a nurse. I came about the furniture."

"*Heh?*" It was as if someone had spiked him with a cattle prod. "Did you come to take more of my treasures away, like that bastard Sakai?"

"I thought you willingly sold to him."

"The only thing I agreed to were appraisals. But living upstairs like this, in bed, do you think I know what's missing downstairs? My *hibachi*, my *tansu* . . . all could be gone, for what that wretch of a woman tells me."

Mr. Ideta's age and illness were leading him into paranoia. I reassured him, "From what your sister told me, the two of you agreed to sell a limited number of possessions. There are many things still downstairs."

"My scroll—is it still safe?"

"The one somebody repaired with tape? That actually was not a good idea—"

"Don't be ridiculous!" He pounded so hard on the little tray by his bed that his tea spilled. "I tell you, it's my scroll and it's perfect!"

"I don't know about that." I rescued the cup and

sat down in his sister's chair. "When you make alterations to old things, they usually lose value. In fact, I wanted to ask you if you remember alterations being made to the metalwork of your Sado Island *tansu*."

"There was no need for repairs. My father kept those pieces in excellent condition and passed them on to me. They're good enough to be placed in the Tokyo National Museum, which is where I may leave them, although my sister will be upset—"

"What upsets me? Older brother, you're getting too excited." Miss Ideta stood in the doorway. I had been so caught up in Nomu Ideta's stormy recital that I hadn't heard her light footsteps.

"We were talking about how nice your family collection is," I improvised. "It's a shame your brother is reluctant to have further appraisals."

"I could have told you that," Miss Ideta said, coolly contradicting what she'd told me ten minutes earlier.

I had broken the rules and was being punished. What could I say?

"No one was at the door, but the nurse is coming any minute. I'm afraid I must get things in order." And with that, Miss Ideta ordered me out.

9

I still had a workout date with Akemi Mihori. I could have canceled, but she would have thought me a coward. Given all that I'd been through in the last twenty-four hours, it suddenly seemed very important to follow through on something I'd promised, to see something turn out right.

I had expected Angus Glendinning to be out of the apartment, but he was on the living room sofa when I arrived home to change clothes for running. He had decided that he wanted to come with me. Thinking of Hugh, I faked enthusiasm, figuring that while I was with Akemi, he could participate in the foreigners' Zen orientation at the temple.

During the hour-long ride to Kamakura, I tried to read a Banana Yoshimoto novel about sexual obsession, while Angus hummed a song by Bush called "Everything Zen" in honor of the occasion. When I asked him to desist, he began pestering me with questions.

"How is Zen different from the original Buddhism? Don't they all worship the same guy?"

"Well, the various sects of Buddhism support the idea that the world and self are just illusions." I tried to remember what I'd studied in my Asian religions class in college. "All Buddhists try to reach enlightenment by ridding themselves of selfish desires. But Zen worshipers work really hard at it, sitting in the lotus position for hours, moving past pain into something else. I've also heard that they think abandoning rational thought can lead to a heightened stage of inner consciousness."

"Oh, like a Zen attitude. Easy come, easy go. That's what I have!"

I shook my head. "Could you sit perfectly motionless in a full lotus position all day, enduring a priest's shouting and hitting you with the discipline stick? Are you humble enough?"

Angus shook his head. "Of course not! I can't believe this judo woman lives that way. Hugh said her family have plenty of money."

"They are wealthy. Consider all the cash donations coming in, and not having to pay taxes. Only one member of each generation actually has to work at the temple. The other Mihoris can dabble in sports, cultural arts, community voluntarism." Like Nana Mihori, saving land for the Kamakura Green and Pristine Society.

"Not bad, but hardly Zen!" Angus snorted.

When the train trip ended, we walked an uncomfortable fifteen minutes to Horin-ji. As we passed under the towering temple gate, I pointed Angus toward the magnificent main hall fronted by hundreds of pigeons and camera-clicking tourists.

"Remember to remove your sandals at the main hall's steps. It will probably be a lot like what you experienced in India. If you get confused, ask the other foreigners for help." I waved my hand at a European tour group.

"But they're German!" Angus protested.

I walked off, reminding myself that Hugh had once irritated me, and I'd grown to adore him. But Angus was not the same. He dismissed people, foods, anything that was different from what he had known. He was into the self, but it had nothing to do with the Buddhist ideal.

I located Akemi, who was twisted into a pretzel-style stretch, on a rubber mat outside her *dojo*. She looked at me sideways and said, "I didn't think you'd come."

I sighed and said, "I should warn you, I've only run once so far. It didn't go very well, and I got shin-splints."

"You did it, though?" Akemi reversed position. "That's really great. Get down on the ground. Ten minutes' stretching before we go."

The trail began straight and wide: perfect, Akemi said, for the sprinting practice I'd want to begin a few months into training. After five hundred yards, the trail narrowed and began to wind through cypress and cedar trees. In Horin-ji's dark brown and green woodland you could almost forget the heat, or maybe it really was cooler away from the steel and cement of Tokyo.

When we started, I expected Akemi to bound on ahead. Instead she jogged backward at my speed for a few minutes, then told me to run more slowly.

"You aren't going at a consistent speed. Too much accelerating and decelerating. If you were driving a car, the police would pull you over." She switched so she was running sideways.

I had been thinking about stopping for a walking break, but now I obediently slowed and matched Akemi's slow, even pace. After a few minutes, my breathing had improved to the point that I could talk.

"Are you sure this is really running?"

"You're too competitive." Akemi chuckled.

"And you aren't?" I shot back.

"Competing against yourself is the issue. If you worry too much about whether you measure up, and set yourself running at a pace that's not natural for you, you'll never give yourself the confidence you need."

"My problem is overconfidence," I gasped as we ran along. "I was too sure about the *tansu*. I didn't make the time to examine it properly."

"I read in the newspaper that the man working at Hita Fine Arts died. It's strange how things turned out."

"I didn't want him to die. I just wanted my money back. He was dishonest, pocketing 1.3 million on a consignment—"

"How do you know that? It wasn't in the paper."

"I met the family who sold the chest to him." Over the course of our conversation, my breath was smoothing out.

"Really? They must be angry!"

"Yes, but there's nothing we can do. I went back to Hita Fine Arts and they refused to be held responsible for Sakai's sales." Feeling depressed, I changed the topic. "Are we safe from your mother? Doesn't she walk here sometimes?"

"I already told you my mother's gone out today, but you'll never need to worry even if you want to practice here alone. My mother once used the teahouse along this way, but after she built our new house with a tearoom inside, she stopped coming."

"This teahouse looks really old," I said, glad for an excuse to slow down as we came upon a building little bigger than a child's playhouse. A few tiles were hanging haphazardly off the roof, and the sliding doors opening the house to the woods were cracked, but there was a charming, round window that looked ideal for moon viewing.

"Watch your pace, and picture your success! On the last lap, you can walk and do your stretching here," Akemi ordered.

We circled the track again before I was permitted to walk. Akemi accelerated, legs flashing faster and faster until she disappeared in a blur. I had been walking only a few minutes when she passed me again.

All the sliding doors were swollen by humidity, so I had to shove hard to enter the small, square room floored in *tatami*. True to Zen style, the teahouse was decorated only with a chest for tea ceremony bowls. A musty smell told me dampness and insects had probably gotten inside the *tatami* and the few *zabuton*, cushions for sitting, stacked in the corner.

"You're not stretching!" Akemi yelled as she passed again, so I went outside and did some hurdler's stretches. What I really wanted was water. A small stream trickled near by, but I didn't trust its cleanliness. I was preparing to head back to the water fountain near the temple when Akemi came around one final time holding two plastic bottles.

"You read my mind," I told her, sucking down the contents of the bottle she handed me.

"Water is very important. I had these chilling in the stream behind the house." Akemi balanced her foot against the teahouse wall and stretched. Her breathing dropped to normal within a minute. I was jealous, because I was as drenched in sweat and as exhausted as during my first run at Yoyogi Park. Still, I calculated that I'd run a mile without stopping. Akemi had shown me I had the strength.

"Has my mother called you?" Akemi finished her bottle and went back to stretching. "She's forgiven you, I think."

"How did that happen?" I was stunned.

"I pointed out how unfair she'd been. It was silly of her not to take what you'd bought for her. It was going into my room, and I don't care at all about its age."

I voiced something I'd been wondering about. "If your room does get redecorated with Japanese antiques, what will happen to your medals, all the things that are a part of you?"

"She wants me to put them in storage. It's silly to keep them around, as I haven't won a match in ten years."

"But you're always training in the *dojo*."

"It's just a hobby. I do a few exhibitions." She shrugged.

"Why don't you work at the temple? You're the only child, so I assume you'll inherit."

Akemi shook her head. "In Buddhism, like your Catholicism, women can't become priests. My cousin Kazuhito gets the temple. I'm sure my parents built me the *dojo* to ease their guilt."

"I'm an only child, too. Growing up, I felt I had everything I could possibly want, except the most important—having someone to play with." I thought about how I'd been taken everywhere by my parents, who taught me all about restaurant and museum manners but nothing about playground sports. Having spent time with Angus, I was pretty sure I wouldn't want a brother, but I would have loved an older sister who could have shown me how to climb across the jungle gym. Someone like Akemi.

"There's nothing worse than having someone forced into your life. Kazuhito came to live with us when we were both twelve. Suddenly he was getting the best pieces of fish at dinner, fantastic gifts, the best position near my father in the temple."

"How are things these days?"

"We coexist," Akemi said tightly.

I listened to a siren ringing in the distance and wondered what would happen to her after her father died. Would she be forced to abandon the spacious house for a small apartment? What inheritance could she carry with her?

"Does Kazuhito work at the temple now?" I asked.

"He's the vice abbot, which means he oversees

the temple's business, our collection of antiquities, and the cultural programs like foreigners' outreach. I don't know why, given that he hardly speaks a word of English—"

"You could do that," I said. "Your English is excellent!"

"Like I said, my sex precludes me from ever being a priest. I could only marry one, but turning into someone like my mother would be like death."

Akemi was getting wound up, and I wanted to keep talking. Too bad it was time for me to leave. I sighed and said, "I have to go to the main hall to pick up Hugh's beloved brother. The foreigners' orientation must be over by now."

"Don't you want to shower first?" Akemi looked at me with concern.

"No! I didn't bring towels or a change of clothing." I'd been in communal showers and baths before, but the prospect of being naked with Akemi made me nervous. She had already commented on my legs; I didn't want to hear more.

"You must not enter a temple dirty. It's against Buddhist etiquette," she said.

"I'll stand outside. I'm sure Angus will be waiting."

"Whatever you want." She wrinkled her nose, making her opinion clear.

"On Saturday I'm having my party. You're still coming, aren't you?" I asked.

"Maybe. It depends on my schedule."

Her schedule seemed pretty freewheeling to me, but I didn't press her. After all, I'd chickened out about the shower.

❊   ❊   ❊

Angus was standing on the wooden hallway that ran around the exterior of the main hall, deep in conversation with a Japanese man wearing long indigo robes. The priest looked ageless, given his smooth, shaved head and lively eyes. To my horror, he noticed me and beckoned.

"Shimura-san, please come up! This young man explained you have been exercising my daughter!"

The priest speaking good English was undoubtedly Akemi's father, the abbot and owner of the temple itself. If he told his wife I was on the grounds, she'd be furious.

"I'm sorry to interrupt you like this," I said, unlacing my running shoes and hoping my socks wouldn't leave damp marks on the smooth cedar steps leading up to the temple.

"We had an emergency!" Angus was looking more excited than I'd ever seen him. "Our priest conked out during the meditation."

"He is talking about my nephew. Angus-san saved his life," Abbot Mihori said.

"Yeah, it was utter madness," Angus rattled on. "We were all sitting cross-legged and staring into our souls or something. It had gotten pretty quiet and I guess all the others were in a trance, because when the priest fell over, I was the only one who noticed. At first I wondered if it was part of, you know, the temple routine."

"Fortunately, Angus-san used his eyes and his common sense. He left the meditation group to summon help," Mr. Mihori said.

So Angus was a hero. I'd congratulate him later; at the moment I was more concerned about Kazuhito's health. Now I realized the siren I'd heard had been for him.

"What happened?" I asked.

"My son had one of the occasional diabetic fainting spells he's suffered since his teens. I keep a special high-sugar drink in my office, and after I administered it, he regained consciousness. The paramedics took him to the hospital. I'm on my way to find my daughter to drive me there."

Diabetes was serious. I thought of Nomu Ideta, the old man lying miserably in bed in Denen-Chofu. Abbot Mihori seemed extremely calm for someone who'd just seen his heir collapse.

"They want me to come back for a wild festival." Angus interrupted my troubled thoughts.

"The Tanabata festival," Abbot Mihori clarified. "Kamakura's celebration is not as big as those celebrated elsewhere, but I think the atmosphere is considerably more scenic. We have a parade of floats along the sea, and archery and dancing at the Hachiman Shrine. . . ."

"Sounds okay, as long as there's not too much religious mumbo-jumbo," Angus commented.

I blushed, embarrassed at what he was saying, but Abbot Mihori took it in stride. "You will be happy that the festival is secular, a mix of Japanese and Chinese legends. It's the story of two star lovers—"

"Do you mean star-crossed lovers?" Angus interrupted.

"That too," Mr. Mihori said, smiling. "The story

begins with the Princess Orihime, who lived on a star, where she worked as a weaver. Her father, the emperor of the heavens, arranged for her to meet a handsome cowherd who lived on a different star in the west coast of the Milky Way. When the two met, they fell so deeply in love that Princess Orihime neglected her weaving. The emperor was furious and did not let them see each other again. The exception is once a year, on the night of July seventh, when birds form a bridge over the river of heaven so the lovers can meet. But you will learn more about that on the festival evening. Will you stay with your brother in Tokyo through that time?"

"I'll be here as long as Rei puts up with me."

"Ah so desu ka?" Is that so? Mr. Mihori's wise eyes studied me. I wondered how much Angus had told him about our communal living situation—and whether he'd approve of my exercising his daughter after all.

10

On the train ride home I rested against the door, watching Angus sandwich himself between two pretty coeds from Sophia University who had been practicing English together. Within minutes they were telling Angus how fascinating he was, a world traveler who looked like Harrison Ford and the lead singer of Simply Red combined. Did he know that band? Did he know Tokyo nightlife?

"Simply Red's a naff band," Angus grumbled, but moved closer to get a look down their halter tops. I wasn't surprised that when we reached Roppongi, Angus foisted his backpack on me and headed off with his new friends for what I guessed would be a night of revelry. I walked home, sweating and brooding. Passing a newsstand on Roppongi-dori, I was jarred by a tabloid with a front-page photograph of Jun Kuroi. Or rather, photographs. A montage had been made from various snapshots of Jun as a young high school graduate, as a smiling salesman at the

Toyota dealership, and finally in a T-shirt and black leather jacket, his Elvis drag. I bought one and scanned the article for my name, one of the few Japanese things I could read.

Blessedly, my name was not there. But I was worried about Jun. What did the story say about him? Was he the victim of circumstances, as I'd insisted to Hugh? Or could Jun be tied to Nao Sakai in some other way? After all, both men were from Hita. They could have known each other and had a relationship that I knew nothing about.

In the apartment, I kept worrying about the situation. I started dinner, and the rice was just beginning to steam when Hugh arrived around seven.

"Where's my brother?" Hugh asked when he found me in the kitchen alone.

"I took him to Kamakura, and on the way back he met two college girls. I'm surprised that he made Japanese friends so quickly." I paused. "Maybe it's a good sign. He's the apple of Abbot Mihori's eye—you will never believe what happened at the temple!"

"How long do you expect he'll be out?" Hugh seemed uninterested in Horin-ji.

"I don't know. It's happy hour for a few hours longer, and then who knows? He might want to go dancing. I hope he can find his way home."

"For a few hours, who cares?" Hugh kissed my neck, and I knew instantly what was on his mind. It had been too long. Maybe this was why we had been bickering so much. Since Angus had arrived, we had been too paranoid to do anything in the bedroom but whisper.

In the bedroom, door firmly locked against any

potential intruders, I turned up the air-conditioning and started unbuttoning Hugh's shirt. His skin was still peeling and required careful navigation. I wasn't that aroused to begin with, but there was something about the way we fit together that made pleasure unavoidable. I adored him, I really did.

Afterward I lay against Hugh's warm, broad back, thinking that the rice would be perfectly done by now. If only I had the energy to get up and put a tray together for us, maybe with some leftover vegetables from the night before.

The telephone rang imperiously on Hugh's bed-side table.

"Ignore it," Hugh murmured, half asleep.

"It could be a client," I said, grabbing it swiftly and answering with my name. It wasn't any of my ladies, though, but a Japanese man who spoke English so fast and slangily I had to ask his identity twice before recognizing him as Kozo, Hugh's favorite bar-tender in days past. Kozo was telling me he'd moved from the late, great English Pub to Club Isn't It. He was telephoning because a customer refusing to pay his bill had asked for Hugh Glendinning.

"Hugh cannot take criminal cases, especially in Japan. All he does are corporate contracts," I said firmly.

"But his brother says—"

"His brother?" I repeated.

Hugh wrestled the phone from my grip, and I got up to dress. I had made sure Angus had five thousand yen when I'd left him at the station. Kozo had said something about Angus trying to walk out on an eleven-thousand-yen tab. Even with the price of drinks in Tokyo, that was something. I didn't want to calculate how much he'd drunk.

Club Isn't It was squeezed into an upper floor of a small high-rise nightclub building typical for Roppongi. We rode up a tiny elevator with a pack of Japanese girls wearing ankle-length dresses with five-inch platform shoes. It was hard to tell who was more out of place, myself in a midthigh-length cotton sundress or Hugh in his classy but corporate Paul Smith suit.

Three burly Americans who looked like marines, save for the earrings, inspected Hugh's leather briefcase for weapons and contraband before letting us in. Admission was free, but every beverage sold cost one thousand yen. Scam, Isn't It? would have been a better name for the place. I pushed my way through a group of green-haired kids gyrating to Prince. I remembered reading in *Tokyo Journal* about a series of drug busts in the place.

Angus was sitting at the bar, and when he saw us, he gave an exaggerated wave. "Dad and Mum. Thanks for coming." He had a little bit of blood running from his puffed-up lip. Someone had hit him.

The bouncer who had been guarding him stepped aside slightly and addressed Hugh. "The bastard who tried to run out on his tab is related to you?"

"I'm here to settle the bill, nothing else," Hugh replied. His grip on my hand had tightened painfully. He was making an effort to control himself.

"He's lucky Kozo knows you. I'd have sent him through the wall if he hadn't stopped me."

"And then you'd be facing a lawsuit," Hugh said tersely. "Your job's done. Why don't you leave?"

"Hugh-san, my apology." Kozo ran up to us and bowed, an incongruous vision of old Japanese etiquette in a strobe-lit jungle. "I am certain your brother did not understand our prices. . . ."

"A bunch of people swarmed around me and started ordering drinks. I assumed everyone was in for himself, but it didn't turn out that way."

"What happened to your Japanese friends?" I asked. The young women had been well dressed; I was sure they had money.

"Who? Oh, you mean those chicks from the train. They went home hours ago, said they didn't like the vibe."

"Kozo, what's the damage?" Hugh asked.

"Eleven thousand yen."

"I'll throw in an extra tenner for the trouble caused to you and any other inconvenienced members of the staff. Excepting, of course, the bastard who hit my brother."

There was some rumbling from the bouncer, but following a sharp glance from Kozo, he went back to the door.

"So, you want a drink?" Angus asked Hugh in a slurred voice.

The show of wrath I expected never appeared. Instead, my lover sighed and said, "Very much so. Let's go to the flat."

All Hugh said to Angus on the way home was that he should put an ice pack on his eye if he wanted to look remotely decent for the party. He said nothing about the debt or how Angus had managed to get himself in such a stupid situation.

"This town is too much—a thousand yen for Budweiser! That's eight dollars U.S. It was fifty cents a beer in Thailand. I should have stayed there. Within a week I'll be skint," Angus complained from the backseat.

"None of that, brother. I'm glad you came." Hugh elbowed me in the ribs, encouraging me to say something. "And as for not having enough money, I'll lend you my cash card so you won't be in an emergency situation again."

"A cash card would be brilliant. What's the code? Could you give it to me now?"

"How long are you staying?" I asked Angus without turning to look at him.

"As long as I'm having fun!"

"Maybe you could get a job." His diction was so poor he couldn't teach English conversation, and he didn't speak enough Japanese to wait tables. But beneath the grime, he had Glendinning good looks. I had it suddenly. "You could model! I have a friend at a good agency, and I bet that Hugh's lawyer Mr. Ota could set up a work visa for you."

"I'm hardly the fly guy type," Angus snickered.

"Don't worry about his working, Rei," Hugh said with unusual sharpness. "Like all men, Angus will have the rest of his life to worry about earning. I'll take care of him for the time being."

Like all men. Were Hugh's words merely sexist, or more of a direct jab at me? Even though I was self-employed, he paid most of the household bills. Feeling both furious and ashamed, I started pulling on my door handle to get out the minute Hugh parked the Windom in its garage space.

"Hang on." Hugh pushed a lever on the door on his side, releasing the lock.

"Neato," Angus said. "The two of you can play all night, but will you let me go?"

"No. You're going to like this, Rei. I've figured something out!" Hugh took me by the shoulders and kissed me, the last thing I expected.

"If you're going to snog, I'm leaving," Angus said, jumping out. I watched him go to the building entrance and get in using the key I'd given him. Now we were alone.

"Rei, don't you see? This could have happened at Ueno Park. Young Elvis—Jun Kuroi, I mean—power-locked the doors, which meant, to him, that Sakai couldn't get out. But while he was left alone in the car, Sakai figured things out. He only had to move the lever on the driver's side to unlock the car."

"And Nao Sakai let the killer in?"

"Maybe. This puts new light on the situation, doesn't it? I'll ring Mr. Ota tomorrow." Sounding satisfied, Hugh flipped the lock so I could open my door.

"Why do you care?" I asked. "Two days ago you said Jun was a fiendish killer."

"Not in those words, and I've been reading about him in the papers. It turns out he's just twenty, Angus's age. I guess the big brother in me is kicking in."

"Or gone into overdrive!" The comparison of my friend to his spoiled brother rankled.

Hugh sighed. "Not having siblings of your own,

I don't expect you to understand. All I ask is that you refrain from trying to discipline my brother."

I was glad that Hugh was going to urge Mr. Ota to help Jun, but I felt pretty injured that he thought I'd been trying to boss Angus around. I replayed how I might have handled the situation better as I lay trying to go to sleep, but didn't get much rest. Awake at 5:30 A.M., I watched the sky outside the window lighten. I imagined the feeling of cool morning air on my skin. Suddenly I had to get out.

I dressed quickly in the shorts I'd rinsed out the night before, plus a fresh undershirt from Hugh's drawer. In the entryway I put on my sneakers and grabbed my Sony Walkman off the coffee table. My Echo and the Bunnymen tape had been replaced with Nine Inch Nails. I didn't want to spend time looking for the right tape, so I went out. When I started moving, I found that the gloomy, industrial beat matched my mood.

The sun was rising over Roppongi—fortunately for me, because the sidewalk was still littered with beer cans, discarded paper fliers, and take-out food wrappers, the detritus of a Friday night. The longer I lived in the neighborhood, the more I disliked its status as the city's nightlife center. When Hugh had first leased his apartment, the area had been known for classy international restaurants and discos, but now you couldn't walk two blocks without seeing an "image club" where men paid for the chance to undress faux schoolgirls. These days, the slogan emblazoned on the overpass at Roppongi Crossing—HIGH TOUCH TOWN—could be read as a nasty double entendre.

After a dreadful sprint to beat the traffic lined up at the crossing, I slowed down on the other side of Gaien Higashi-dori and fell into a meditative state. Tonight was my big cocktail party. At six o'clock the hordes would descend. I would greet them all by name while supervising the caterers and trying to sell my wares. "*How are you?*" I imagined people asking. I couldn't tell them how bad things were.

Approaching Nogizaka Station, I had to dodge early commuters. Most of Japan worked at least a half day on Saturday; I thought about the Middle Eastern man who had lent me the telephone card in Ueno. Maybe he slept there at night. If I could find him, I might learn something that could help Jun. Glad for an excuse to stop running, I reached into my shorts pocket for change and headed down the subway stairs.

To my disappointment, Ueno Park was deserted except for foreign backpackers sleeping on benches and a group of senior citizens performing *tai chi* exercises. My antiques-dealing friend Mr. Ishida was in their midst; I waved, but he didn't break his pose.

I wasn't going to find the man in the park, so I decided to head into Ameyoko Alley to buy a cup of coffee. Since it was now past 7 A.M., a few places had their doors open. I wandered awhile, looking for the cheapest menu, when I was startled by one called Old Tehran that was decorated with a red and green flag.

Inside, four dark-haired, foreign men sat at a vinyl-covered table. In front of each was a super-tiny coffee cup. A thick, almost chocolatey aroma wafted toward me, and I felt my stomach growl.

I didn't remember much about the man who had

helped me except for his scar. I made a slight bow to
the group and began speaking in slow Japanese.

"Telephone cards? I don't know what you mean.
I'm just here having breakfast." A lean young man in
his early twenties ran his hand through his short,
curly hair and looked at me. I could swear he was the
man who had offered me ten cards for two thousand
yen, but I didn't have the nerve to say that.

"This man was very helpful to me, do you understand? He lent me his telephone card, and it's still got
forty units on it." I fished the card out of my pocket
and stretched it out, a slim piece of plastic decorated
with two cuddling kittens.

The young man took the card in hand and looked
it over quickly. "It's a new card, not recycled. I can
tell from where it's been punched along the side."

"Good. I just want to give it back to the right man."

"Everyone carries telephone cards. How do you
expect us to know who had this one?" one of his
companions grumbled. "And how do we know
you're not police?"

"They aren't forced to carry ID like this." I offered
my alien registration card, and as it passed from one
work-weathered hand to another, the thought flashed
through me that I might not get it back. Legitimate
registration cards allowed you to work, and were cov-
eted by those the government would rather keep out.
Maybe someone's wife or girlfriend would wind up
with my card. Where was the shop's proprietor, anyway? In the two minutes I'd been in the brightly lit
café, I was getting spooked.

"So you are also a foreigner? Your name is

Japanese." The oldest man in the group cocked his head and looked at me more closely.

"Yes, I'm from the States," I said, keeping my eyes on my card.

"Which part? My brother has a Persian restaurant in New York, Upper East Side."

"I don't know New York. I'm from San Francisco." This elicited some discussion among the crowd, none of which I understood. My registration card traveled back though the rough hands and was placed in my palm.

"The telephone card—you say someone lent it to you? On which night?" someone else asked.

"Last Wednesday night," I answered.

"The night of the killing. It was bad for all of us. Hassan was kicked around by a fascist policeman."

The wide blue curtain that had obscured the café kitchen from view moved, and a voice said in English, "I remember her."

The scar-faced man emerged wearing a clean white apron over a short-sleeved shirt and blue jeans.

"My name is Rei Shimura. Are you Hassan?" I asked with a tremendous rush of guilt.

"No, I am called Mohsen. It was not necessary for you to return my card, but thank you anyway."

"I needed to call the police. I never expected them to hassle any of you. I wish I'd gone in the other direction. . . . I'm sorry."

"Where else could you have gone?" Mohsen asked wryly. "That street had no exit. Everyone who comes and goes must pass the park."

"Do you recall seeing anyone walking that way before I did?"

"Sure. But no one who looked dangerous."

"Would you tell me what they looked like, anyway? This is worth a lot to me." I lowered my voice, although there was no escaping the attention of the men at the table.

"What are you going to give? Five thousand yen, what I earn washing coffee cups twelve hours a day?" He laughed bitterly.

"I don't mean to offend you—"

"There is no secret! I had nothing to do with it!" Mohsen sounded exasperated.

"My friend is in trouble. I need to know who you saw for his sake."

He hesitated, then said, "I saw an older man I recognized from the neighborhood because he spits at me. There were three children, all in school uniform. There was also a Japanese woman. She was odd—she wore a bright *kimono* and an old-fashioned hairstyle like the performers in the music groups that walk around sometimes."

"*Chindonya*," I said, thinking of the traveling band I'd seen on Thursday. "Did the woman have a mole?"

"There was no pet with her."

"I mean a black birthmark. On the lady's nose." I pointed to mine for emphasis.

"Who could tell? Her face was covered with white makeup. That's why I could not tell the age."

The costume made complete sense; in this old section of Tokyo, whoever had worn it could pass as someone working in a tourist shop or restaurant or even, as Mohsen suggested, a musician.

"That's interesting information. I wish I could do something for you," I said to Mohsen.

"Why? You have returned my card. Your mission is complete."

Something about his excellent English and his manners made me hesitate. "You are from Iran? What kind of job did you have there?"

"I studied accounting. After university I had hoped to work for a firm in Tehran, but our economy was very bad. There were no jobs, so I came here."

He came to sweat through life as a 3K worker, enduring insults and spitting from locals. It wasn't fair. "Mohsen, how late do you work tonight?"

"The café closes at seven. Why?"

"I'm having a party. There will be a number of businessmen, Japanese and foreign. Maybe . . ."

"You think they may decide they like me and offer to sponsor me for the work visa? You really are a crazy girl."

I shrugged. "There are no guarantees. If worse comes to worst, you'll have a nice *sashimi* dinner."

We were teetering on the edge of something, our roles as legal and illegal foreigners transcended. Having talked with Mohsen and his group, I would never again automatically use my hands to give the X of refusal when approached. I would listen to them, as they had listened to me.

"*Sashimi*. I've never had it." Mohsen sounded thoughtful.

"You either love it or hate it!" I said, knowing now that he'd come.

11

There are only so many ways to carve an ice fish. I said as much to Miss Wada, who was still tinkering with the tail of the frosty centerpiece at six o'clock. The concierge had telephoned that the first wave of guests was on its way up, and I was on the sofa, drinking my first glass of wine and trying to forget an argument with Hugh.

"Where's your new dress?" he had asked when I'd come out of the bedroom in a little black crocheted cocktail dress I'd worn a million times before.

"Sorry. There wasn't time to have it made." The truth was I had forgotten about the luminous red silk he'd brought me from Thailand.

"I gave you Winnie's seamstress's number. Did you even call her?" Hugh leaned against the counter in gray flannel trousers and a starched Turnbull and Asser shirt with one button undone, his only concession to the supposedly relaxed nature of the evening ahead.

"You know I love the idea of a new dress," I soothed. "I'll go to the seamstress when life isn't so crazy."

"What is that thing you're wearing, vintage?" His lip curled.

"It's from Joseph Magnin, and my mother paid a small fortune for it in 1968! She wore it to some big parties."

"Don't tell my colleagues, okay?" Hugh snapped before going to open the door to the first guests, a group of Sendai executives—salarymen, as they were called in Japan—and a few wives. It turned out that a number of couples had fibbed to their baby-sitters that they were going to a wedding, as it was considered terrible for a wife to abandon care of her children for any other kind of social engagement.

"I don't know how you'll like the food, but please try something," I said, urging them toward the buffet. In addition to *sashimi*, the table was loaded with ginger-marinated shrimp, a salad made from rice noodles and slivered vegetables, and various pickled vegetables arranged on perfect bamboo leaves. As I'd expected, the item the women liked most was a *trompe l'oeil* country landscape—a bed of vinegar-flavored rice garnished with grilled eel and lotus root mountains, and cherry trees made from pink ginger slices and black seaweed. Later, Miss Wada and her assistants would serve coffee, tea, and honeydew melons stuffed with strawberries, kiwi, and mango, as well a tray of cream puffs my aunt had dropped off earlier in the day, and some brownies that Angus had spontaneously baked during the afternoon.

"No meat? The Japanese expect you to spend

some money." Winnie Clancy delivered her opinion over my shoulder. I turned around and took in her tasteful but boring blue silk sheath, feeling glad I hadn't gone to her seamstress after all.

"You fixed roast beef for Hugh while I was out of town, didn't you? There's plenty left in the fridge, but I was afraid it wasn't fresh enough to serve." I stared her down, giving as good as I got.

"I'm surprised any of the roast is left! Hugh and I ate supper together—just the two of us, such a shame that Piers was in London—and he asked for a second helping. If I were you, darling, I wouldn't deny him."

I had a good escape when I saw Mohsen, the Iranian immigrant from the coffee shop. He must have borrowed a business suit from someone. The sleeves were slightly too long, but it was immaculately pressed. He looked every bit the southern European professional.

"You look different, Miss Shimura." He smiled when I greeted him. "I think you should wear dresses instead of gym shorts."

"I agree with you." Hugh had come up behind me. "I'm Hugh Glendinning, Rei's partner and a lawyer representing Sendai Limited, where most of the Japanese chaps standing around here work. You must be Mohsen."

"My full name is Mohsen Zavar." He looked startled at Hugh's outstretched hand, but took it, adding, "I am currently looking for meaningful employment."

"Rei told me you're an accountant—with your excellent language abilities, I don't see why you couldn't be hired by one of the multinational oil companies. Piers

Clancy, the pale fellow arguing with his wife by the window, knows the managing director of every British company in Tokyo, at least. Let's go over for a chat."

Hugh liked getting people together, redefining lives. It often worked. He bore off Mohsen as his latest offering to international commerce, and I got another glass of wine, breathing easily for the first time that night. Then I realized something had changed: the subdued Holly Cole jazz ballads I had slipped into the tape deck had given way to the gritty, anguished growling of Nine Inch Nails. Angus was slumped against the balcony railing, smoking a cigarette and talking with a group of young people in dark clothing and hairstyles ranging from a green crewcut to long orange dreadlocks. As I moved toward them I recognized a few European faces from Club Isn't It, including a pale, drugged-out-looking girl from New Zealand who often stood outside a strip club trying to recruit customers.

Hugh's corporate guests weren't mingling with these ragged newcomers, but they definitely had noticed the change in music. Masuhiro Sendai, the company chairman, was tapping his foot, and a few of the Sendai wives had started to dance. I had been planning to tell Angus to put the jazz back on, but I changed my mind, deciding the edgy music wasn't all bad. It was waking up the party. Akemi Mihori, who had just walked in, waved at me with a delighted expression. I headed for her but stopped dead when I saw Nana Mihori standing beside her. One of the Sendai executives approached Nana, who smiled and greeted him. Old friends. In the instant that she

began a conversation with the man, Akemi slipped
away and joined me.

"Sorry about coming late, and with my mother."
She tugged a bit nervously at her body-hugging red
jersey dress. It suited her, revealing every muscle in
her body. "She found out where I was going and
insisted she come along. I'm sorry."

"I'll survive." I wiped a hand over my damp brow.
"What do you want to drink, green tea or lemonade?"

"I want something stronger. Oh, super! You have
Guinness stout."

"You drink beer?" I had thought Akemi was a
health food freak. I poured the Guinness, which
Hugh had taken pains to serve cool but not icy cold,
into a tall glass. I started my third glass of wine.

"Stout is rich in iron, did you know that? Very
healthy for women." Akemi said. "Hey, is that your
boyfriend on the balcony, the long-haired one?"

I laughed shakily. "No, that's the younger
brother. Angus."

"A woman living with two men . . . it's almost like
a fantasy, isn't it? Your Angus resembles the lead singer
of Simply Red. Still, he doesn't look strong enough to
please me." Akemi took a generous sip of her beer.

"I thought you hated men!" It flew out of me
before I could think.

"I might sleep with a man, but I wouldn't be kept
by him. There's a difference."

A clutch of Sendai salarymen came up to ask for
autographs. Akemi signed dutifully, a mask falling
over her strong features as she answered their giddy
questions in polite Japanese. Yes, she was a friend of

mine. No, she wasn't competing again. It was time to let the younger generation have a chance.

The caterer sidled up to ask if I wanted her to send someone for more alcohol; it was just seven, and three quarters of the wine was gone.

"More wine, definitely," I said, thinking I needed another glass. Out of the corner of my eye, I saw that Akemi had walked away from the salarymen and was talking to Angus. She seemed to be taking the offensive; I was amused to see him backed up against a wall, trying to explain something with a lot of hand movements. What was she trying to get out of him?

I shook myself. What I needed to do was make some kind of peace with Nana Mihori, who, after all, had gone to the effort of coming to the party. I watched her talking with people and sprang in when she was briefly alone, standing by the glass wall in the living room that had a view of Tokyo Tower's steel fretwork lit up brightly against the night sky.

"It's funny to think that Tokyo Tower is a copy of the Eiffel Tower," she said to me when I joined her. "When my husband and I were in France on our honeymoon, I was shocked to find the original."

"Tokyo Tower is an excellent copy. Just as the *tansu* I bought for you was," I added.

"My daughter has explained how badly that purchase has turned out for you. Perhaps I should have taken it."

I shook my head. "Every dealer has to face up to her mistakes. It's part of the learning process."

"That's mature of you." Mrs. Mihori smiled, and I sensed that she was relaxing. "It's like Zen. Our novices make many, many mistakes on the path to enlightenment. But along the way they come upon small blessings, such as your friendship with Akemi."

"Really?" I had the thought our running together was secret, but maybe it wasn't anymore.

"My daughter does not have many appropriate social contacts. It is refreshing for her to have a young woman friend."

"Is that so," I said, mind racing.

"I want you to know you are welcome inside the house as well as on the grounds. Next time, I insist that you bathe after running! The water in Akemi's shower and bath is piped in from a hot spring—"

The sound of breaking glass interrupted Nana Mihori's speech.

"Please excuse me," I said, putting down my drink.

"Rei-san, you have caterers to handle those things!" Mrs. Mihori said. "As a hostess, you must learn to delegate responsibility to others."

"I'm not very experienced." I jumped at the sound of a slamming door. The guests stopped talking, and I pushed through them toward the study. As I stepped through the doorway, I saw two beer glasses lying smashed on the parquet floor.

"A simple cleanup job. Ask a servant to bring a towel," Mrs. Mihori advised.

Hugh was there, too, trying unsuccessfully to shoo people back into the living and dining rooms. As a few bodies parted, I saw Akemi Mihori lying on Angus's futon. She was fully dressed but looked dead. The horror of Nao Sakai's corpse came back, and I felt myself grow dizzy.

"What did you do?" Hugh asked Angus, who was picking up the broken glass.

"Nothing. How was I to know she'd react like this?"

Somehow I got to Akemi's side. I touched her wrist. It was warm, and the pulse drummed against my searching fingertip, relieving me greatly.

"What's happened to you? Can you hear me?" I asked softly in Japanese.

"Mmm." Akemi's eyelids fluttered.

"Is she diabetic, like her cousin?" I asked Nana Mihori, who was trying to shove me aside.

"Absolutely not." Nana Mihori gathered her daughter in her arms.

"She just passed out," Angus said, nevertheless sounding nervous.

"The colors . . . get these colors out," Akemi croaked in Japanese.

Nana Mihori said tearfully, "My daughter has become very ill. I apologize for upsetting your party."

"Take me away from here," Akemi moaned. "The colors, they are inside my head. Please . . ."

"I'm calling the doctor who lives on the tenth floor," Hugh said in his most authoritative voice. "In the meantime, it would be really considerate if everyone could leave Akemi in peace."

Still shaking, I helped him usher the gawking guests past the catering assistant who was sweeping up the shards of glass and mopping the puddle of beer. There were a number of backward glances, but finally people were out, and the door closed. Already the rumors were starting. A salaryman's wife was reprising what I'd said about diabetes. One man suggested that Akemi had been training hard for a comeback but was obviously too old and weak. Somebody else blamed alcohol—why else would she have dropped the beer glass?

When the doctor arrived, I showed him into the study and then went to the living and dining areas to see what had happened to the party. People were talking in lower voices, and the ragged group of Angus's friends had gone. I saw Hugh talking to Angus on the balcony, so I stepped out to join them.

"All she had were two brownies. I had no clue she'd freak out!" Angus was laughing uncontrollably, a sign of his own deterioration.

"Those brownies . . . you baked pot brownies?" I tried to keep my voice from screeching.

"Hashish, actually. It wasn't going to be for the masses, but Rei asked me to put them on the dessert tray!" Angus was in stitches.

"Did you import it from Thailand or buy it from your creepy new friends?" I asked, thinking back to Club Isn't It, where he had suddenly run out of cash.

"Hush, Rei," Hugh said. "I'm trying to find out from him whether the brownies are still accessible to others."

"I was going to yank them from the tray, but Akemi had just eaten two and I couldn't very well do that in front of her," Angus said.

"You've got to stop those caterers," Hugh directed me. "Mr. Sendai is keen on chocolate. God knows who else is!"

Everyone, I thought, sprinting to the dessert

table and grabbing the brownie tray away from outstretched hands. The Japanese had a strong fear of food poisoning, given a wave of deaths from mercury-tainted fish in the 1960s. Foreign foods were widely believed to be contaminated, so if any-one got sick at our party, accusations would be quickly made.

"The brownies are bad," I told Miss Wada when I started dumping them in the kitchen trash bin. "Please send your staff around to take any that might be on people's plates."

"That's a bit unusual, as we did not prepare those cakes. We only prepared Japanese food," Miss Wada insisted.

"That's not what people will think," I warned her. "If anyone else takes ill the way Akemi Mihori did, your business could be ruined."

Leaving Miss Wada sputtering, I hurried to the living room with an extra tray of Aunt Norie's cream puffs. Unfortunately, Hugh's worst nightmare had come true. Masuhiro Sendai had a brownie on his plate with a bite taken out of it.

"Sendai-sama!" I greeted him with a supremely polite honorific. "Please excuse me, I need to replace your brownie."

"Whatever do you mean? This is quite tasty!" Mr. Sendai, whose rotund shape suggested he loved desserts, lifted the brownie to his mouth. I bumped his hand so the soft dessert fell to the floor.

"I'm so clumsy!" I apologized, scooping it up with a napkin. "I will have Hugh bring some extra brownies in his lunch box next week, so you will have a custom order. Until then, you must try a cream puff made by my aunt."

Miss Wada instructed her catering assistants to tell people that the tray of brownies had been inside the room where the accident had taken place, and therefore might have been sprinkled with glass shards. Winnie Clancy popped over to her apartment to fetch a few packs of Cadbury's Chocolate Fingers as a substitute dessert, and for once I was grateful.

"A hostess is always prepared for emergencies," she lectured me. "One should keep a generous supply of nonperishable foods. Remember that for your next party."

Mrs. Mihori remained closeted with Akemi, but the doctor eventually emerged for a cup of coffee. "Miss Mihori fainted," he announced to the guests who had crowded around us. "A common occurrence when going from the hot city streets to a very cold place such as this apartment."

"Yes, air-conditioning is unhealthy," Winnie Clancy said. "In England, nobody has air-conditioning. We're all better off without it."

"*So desu neh!*" Mr. Sendai agreed, and the cover-up was complete. Hugh had suffered no loss of face, excepting the rumor his apartment was too zealously air-conditioned. And I even had a prospective client, a friend of Nana Mihori's called Mrs. Kita, who wanted a pair of old porcelain *hibachi*.

"Despite the drama, it wasn't that bad. My colleagues learned to dance to Nine Inch Nails, you've got yourself a new assignment, and Piers is setting up an interview for Mohsen." Hugh yawned after we'd seen off Nana Mihori and her laughing daughter in a limousine headed for Kamakura.

"Did you see the look on Mrs. Mihori's face as she left? It was positively lethal. She didn't buy that stuff about air-conditioning, not with Akemi talking about colors moving behind her eyes." I slid down on the sofa and put my head in my hands.

"Mrs. Mihori is grateful her daughter's alive. And thank God Angus didn't let Akemi have more brownies. She'd be headed for the hospital if she had five or six of the things."

"Are you going to talk to your brother about how he got the hash?"

"Later. I don't think he's capable of talking about anything until tomorrow."

"You will talk to him?" I prodded.

"I'm not the father figure, okay? If you have a problem with him, speak to him yourself. I'm sick and tired of being pulled between you both."

"Last night you told me not to discipline him," I protested. "You're always blowing hot and cold. Why is that?"

"Sorry, but I have zero energy for one of your therapy sessions tonight," Hugh shot back. "Coming to bed?"

"I don't think so." I was too filled with anger and frustration to lie down. I would clean the kitchen which the caterers had rushed away from, rearrange the furniture, drink another glass of wine. I would rearrange the surfaces of things, although I couldn't do anything about the chaos underneath.

12

Sleeping on a sofa is a particular kind of hell. My body was half paralyzed by the time I woke up the next morning. I had forgotten to take my usual glass of water with aspirin, so my throat was a desert and my head vibrated with pain.

What had woken me? A whining appliance in the kitchen. And now Hugh was coming in, bearing a tray laden with orange juice and tea and a piece of toast with scrambled eggs spread neatly across the top. My favorite Sunday morning breakfast. This had to be a joke.

"Sleep well? The kitchen looks like it was cleaned to within an inch of its life." Hugh towered over me, a crisp vision in a white polo shirt and khaki shorts.

"I can't even remember doing it." I reached for the juice, which had suddenly become the object of my deepest desire.

"I didn't expect you'd stay here all night. I would have carried you in if I hadn't fallen asleep myself. When will you be ready to go to the shrine sale?"

"I'm not up to it." The thought of indulging in my usual Sunday morning antiques-shopping routine was anathema this morning.

"When I have a bad day, I still go to work," Hugh reproved.

"Don't push me," I warned. "I don't want Angus to hear us fighting."

"Don't worry about my brother—we're the only ones who should matter in this relationship. I can't stand the way you withhold yourself from me! Why didn't you come to bed last night? Honestly."

"I wanted to be alone."

Hugh laughed shortly. "Well, then, Greta Garbo, I'll leave you to your own devices. And since you can't bear my company, I'll take my brother golfing."

Hugh had to drag Angus out of bed, and the two of them left an hour later, still arguing about whether Angus really would have to wear Burberry shorts on the course. I put the breakfast dishes away, showered, and made a telephone call to the Mihori household. The phone rang eighteen times without being answered. Feeling restless, I decided to get out of the apartment and go to the shrine sale after all.

It was 10 A.M. when I arrived, too late for anything really good to be left along the steps and court-yard outside the historic Nogizaka Shrine. I went to the outlying area where furniture dealers sold their larger pieces. I didn't expect to find a real Sado Island *tansu*, but I'd keep my eyes open. I was heart-ened when Mr. Ishida crossed my path, his slight frame weighed down by heavy bags. He had been at the party last night, but I'd been too busy to say more than hello to him.

"Let me help." I was stiff and headachy, but I was forty-seven years younger than my friend.

"It's too much for a young lady," he apologized, nevertheless letting me take hold of a large bag that felt as if it contained ceramics. "Thank you for yesterday evening. What a lively event it was!"

"The party was a disaster. So, what you have bought this morning that's pulling my arms out of their sockets?"

"A set of Imari bowls painted with a carp design. I'd like to show you, but unpacking them now would increase the chance of breakage. There's a new porcelain dealer on the other side of the steps who gave me a dealer discount. You should introduce yourself."

"I will. Did you see any matched pairs of *hibachi*?" I asked, remembering Mrs. Kita, the guest from the party who had made the request.

"Those are hard to find, *neh*? I saw a pair but passed because they had a Mount Fuji illustration, a bit too ordinary for my taste. They're also too big for you to carry without Glendinning-san."

"I have to see them! I have a client who's interested."

"Nana Mihori? I saw you speaking together last night and was very relieved. How did you handle that problem, anyway?" Mr. Ishida put down his bags and leaned against a gnarled old gingko tree.

"It's a new client I'm talking about. Unfortunately, Mrs. Mihori is pretty much lost to me." I filled in the details of Nao Sakai's death and Jun Kuroi's imprisonment.

"If only you'd allowed me to help." Mr. Ishida grumbled. "Had the *ya*-san stolen the *tansu* from you, your renters' insurance would have covered the loss. You'd still have your client, and none of this humiliation!"

"Where did you say your van was parked?" I tried to change the subject.

"In the next street." Mr. Ishida's voice softened. "You should not forget about the porcelain dealer. If you like the *hibachi*, get one of the Morita boys to help you carry them to my van. I can hold them for as long as you need."

The *hibachi* were just right. Painted in soft blue and orange strokes on creamy porcelain, one of the pair illustrated Mount Fuji at sunrise, the other at sunset. The set clearly belonged together and was worth investing in even if Mrs. Kita didn't like them. I got the dealer to put a hold sign on them while I raced first to the bank machine and then to a pay phone to telephone Mrs. Kita. As I'd hoped, she was charmed by the sunrise-sunset motif and wanted the *hibachi*.

"The total cost, including my dealer surcharge, is one hundred and twenty thousand yen. Is that agreeable with you?" I asked carefully.

"Certainly! As long as it covers the cost of delivery—"

"That will be no problem." Ordinarily I'd have run the *hibachi* over to her house in Yokohama using the Windom, but Hugh had driven to the golf course. Mr. Ishida would probably lend me his van if I made sure to refill the gas tank.

"Miss Shimura, I am so glad I met you," Mrs. Kita enthused. "I have never been invited to one of my husband's colleagues' parties before. Until the last minute, my husband was saying that nothing would be of interest to me, but that certainly was wrong! Although poor Miss Mihori had a different experience. I have been worrying about her health."

And searching for some gossip. I said, "It's very kind of you to worry, but Miss Mihori will be fine. The doctor told us all she needed was a good night's rest."

"Is he checking on her today?"

"Now she's in the hands of her own doctor." I was not going to tell her I'd called myself and found no one at home.

"*Ja,* I'm sure you will be in touch with that doctor. Give me the latest news when you bring the *hibachi,*" Mrs. Kita said firmly, and rang off.

By late Sunday afternoon, the drive back from Yokohama was very difficult. The freeways were packed with people coming home from excursions to the beach. I remembered my time on the expressway the week before—when I'd taken my attention away from the road for a few seconds and smashed Hugh's car. I was seized with a panic that something might happen to Mr. Ishida's van, so I kept the radio off and my tired eyes open. By 7 P.M. I was home, utterly exhausted. I lay down on the sofa where I'd slept before and closed my eyes. It seemed like a few minutes later that a light was shining down on me and a voice was cutting into my dreams.

"Where's my brother?" It was Hugh.

I struggled to make sense of this. "He's with you. You were playing golf."

"I dropped him off here at five, and it's now half eleven. Where could he have gone?"

"No idea. And where were you?"

"I had an appointment with Mr. Ota. We were trying to decide how to evade potential lawsuits from the Mihori family. Tomorrow he's going to deliver a cash offering as an apology for what happened to Akemi."

I sat up at that. "Doing that will make us look tacky and guilty. Besides, you know how rich the Mihoris are. As nice as your stock portfolio is, you couldn't possibly give them anything of significance."

"It's not the amount that matters, it's the gesture of caring. Mr. Ota says it's the Japanese way."

"You're worried the Mihoris will tell the police to go after Angus," I said, finally understanding that Hugh was worried his brother could be arrested for pushing drugs. Given that Mr. Ota had suggested a payoff, the threat was probably very real. "Maybe I could try to smooth it over with the Mihoris—"

"Forget it. This is my problem."

"Only because you want it to be." I felt a lump rising in my throat, thinking of how I'd helped him in previous months with Japanese telephone calls, and how in turn he'd set up the legal documentation for my antiques business. Leaning on each other had made us close.

"Listen, Rei, the deal is all set up. Mr. Ota knows what he's doing." Hugh gave me a final angry look and went into his bedroom, closing the door behind him. I did not follow.

Angus showed up at seven o'clock the next morning, his eyes bleary and his mouth shut. All he would say was that he thought he'd misplaced his key somewhere and had stayed out to give us a chance to sleep.

"I was worried about you, lad. You should have come back, no matter the hour," Hugh said.

Angus shrugged. "I'm here now, aren't I?"

"We should perhaps try to put some shape to this visit of yours," Hugh said. "To start, I think I'll take the afternoons off this week in order to really spend some time with you. We can play more golf or swim, whatever you want."

I stared into the *Japan Times*, trying to hide my shock. Hugh never took time off. As it was, his hours of nine to seven were considered light for a multinational executive.

"I hate golf," Angus said. "But I wouldn't mind getting around. There's that festival in Kamakura. Remember, the one Akemi's father told me about?"

Hugh dropped his butter knife at that. "I think it's wise to let the Mihoris take a break from us."

"There's a luxury car show coming up in Yokohama." I scanned the newspaper's inside pages for something that might inspire male bonding. "You could go to that, then eat some *dim sum* in Chinatown."

"I have been thinking of trading the Windom in." Hugh sounded thoughtful. "It might be worthwhile to look at the new models."

"It's at the Shin-Yokohama Prince Hotel tomorrow. Let's see, what could you do in Tokyo today? . . ."

As I ruffled past the obituary section, I spotted an oddly familiar face—an old Japanese man with glaring eyes. I looked more closely at the black-and-white photograph and the caption below.

Nomu Ideta. My eyes flicked over the article about the longtime art collector in Denen-Chofu who was survived by his younger sister, Miss Haru Ideta. He had passed away due to complications from diabetes.

"No," I said, clutching the obituary page in my hand, the rest of the paper falling to the floor. It had been just a few days since I'd seen the old man. He had been lively and full of arguments. Nowhere near death.

"Nothing's on today? Like I said, we could go swimming. Rei, you're welcome to join us."

"I can't! I mean, sorry, I'll be busy." I went into the bathroom, the only place I could be alone for a few minutes, long enough to decide why the newspaper obituary troubled me, and why I was going to Denen-Chofu.

In Nomu Ideta's neighborhood, it felt as if people knew about the death. A group of boys halfheartedly kicked a ball among themselves, and housewives had stopped their driveway sweeping to chat in low voices, casting glances at the cars that pulled up to the Ideta house. They looked at me, too, in the black dress I'd worn to show respect for the occasion.

This time the house's bamboo gate stood haphazardly open. I slid into formation behind two women who marched inside without regarding the doorbell.

"When will the funeral take place?" I asked, following them into the kitchen, where they began unloading lacquered containers of food.

The younger of the two, wearing a pink and white T-shirt that read BUTTERFLY C'EST LA VIE, smiled at me as if I also had come to help in the crisis. "Ideta-san is making arrangements with the priest at the temple. We will know soon. You are? . . ."

"I'm here about the furniture," I improvised, not wanting to give my name.

"Of course, all the antiques!" said the older woman, whose round face was so similar to Butterfly's that I decided they were mother and daughter. "The first floor will need to be cleared for the ceremonies, won't it? I must say I expected you to come in a uniform."

"I'm actually here to appraise things. I just learned about the death this morning."

"It was sudden, instead of lingering, which was not the way we expected it," the mother agreed. "The hazards of those new machines . . ."

"Which machines?"

"Mr. Ideta used a dialysis machine for treatment of diabetes. There was a tube that went from his arm to the machine, and every several days his blood underwent a sort of chemical rinsing in the machine."

"Like a washing machine," the daughter added, and her mother shot her a reproving look before continuing.

"Normally, the blood would flow in a nice circuit from him through the machine and then back to his body again. But the last time—" Here the mother gulped. "The blood was pulled out but did not return. It stayed in the machine."

"He died with no blood in him, then." I was feeling queasy. "How could that happen?"

"A jammed switch. Poor Miss Ideta blames herself, which is unfair. She devoted her life to that old man!"

"She should be finally at peace, ready to go on with her life, and now it's so awful," Butterfly agreed.

"Wasn't it the nurse's fault?" I asked.

"The nurse was not in the house. Miss Ideta learned how to use that machine ten years ago to save the cost of having someone come in. It was very easy for her, like clockwork. She set the machine to process and went out to the garden to hang her laundry. By the time everything was pegged up, her brother was dead." Butterfly ended her macabre description in a whisper.

I wondered if the doctors who had performed the postmortem were thinking about what I was. Japan, like most countries in the world, banned euthanasia. But there were too many old people living on a shrinking socioeconomic tax base, which had led to some assisted suicides. It was an issue that Japanese society had as much trouble grappling with as the United States did.

Moving into the cramped living room to look at the furniture, I found myself doubting that Nomu Ideta had asked his sister to help him die. He had talked about trying to keep his antiques, which surely was a sign he wanted to live and enjoy them. Maybe Nomu had been right that someone was stealing his treasures. Haru Ideta overheard him telling me these things . . . could she have killed her brother to shut him up?

New voices in the entryway reached my ears. From the greetings uttered by Butterfly and her mother, I knew Haru Ideta had come back. I'd traveled to Denen-Chofu wanting to talk to her, but now I was scared. I couldn't let her find me. Unlatching the floor-to-ceiling window in the living room, I squeezed my way out into the garden. Forgotten laundry still hung from the day before, a collection of long, old-fashioned men's undergarments that must have belonged to Nomu. The long pants flapped forlornly in the wind, and I hoped Butterfly and her mother would remember to bring them inside.

At the apartment, I checked the answering machine and found a message from Hugh saying that he and Angus were swimming at the Tokyo American Club. They'd probably stay for drinks and dinner. Bully for them. I pressed erase and went into the bedroom, where I slipped off my dress and lay down on the bed and closed my eyes.

What would it feel like to have the blood drained out of you? Would you slowly go numb, or might the lack of blood flowing to the brain mean you simply went to sleep? Nomu Ideta had died slowly, while Nao Sakai's death had been sudden and violent. Still, it seemed likely that both deaths had come about by the same hand. Who would die next? When Akemi had suffered such a strong reaction to the hashish, I'd thought it was all Angus's fault, but now I couldn't be sure. Somebody within the group of ragged strangers who'd come to the party might have sprinkled something more dangerous over the brownies, heightening the effect. But had that been done for the purpose of knocking us all out?

I was getting so wound up that I couldn't sleep. I tossed unhappily between the smooth cotton sheets for a while before raiding the medicine cabinet for NyQuil. It was ironic how I couldn't tolerate Angus's mood adjusters, although I felt free to use one when I needed it. Lying back down, I did not have to wait long for blackness to overtake me.

I was dreaming that I was running. The faster and louder my feet fell on the track, the more effortless moving seemed to be. *I can't believe it,* I shouted, looking back at Akemi Mihori, whom I'd eclipsed. Running was like flying; it was what I had been born to do.

A roaring in my ears broke the rhythm; I felt myself falling through a fog and into Hugh's voice.

"All knackered out from your house wrecking?"

I mumbled something, keeping my eyes closed and trying to fall back into my dream.

"Why'd you do it? It looks bloody terrible."

"Hey!" I opened my eyes and beheld him fairly glowing with rage.

"Don't look at me. Look at the room!"

I saw the source of his anger: the wall-length wardrobe standing open, his precious English shirts and suits lying willy-nilly on the ground. My clothes were mixed in the heap, as well as every volume from the bookshelves. The Turkish rug had been turned over, and my wood-block prints were hanging askew on the wall. I sat up, the sheet falling away from me. While I had slept, something terrible had happened.

"I didn't do it," I said, fear breaking through my sleepy haze. "Someone must have come in."

"The whole flat's like this." Hugh's voice shook. "God, to think you were lying here undressed—think of the risk to you—"

Angus appeared in the doorway, and Hugh whipped the sheets up to cover my bare body.

"So, who's leading the cleanup?" Angus cackled. "Not her, I hope."

"Is the *tansu* still in your room?" I asked, flashing to the item that tied together Nao Sakai, Nomu Ideta, and me. Obviously this was why the burglars had come.

"That beat-up old chest? It's there, but everything's been tossed out. It'll be hours till I get my cassettes alphabetized again!"

"Angus, could you leave the room for a minute? I need to get dressed." I couldn't wait to get to the *tansu* and make my own examination.

Swearing about his cassettes, Angus went off, and I slid unsteadily out of bed and rushed into some clothes. Hugh picked up the bedside telephone, held it for a second, and then followed its cord around to the plug point. "The line's been clipped. Great. If you'd awakened, you would have been powerless." He rummaged around the room. "And my pocket phone's gone!"

Once my dress was buttoned up, I went straight to the *tansu*. As Angus had said, every drawer had been pulled out. I pawed through Angus's filthy garments on the floor, wondering whether there had been something of value in the *tansu* that had been found and removed. In that case, our troubles should be over.

But they couldn't be, I realized with a mixture of nausea and terror as I left the bedrooms and went into the rest of the apartment. It had been completely trashed. I walked through the living room and kitchen, seeing every cabinet flung open and all the books left facedown on the carpets. I didn't know how I'd put away the things I'd loved, which now seemed tainted by an unknown intruder's touch. All of a sudden, I hated Roppongi Hills. Despite its high-class fees and doormen, I was no more protected than Nomu Ideta had been in his high-walled house, or Nao Sakai in a power-locked car—although they had been killed and I had been spared, for reasons I didn't want to begin contemplating.

13

The police arrived within minutes, filling the circular driveway of Roppongi Hills with their blue and white motorcade. From the window, I stared down at their cars and Winnie Clancy buzzing about in a fury of excitement. She was in leotard and tights; obviously she'd run from her video workout to see what had happened. I was almost glad the telephone was out of order, given that it might slightly delay her interference.

For now, the apartment was filled with blue-suited men crawling on the carpet collecting samples of dirt or dusting the *tansu* for fingerprints while I explained to Lieutenant Hata, the young officer in charge, about the fifty-odd people who'd attended our cocktail party.

"So there's not much use dusting for fingerprints, given the number of our guests—oh, and the caterers as well—"

The officers dusted awhile longer before deciding to focus on an inventory of missing possessions. Locating the television and CD player and valuable furniture was easy; what I struggled with was trying to remember exactly how many Imari plates had been in the cabinets. In the end, we still had no idea what was missing beside Hugh's pocket phone.

"There's the possibility the break-in was some kind of warning. The work Mr. Glendinning does for Sendai—is it of a confidential nature? Can you ask him if he can think of any enemies? Any trouble you've had over the last several months?" Lieutenant Hata asked me.

I translated for Hugh, and he shook his head. "My laptop—which has everything on it—is still here. Besides, I have good relations with everyone."

"The burglar could have been at our party." Angus lazily dropped onto the sofa next to me. "I mean, I thought I lost the flat key, but I don't know. Maybe someone nicked it."

After I translated, Hata nodded at Angus, as if respecting the opinion of a sage. "That is a good thought, because the door shows no signs of forced entry. It is possible one of your guests removed it for his own use."

"I doubt it," Hugh said. "Our friends are good people. Tell him, Rei!"

I thought of Angus's sinister friends who'd dropped in, but I was sure they would have been more interested in Hugh's fancy stereo than an old wooden *tansu*. And that, I reminded myself, was the root of all the trouble.

"Actually, there's something you should know, Lieutenant. It concerns a *tansu* I bought last week."

"Rei, the *tansu* is still here. Now is not the time to bring it up," Hugh said.

"Please. I am here to try to help." Lieutenant Hata looked at me intently.

"Does anyone want a cup of tea?" I asked. "It's a complicated story, but I've been waiting for someone who wants to listen."

It was hard to figure out why I trusted Hata. He wore the same dark blue uniform as all the others. He was young—somewhere in his thirties, with kind eyes. He was also a good, uncritical listener, allowing me to slow the story down and add in details that I'd almost forgotten. I spoke in Japanese first, and then in English, so that Hugh, who was glowering at me from across the table, could understand everything.

"To sum it all up, Miss Shimura, you think your burglar had something to do with the murder of Nao Sakai? And the accidental death of the diabetic man in Denen-Chofu?" Hata asked after half an hour.

"That's right. It's the *tansu* that links the three of us. What I can't understand is why it's so important! Supposedly it's only worth a fraction of what I paid."

"Before we go further, I should really ask my Japanese lawyer to join us," Hugh interrupted. "He's more familiar with the situation."

"More familiar than me?" I shot back.

"Please have him telephone me, if it's not too much trouble." Hata, the peacemaker, smiled slightly at Hugh. "I'm grateful for the frankness of Miss Shimura. She has construed many things, but it is still worth writing a memo to my colleagues."

"A memo to your colleagues?" I repeated, upset not only with Hata, but with myself for being naïve enough to believe he was going to take over.

"Yes. I work for the Roppongi police department, which means I'm responsible for investigating crimes in this neighborhood, not Denen-Chofu or Ueno."

"You mean you can't order a new investigation?" I was appalled.

"The Japanese police force is very—how shall I say?—territorial about work. I will endeavor to apprehend Mr. Glendinning's apartment intruder, but I can only share information with the officers handling Mr. Sakai's death. I cannot investigate it myself." Lieutenant Hata capped his ballpoint pen and returned it to his breast pocket.

"If everyone works in their own tiny patch of Tokyo, how d'you solve crimes?" Angus interrupted, for once speaking my mind.

"Through cooperation," Lieutenant Hata said, smiling wryly. "Another Japanese custom."

Try as we might, Angus, Hugh, and I found it impossible to cooperate on the apartment cleanup. I had to invade Angus's quarters to look for my business files, and he went crazy when I overturned a case of already jumbled cassettes. Likewise, I found myself snapping at Hugh when I discovered he'd arranged my side of the clothing closet according to his taste.

"Let's leave the cleanup to the maid," Hugh said at last. "She's scheduled for Wednesday, but if you call her, Rei, I bet she'll come tomorrow."

"Fumie couldn't possibly help. What would she do with all the papers?" I objected.

"Put them in one big stack, I suppose," Hugh said. "Later on you'll sort through yours, and I'll sort through mine."

"I don't want any more Japanese going through my stuff. *She's* bad enough," Angus said, sneering.

Hugh turned from the books he'd been reorganizing to face his brother. "I'm your brother, so you can vent on me. But you won't speak to Rei like that."

Angus's face reddened with outrage. "I should just get on the plane again, for all you've done to make me feel welcome, you and that bitch!"

As much as I'd dreamed of seeing Angus getting dressed down, I suddenly didn't want it. Not with all the tensions I already had. In a low voice, I said, "Just stop. The apartment's just too crowded. One of us needs to go, and it'll be me. I can stay with my relatives in Yokohama."

"Don't you dare." Hugh turned on me fiercely.

"What's wrong with my relatives?"

"Run to them and they'll think I'm a bastard. After the gossip mill feeds them the story of what happened at our party, they'll never let you come back."

"What do you mean, not let me come back? I'm twenty-seven years old!"

The door chimed, as if to punctuate my rage. I went to open it and found Winnie Clancy standing in a powder blue leotard with matching headband and tights.

"Oh dear, your flat is in a jumble. You'll need to get sorted—"

Without saying a word, I fled.

The glass-enclosed telephone booth halfway down the block was well over 100 degrees Fahrenheit when I squeezed myself in and punched in Mr. Ishida's telephone number.

"You said the *tansu* is still there?" Mr. Ishida asked. "Obviously it was not my friend who did the burglary. Stop whispering like a ghost and come to my shop. I will help you locate an apartment in a safe neighborhood."

"I don't have time today," I said, and apologized for having to end the call. I dialed the Mihoris next, hoping I'd get through to Akemi. Unluckily, my call was answered by Miss Tanaka, the household retainer. Trying to cover up my disappointment, I said, "It's Rei Shimura. I'm so glad you're home, Miss Tanaka. Yesterday morning I tried calling."

"We spent all day Sunday at the temple. I thought you knew the family worships there." Her tone was slightly starchy.

"How is Akemi-san? I called to speak to her, if she's well enough."

"Of course she's healthy! At the moment, though, she is practicing in the *dojo*. May I ask her to return the call?"

"Actually, my phone is out of order and I'm calling from the street—"

"Is that so? I will interrupt her practice, then."

"If it's not too much trouble," I said, sensing Miss Tanaka's displeasure.

"It's no trouble." She dropped the receiver with a loud bang and shuffled off while I scrambled to stuff yen into the complaining telephone. Too bad I'd given back Mohsen's phone card.

"Rei? Are you still there?" Akemi came to the phone, sounding breathless.

"I'm sorry I interrupted your practice," I apologized.

"It's okay. I'm sorry I was so crazy the other night. I don't remember half of what happened, but my mother says I was an embarrassment." She was speaking English.

"It wasn't your fault. In fact, Hugh's lawyer should have telephoned your family with an, uh, apology." I had to broach it sooner or later.

"I'm okay now and back on my regular regimen. When are you coming to see me?"

"I don't know. Things are pretty tense around here." I leaned against the glass door, then sprang back from the burning heat.

"That's why you need to run," she said with a hint of impatience. "I'll be done with practice soon. We could run after that."

"I'm not fit to do that. I took something that's left me in a fog."

"Are you well enough to meet for dinner?"

"Do you want to ask your mother first?" I winced, thinking how much it sounded as if we were two ten-year-olds arranging a play date.

"I think that would be . . . awkward," Akemi said. "In fact, let's not even meet in Kamakura. I don't have the time to come all the way to Tokyo. Can we meet somewhere in the middle?"

"Yokohama? I could be there by, say, six-thirty."

"Excellent. I'll meet you at Yurindo Books inside Lumine at Yokohama Station. And don't tell your boyfriend." Akemi hung up before I could ask anything else.

The Toyoko express to Yokohama had a big problem: broken air-conditioning. The windows were propped open, but the heat from the hundred-plus packed bodies made the car I rode in unbearable. Pinstriped businessmen and nylon-clad matrons waved themselves with traditional paddle-style fans, while those younger and less prepared pressed cold soft-drink cans to their foreheads. I stared at advertisement for an Alaska tour, only $1,600 for five days on a glacier. The prospect of being both cold and away from all my fears was suddenly alluring; too bad my bank account was so piddling. A year ago, when I'd been teaching English for a salary, I could have done it.

Entering Yokohama Station's icy air-conditioning was bliss. I went through the Lumine mini-mall to Yurindo Books, and, not seeing Akemi, wandered into the foreign-books section. I was paging through some English mysteries, noting that the NyQuil had made me unable to read small print, when Akemi tapped me on the shoulder.

"Great weather," she said with not a trace of irony. "I love summer evenings. Shall we walk to Chinatown?"

It was such a short train ride to Yokohama's Chinese neighborhood that I would never have chosen to walk, but I nodded and followed my athletic friend out into the humidity.

"Your eyes look terrible, all sleepy and vague. Did you eat one of those small chocolate cakes that Angus prepared?" Akemi asked as we began walking toward the river.

"No, I took NyQuil. An over-the-counter medicine for sleeping." I was surprised at her ease in talking about her collapse; what exactly had her mother told her?

"I thought you'd want to eat a big dinner, because when I woke up after the drugs, I was starving. I made the car stop at Family Mart so I could buy snacks. I would have enjoyed more of those chocolate cakes, but Angus had taken them away."

"So you know?" I didn't know whether to be horrified or relieved.

"Of course! Angus explained them to me, and I ate out of curiosity. I'm interested in drugs. I've taken steroids, you know."

"I didn't. Surely not at the Olympics—"

"Yes. Unfortunately, my stupid coach had me on the wrong kind, the ones that show up in testing."

I looked around nervously, but none of the masses appeared much interested in an English conversation going on between two sweaty young women.

"There was an agreement. I was allowed to compete on condition that I lost my matches. If I didn't, they would have told the judo committee about the drugs."

"How many people know this?" I was appalled at the easy way Akemi was telling her story.

"My former coach, the doctor, and my parents, who thought it more face-saving for me to perform and lose than to be thrown out for cheating."

"So you never tried at all?" Somehow this made

me angry. I'd watched the Seoul Olympics largely to root for the Japanese athletes and had been heartbroken when she'd been defeated so easily.

"I rolled over and played dead for the Koreans and Chinese," Akemi said in a voice that seemed to come from somewhere outside of her. "No one could understand the breakdown of the top-ranked middleweight woman. It got easier with time. I fell so stupidly in the second match, I had a genuinely sprained shoulder to add to my pain."

"And you never made a comeback," I said, thinking about what had happened in the Pan-Asian Games and other matches over the following years.

"I left my coach, of course, and went completely off all the pills and vitamin supplements, trusting nothing. I tried to get my strength entirely from food and became a macrobiotic vegetarian." She made a wry face at me. "Something was lost. I became weak . . . the fighting spirit inside me was gone."

"Adzuki beans can give you only so much energy," I said, hoping to make her laugh. She didn't. An hour after we had started walking, we passed under the gaudy red gate leading into Chinatown. Rich smells of steaming pork buns and barbecued chicken began curling into my nose. I wondered if we would be able to find vegetarian food.

"So you can see why I tried the hashish?" Akemi fixed me with her tough gaze.

"Not exactly."

"I gave my youth to judo. In my teens and twenties, I was just a workout girl bulked up on drugs and exercise. I had no friends. I didn't even know which bands were in the top ten!" She laughed shortly. "Angus is an interesting boy. We ate the chocolate cakes together and I told him so much. It was a mind-opening experience."

"You fainted," I reminded her. "You had too much—"

"It was stupid for me to do something like that with my mother around. Now she's going through some kind of crisis, deciding whether to take the money your boyfriend's lawyer sent us."

"It looks bad, doesn't it? Like we're trying to buy you off."

"The river washes everything away. Things are forgiven. My mother will not contact the police. She is not even around to worry about me because she's gone to Kyoto for a tea ceremony convention." Akemi steered me into the doorway of a small, homey place where a Chinese woman owner greeted her like an old friend. We sat down, but I was unable to concentrate on the menu.

"Why did you ask me to keep this dinner secret from Hugh?" I asked.

"He doesn't trust me. He'll be upset."

"What gives you that idea?" I asked, my stomach doing a funny skip when Akemi laid her hand over mine. She laughed at my obvious nervousness.

"What do you think? At your party, he introduced me to women but no men. He thinks I like girls, doesn't he?"

With mighty concentration, I forced my hand to lie still under her caressing fingers. "Do you?"

"I told you already that I enjoy men. In limited

doses, which is something you should consider." She freed my hand. "You should leave Hugh. Angus said the two of you have been fighting."

So Angus had been listening in. I said, "When you live in close quarters, a little misery is part of the package."

"It is a shame to live in such a way when you're not even thirty."

"Spring roll for an appetizer?" the restaurant owner cut in as I began casting about for a defense.

"Two, with hot mustard on the side," Akemi said without consulting me. "And for the main course, what are your noodle specials? We both need to carbo-load."

It wasn't until the lychee pudding arrived that I had calmed down enough to tell Akemi about the apartment break-in.

"So you think the criminals came because of the *tansu*? Even though it wasn't stolen?"

"It's a sense that I have, although Lieutenant Hata said that the break-in could have been a personal attack. A warning to me, Hugh, or Angus, whose friends seemed pretty unsavory—did you notice them?"

"A bunch of idiots, those kids. I'd like to see them thrown into a Zen monastery for a few weeks' training," Akemi snorted. "You should move out of the apartment. If you don't go to your cousin's, maybe I could help you."

"No!" I said a little too loudly. "I mean, no, thank you. If someone's after Hugh, I can't leave him alone."

"But you told him you *wanted* to live with your cousin."

"I didn't really mean it. That's just the way I tend to fight." Akemi looked at me uncomprehendingly, so I pressed on. "I want to be with Hugh. This thing with Angus—if I can just get through it, take a Zen attitude toward his unending visit—"

"Zen's relaxing, but it can't save your life." Akemi licked the last of the lychee pudding off her spoon. "Come to the *dojo* and I'll teach you a few self-defense moves. Seriously."

"I shouldn't go to Kamakura anymore."

"But my mother's in Kyoto. And don't worry about Miss Tanaka."

If that were the case, I couldn't understand why Akemi had spoken to me in English over the telephone. And why couldn't I have come to Kamakura for the evening? She didn't trust Miss Tanaka.

I rode the Toyoko train back to Tokyo, changing at Shibuya for the Hibiya subway line home. I emerged in Roppongi just after midnight, walking through hundreds of young and happy drunks. Then the streets were quiet, and I walked faster, thinking about the apartment burglar who hadn't been caught. If I were the target, the intruder might not stop with the burglary. He could be watching me come down the street and have something else in mind.

I half ran into the apartment building, and as the elevator took me up I felt myself yearning to go faster; now that we'd been robbed, being alone anywhere in the building gave me the willies.

Opening the apartment door, I stopped dead. A hurricane had swept the apartment again—this time, it was one of order. Winnie Clancy must have gone on a cleaning rampage. Every piece of paper or book had been returned to its place, and the horrifying centerpiece was the sofa already made up for me with pillow and sheets. Had she done that? Would Hugh have announced to her that we had stopped sleeping together?

I picked up my pillow and tiptoed through the darkness to the bedroom, where Hugh was tossing in his sleep. He was feeling as unhappy as I, probably. I went to his side of the bed and crouched down, lifting the sheet away to study him in the room's half-light. Even with his eyes closed he was handsome, but there was a tightness in the sleeping face that bothered me. If only I could erase the lines of tension.

As I lowered my face to kiss him, he jolted upward, moving his arm in a fast arc. A fist slammed against my cheekbone. I fell backward from the bed, landing on the steel rowing machine.

"I'll kill you, damn it!"

I pressed my hands against my cheekbone to dull the pain spreading across my face. Hugh grabbed my hands away, strapping my arms under his. Within seconds I was pinned to the floor. I hadn't known he was so strong, so violent. I whimpered slightly, hating myself for it.

"What in hell?" One arm lifted off me, and I sensed him groping for the bedside light. "Rei, I thought—"

"That I was a burglar?" I whispered.

"Yeah, I thought someone had come back. It was part of a dream, I guess, and I woke up and felt someone inches from my face. I panicked."

"I'm inches from your face every night. I mean, I used to be." The tears were coming fast now, and Hugh wiped them away with his finger.

"Let me look at your face. Oh, God. I didn't expect you to come in—didn't you see I fixed the sofa for you?"

"So it's my fault this happened?"

"No. It's mine alone. To have hit you . . ."

I understood what had happened. Deep down, his anger must have grown so exponentially that his subconscious wanted to punch the lights out of me. The organized, conscious Hugh never would have; but at night, in a dreamlike state, things like this could happen. What would my psychiatrist father say? I wondered, before realizing I could never tell him what had happened. My boyfriend had hit me. A terrible boundary had been crossed.

"I'm getting an ice pack." Hugh stood up and pulled on his robe before heading out the door. Dimly I heard Angus in the hall; Hugh said something that sent him back to bed. Good—I didn't want him seeing me freshly battered.

I'd crawled under the covers when Hugh returned with a frozen gel pack wrapped in one of his handkerchiefs. He was the only non-Japanese person I knew with a drawer full of ironed handkerchiefs. I sniffled into the soft cotton.

"Do you want me with you tonight?" He stood at the edge of the bed, looking wary. I nodded. He lay down, but stayed so far on the other side, I might as well have been alone.

14

My Shiseido cover stick covered the stress pimple erupting on my chin but was not thick enough to camouflage the beginnings of my black eye. I plastered it on anyway. I was in serious pain; at breakfast I had to chew slowly so as not to jar my sore cheekbone. Hugh sat across from me, not saying anything.

When Angus trailed in wearing just a pair of ancient bikini briefs, I exploded. "Can't you find anything to wear? There's plenty of clothing strewn on your floor."

"Don't blow a gasket." Angus looked from my face to Hugh's. "Got into some S and M?"

"I fell on the rowing machine," I said quickly. Well, it was partly truthful.

Angus moved closer, as if to examine my eye.

"Put some trousers, on, man. Now!" Hugh barked at his brother, who unaccountably obeyed. When we were alone, Hugh spoke again. "I'm going to work now, but this afternoon I'm cutting out early to fly with Angus to Okinawa. He's been asking to go to a white-sand beach."

I stared down at the toast half left on my plate. I could shove the whole thing in my mouth and swallow it without feeling a thing.

"Is there a problem?" he said after a minute.

We'd never taken a vacation together. But I guessed that was my fault. I had rejected a trip to Thailand in order to search for a *tansu* that had brought nothing but bad luck.

"I didn't think you'd want to come, given you've done nothing with my brother and me to date."

"I'm sorry you feel that way," I said carefully. Obviously he was fleeing his expensive, air-conditioned tower because he couldn't stand seeing me another day.

"It's best for all of us, isn't it?" Hugh said. "Hey, I meant to tell you that Lieutenant Hata called when you were in the bath."

"I didn't know the phone was working?"

"The police arranged to have NTT fix it yesterday evening. I have a new pocket phone, too."

"What about the burglars? Is there any information on them?"

"Unfortunately not. He wants you to stop by the Roppongi police station this morning. I suggested you delay the appointment until I could be there, but he wouldn't hear of it." A muscle twitched in his jaw, signaling how annoyed he was.

"I can't think why he wants to see me. It's not even my apartment," I said.

"He probably finds you very charming. And he knows we're not married."

"You sound possessive, which is pretty inappropriate, given the circumstances—"

"Possession is what sadomasochism is about, guys! Was it fun? Where are your bruises, Shug?" Angus came back wearing my cotton *yukata*, which barely hit his knees.

"Too buried to be seen," Hugh muttered, putting down his cup. "I'll be late if I don't leave now. I'll call home when I get the flights arranged."

The Roppongi police station also kept caged canaries. After watching them chirp for a while, I switched my attention to the walls, papered with public service announcements. I was working through a police bulletin displaying an image of a wanted cult member with his hair color changed to red, thinking it could be a Japanese version of Angus, when Lieutenant Hata's soft voice made me jump.

"You have seen him, Miss Shimura? The criminal in the poster?"

I guessed he was making a joke, so I relaxed slightly and said, "I'm practicing my reading."

"A good idea, but won't you come with me to a quieter place?"

Inside the small conference room, fitted with a plain wooden table and a few plastic chairs, Hata closed the door. He sat down across from me and leaned forward, taking out his notebook. I saw a flash of dull gold on his left hand as he pulled out a pen. So he was married. I couldn't wait to tell Hugh.

"I overlooked your injury yesterday," he said, his

eyes on my face. "Did you go to the hospital? If an intruder assaulted you, it's a very serious charge."

"They didn't. I had a small accident after you left last night."

He was silent for a moment, then said, "You should not have to live that way. There are laws against it in your country and ours as well."

"It's not what you think. I fell in the dark."

"Face first? Your whole left side should be bruised, then." His eyes traveled over my unmarked shoulders and arms.

"This isn't why you called me in. What can I do for you?"

"I have some news that I think will please you, Miss Shimura." He paused, drawing out the suspense. "Your friend Jun Kuroi has been released."

"How?" It was too good to be true.

"I asked my colleagues in Denen-Chofu and Ueno to compare notes about the two deaths you told me about. Early this morning I was informed about laboratory results that made things certain."

"And?" I gripped the edge of the table so hard it cut into my palms.

"When the police reexamined the kidney dialysis machine with more care, they found evidence of tampering. As you suggested, Nomu Ideta's death may not have been accidental. The dialysis machine switch was jammed. And the invalid's room bore signs that also appeared in the car where Nao Sakai died."

"What kind of signs? Fingerprints?"

"I'm sorry, but for the moment that must remain confidential."

"Were these signs in our apartment, too?"

"Now that we know what to look for, we would like to go inside again," Hata said instead of answering directly. "But before I do that, Miss Shimura, I wanted to show you something."

He withdrew a brown envelope from the folder of papers he had brought in. Angus's stash. God help me, we'll all be sent to prison as drug traffickers.

"I think you know what this is, don't you?"

I shook my head vigorously while he extracted a plastic bag from within the brown envelope. When I saw its contents—a few dozen plastic cards decorated with pictures of fuzzy dogs, Mount Fuji sunsets, and the like—I smiled in relief.

"Telephone cards?"

"Black-market phone cards," he corrected. "I found this package in the bedroom with the futon and fax machine. I didn't bring them to your attention then because I wanted to test them first."

I had a sense where he was headed and didn't like it.

"You can see from the tiny holes punched along the side of this card that all one hundred units have been used. However, when I fed the card into a pay telephone booth, it worked perfectly. The magnetic strip has been recharged."

"They're not my cards, and I have no idea who they belong to. Maybe someone unfamiliar with the black market bought these cards innocently?"

"You cannot buy used telephone cards at any legal outlet in Japan. You know that." He paused. "One theory is that the person selling these cards might have dropped them in your apartment. By accident, or because he was making an exchange with someone."

Mohsen immediately came to mind. I could swear he'd been in the living room the whole time, but I'd been too busy to keep my eye on him once Hugh had taken over. Could Mohsen have come to the party to sell phone cards? I didn't want to believe it.

"I called you in, hoping you could give me your party guest list." Hata wrote a heading on his notebook page.

"I can't remember all the names. It was the biggest party I've ever given. I have to pull it from the computer." Hugh's laptop contained the master list of guests he'd used to address the invitations. He'd written it up weeks ago, so there was no way Mohsen's name would be listed.

Lieutenant Hata sighed. "Please fax it to me when you get home, and don't forget to ask Mr. Glendinning about when we can return for our search."

"It might be a little difficult, since he's going out of town this afternoon."

"Where?" He sounded suspicious.

"Okinawa." I rolled my eyes. "I know nobody goes to Okinawa in July. But his brother wants to see a white-sand beach."

"You will stay alone in the apartment, Miss Shimura? I would think a police presence would be welcome for you."

"Oh, I'm going away, too," I improvised.

"*Ah so desu ka!*" Understanding dawned. "You are doing the sensible thing. Leaving so he cannot find you."

There was no point in arguing. "I promise I'll ask Hugh about the apartment search, but I can't guarantee he'll let you go in if he's not there. Being a lawyer, he's uptight about things like that."

"I don't want to cause you to have trouble," Lieutenant Hata said. "Please just concentrate on leaving. I will ask him about the search myself."

"Are you sure it's okay?" I couldn't believe I was off the hook.

"Just telephone me when you are safe. I will need to know where you are."

I left the station feeling as if I'd taken advantage of Hata, who now believed I lived under the thumb of a violent man. I'd have to warn Hugh to be well behaved with him and to wash all the baking dishes. If any shred of Angus's recreational substances were found, he would be ruined.

The apartment door was unlocked, something that made me hold my breath as I swung the door open.

"Oh, it's you." Angus looked up from the backpack he was stuffing with clothes and cassette tapes.

"Who were you expecting, your underworld friends? Is that why the door's open?"

"Say what?"

"Frankly, I don't care what you do to your pitiful mind or body, but by the time you leave for Okinawa, I want everything illegal gone."

"Sorry?" Angus raised one sardonic eyebrow in the manner of his brother.

"How do you do it?" The anxiety I'd felt during the police interview sizzled like tempura thrown into hot oil. "In the space of one week you've racked up bar tabs you can't pay and brought drugs and black-market phone cards into this place along with those horrible people. Given that you can't speak a word of Japanese, your accomplishments are truly amazing!"

"Do you have my phone cards?" He brightened. "This morning I was going through my gear and couldn't find them. I thought they'd been nicked."

"You admit it, then." I fell onto the couch, closing my eyes.

"They were a gift! I was hanging in one of the parks when a guy asked me for a fag. I gave him two, 'cause he seemed to be on some kind of bender. The cards were his way of saying, like, thanks."

"I don't believe you. There must have been two dozen cards in Lieutenant Hata's evidence bag—"

"Seventeen," Angus said mournfully.

"You call that an even exchange for two cigarettes?"

"I don't know. I just want the bloody cards back!"

I'd done everything I could to save Angus from the police, and he was being insolent. I felt myself start to shake as I said, "If you want to retrieve them, you'll have to give the police the same pack of lies you're feeding me."

A door slammed, and Hugh was there.

"What lies?" He was shooting daggers at me, not Angus.

"Your brother just gave me a ridiculous excuse for possessing a cache of illegal telephone cards. Lieutenant Hata assumes the burglars dropped them, but if he knew the criminal actually lived here—"

"Apologize to my brother, Rei. He's not a liar, and you're out of control."

I struggled to steady my voice. "I was actually warning him, since the police are coming back to make a second check."

"Oh, God. When?"

"I don't know, but he should be calling you very soon. Oh, and I'll need to get the party guest list off your laptop. Do you suppose he'll ask each of our guests whether they lost any telephone cards? Mr. Sendai, even?"

As the telephone rang, Hugh groaned. "I should never have had the line fixed."

"It might be for me," Angus yelped, and ran to get it. A second later he was chuckling into the phone.

"Why don't you just get him a pager?" I asked. "All the drug dealers have them."

Hugh gripped my elbow and steered me into the kitchen. "Aren't you listening to me? I want you to lay off my brother. You've become so vindictive—so bitchy—you're not the person I met six months ago. I don't know who you are anymore."

Hugh let go of me so abruptly I had to clutch the counter for support.

"Rei, I think we need some time apart. To think."

"Blood is thicker than water, isn't it?" I said, staring hard at a cutting board littered with bread crumbs. I could not let myself break down.

"My brother has nothing and no one. He's crying out for help, and at the moment he needs me more than you do."

"I'll be out of the apartment as soon as I can."

"There's no reason why you can't stay here—"

"Forget it! Do you have any idea how humiliating it is that I've driven you from your own apartment?"

"Hold on, it's just a short holiday I'm taking!"

"A holiday from me. Have a damn good time," I said, and slammed out of the room. I could hardly see through my tears but was aware of Angus leaping out of my path as I went to the bedroom and began tossing clothing and my address book into a duffel bag. Getting out fast was important to my dignity, but I still had to run a business. Which brought up a problem: if I left the apartment, I would be unable to communicate with my clients.

Ignoring Hugh's pounding on the locked door, I snatched his new pocket phone and instruction booklet from his dresser and opened the sliding glass doors to the balcony. It was fourteen stories to the ground, but only three feet to Mrs. Ito's apartment. My neighbor wasn't on the balcony, and her glass doors to the apartment were open, perfect for a discreet exit. I didn't want to go past Hugh, especially if his pocket phone started ringing.

Could I make it? I lobbed the duffel over to the other side, then considered things. I was too much of a wimp to stand up on the cement edge of the balcony. If I could sit on the edge and somehow swing my body over . . .

Hugh's knocking at the door was increasing my nervousness. I sat on the balcony, drumming my ankles against the railing. A glance down at ant-sized people on the sidewalk gave me a nauseating case of vertigo. I looked up at the sky and pretended Akemi Mihori was coaching me: *You can do it. Picture your success.*

A three-inch cement ledge ran along the outside of the balcony railings, just wide enough for me to perch on if I stood on my toes. Then I could step across to the next balcony.

People on the street pleaded with me not to jump, to stay until the fire department arrived. I forbade myself to look down at them as I straddled the balcony and stepped over onto a skinny ledge bordering it. I rotated around with tiny tiptoeing steps until I was facing the Ito balcony. *Picture success.*

Taking deep breaths, I stretched my right arm, and then leg, to the other side. As I paused, spread-eagled between the two balconies, a rough summer breeze whipped up my dress, giving me an embarrassing incentive to finish my travels. Swiftly I moved my left hand and leg to join the rest of me. Then I threw a leg over the railing and launched myself into Mrs. Ito's tidy laundry racks. I went over with a row of shirts and underpants, wet but safe.

15

Getting out of Tokyo would have been easier if I'd had shoes on. But in a shoes-off household there was no footwear stored in the bedroom, so I wound up going barefoot through Mrs. Ito's apartment. Mesmerized by a television game show, my neighbor never saw me. I ran down the building's emergency-use-only staircase, slithering out the side exit and past the Punk Rock Coffee Shop to Roppongi-dori. The first shoe store I found sold only athletic shoes, and an ugly pair of Asics was the sole thing they could pull up in my size.

I was tying the shoes when the pocket telephone began ringing in my duffel bag. I hastily dug it out and said hello. It was the Roppongi Hills concierge, who liked to practice English.

"Miss Shimura, are you safe? People were reporting a suicide girl on the balcony of the fourteenth floor. After your recent burglary, I was worried."

"Of course I'm safe! I was just, ah, doing some gymnastics."

"You were? Ah, here comes Mr. Glendinning from the elevator. He looks very upset. Will you kindly wait?"

I hung up immediately and bought the shoes. I was ready to run for it, but first I would make a free phone call. Leaning against a newspaper kiosk, I dialed my aunt in Yokohama. Her answering machine told me what I'd forgotten; the whole family had gone on vacation. Their house in Yokohama was locked up, and there was no way I could take shelter.

I dialed Information and got the number for Asia Center, a budget hotel I'd stayed in during my first month in Tokyo. The desk clerk told me every room was booked, which I should have expected for mid-summer. I hung up and considered trying to negotiate an all-night rate in a love hotel, but being nestled in the midst of lovers would be too depressing. In the end, I did what I'd been thinking of all along: I called Akemi Mihori.

We met an hour later outside the west exit of Kamakura Station. Akemi was stretching her legs at the taxi stand, wearing a Simply Red T-shirt and athletic shorts.

Akemi's expression hardened when she looked at my puffy eye. "You won't have to worry about him hitting you once I've started your self-defense training."

"Like I told you on the phone, he thought I was a burglar. It wasn't intentional." I couldn't tell her how much more painful it had been when Hugh scrapped our relationship in favor of Angus. She wouldn't understand.

"Today's a *tomobiki,* which actually makes it fairly

convenient for you to move in." Akemi started walking up Komachi-dori, Kamakura's tourist-packed shopping street.

"What's that?" I asked.

"The priest's day off. It comes every six days or so, and gives my father and Kazuhito a chance to leave the grounds and take care of personal business. Many priests play golf, but my family went to"—she made a face—"a museum. Miss Tanaka's still in the house, though, so we can't eat there. I thought we should go out to eat."

"Dressed like that?" I inclined my head toward her skimpy gym outfit.

"It's my coach's sister's place. She'd be honored to have me any way I'm dressed." Akemi spoke without arrogance, and as she swung through central Kamakura I could see how she was considered a neighborhood girl. A rumpled grandfather type selling postcards called out to her, two women in an incense shop waved, and a young man roasting rice crackers offered her a freebie. For someone who had declared herself friendless, she certainly knew a lot of people.

"Aren't you concerned about being seen with me? They must know your mother, and even though we started to make up at the party, I'm sure she hates me now."

"Nobody talks to my mother," Akemi said shortly. "They say my mother wants to kill the town of Kamakura."

"But that doesn't make sense! She's president of the Green and Pristine Society."

"That's where the trouble began. She cannot

stand what's happened to the town. Every hectare of land is being used for houses, and now the real estate developers are going after the hills, tearing up the old caves and burial grounds. My father was thinking about selling some of our mountain property, but my mother said no. The land is holy and not for anyone to sell."

Converts were always the most zealous. I cared about Japanese traditional arts more than any of my Yokohama-born relatives. It sounded as if Nana, who had married into an old Kamakura family, had become the standard-bearer. I liked her a little more, knowing this.

"She pressured all the families who own mountain land not to sell," Akemi continued. "Of course, all that's done is drive the bidding higher. So when somebody finally gives in, they'll be even richer."

"How can you fault her for wanting to save the land?"

"Well, she and the other Kamakura millionaires can afford to be high-minded, can't they? That's what people in town said. The real battles started last fall, when she proposed a ban on all private cars in the city."

"For tourists I can understand it, but for locals?" I was amazed.

Akemi nodded. "Under her plan, only official city vehicles and minibuses would be allowed on the streets. She thought it would eliminate traffic jams and preserve Kamakura's old-fashioned character. Of course, the shopkeepers screamed that her preservation would kill their businesses, and the residents who use cars to drive to work were upset, too. The motion was shot down within a few weeks, but people have never forgotten. Hey, this is where we go in."

I'd been to the Zen Café before for its slightly trendy macrobiotic menu. I'd been treated in a polite but distant manner, so it was nice going in with Akemi, who received warm hellos from every waitress and inspired the old man who'd been washing pots in the open kitchen to come out and pinch her cheek. As early as it was for dinner, most of the tables were already gone. We took seats at a table underneath a tiny speaker playing the latest Akiko Yano disc. I should have felt tranquil, but Akemi's story about her mother had disturbed me.

"Sake?" Akemi poured without waiting for my answer.

"I actually sold two *hibachi* yesterday. I'm paying for my half of dinner." I decided to speak up before she threw more hospitality moves at me.

"Don't say that until you've tasted it. Westerners usually have problems with Zen cuisine."

"I'm a vegetarian just like you," I reminded her.

"You won't be able to cook in the teahouse, or use the toilet or wash. I don't know how a person could live there."

I'd had the idea to stay there when I'd telephoned Akemi. The rickety teahouse was buried so far into temple grounds that no one knew it existed. It would be the perfect place for me to stay while I worked to find more permanent housing.

"I'll use the public toilets near the temple's main hall, and I can get my water from the drinking fountain,"

I suggested. When I was young, I'd read a marvelous novel about a girl who, with her little brother, moved into the Metropolitan Museum of Art and lived undetected for weeks. Part of me had always wanted to have such an adventure.

"Don't wander too far," Akemi said abruptly. "In the mountains there are some caves that are the old burial places for monks. Every ten years some fool wanders up there and gets lost in the tunnels. I know your interest in history, so I'm warning you."

"I won't go there, and I'll be out of the teahouse in a few days, I promise. I'm so grateful to you. I'll use this time to work so hard, I'll never need to depend on anyone again."

Adding emphasis to my statement, the pocket phone rang inside my backpack. "Rei Shimura Antiques!" I answered brightly. All I heard was breathing on the other end and then a click. Typical. When Japanese people dialed a wrong number and heard someone answer in English, the experience was usually so shocking that they either fell silent or giggled uncontrollably. I turned my attention back to my friend. "Once again, I really appreciate your help. I'll stay out of your way and try not to be the guest from hell."

"I'm afraid you'll be more like the guest *in* hell. Did you bring mosquito repellent?"

Akemi found a citronella candle tall enough to burn all night, but that wasn't any barrier to the cicadas, the centipedes, and the *tanuki*—a dark-eyed, spooky Japanese species of raccoon—who all came to inspect

me. I had not thought about how dark the forest
would be, nor how the wind and forest creatures
would stir all night long. Every time I started to drift
off, I would awaken to a subtle sound that set my
heart pounding.

No one outside of the Mihoris and their monks
knew about the teahouse, but it didn't feel secure to
me. Now that I was alone, the rashness of my decision
hit me. The sliding wooden doors that formed the four
sides of the simple house had no locks, and the window
areas were weakly shielded with old, partly torn paper.
Lying on the aged, mildew-reeking futon Akemi had
dragged out from somewhere, I concluded the teahouse was about as secure as the cardboard boxes the
homeless lived in around Shinjuku Station. Then again,
the homeless had overzealous police protection, while
my only link to civilization was the pocket phone.

It was fairly ironic that I had climbed like a mon-
key fourteen stories over Tokyo and was succumbing
to terror of Mother Nature. Hugh would tease me
about it, I thought before remembering he was the
cause of at least half my troubles. It was not a good
idea to think about him tonight, not even to take my
mind off of the creepy-crawly things just inches away.

Running in the rain the next morning was a disaster.
I was so exhausted I could barely keep my feet moving, and every time I moaned about it to Akemi, she
told me to visualize my success. When a lashing rain
started, I took cover under a canopy of wisteria, but
watching Akemi press on made me feel so guilty I
started up again. Akemi didn't look back but must

have heard me squelching along the trail, because she slowed enough for me to catch up.

"The most difficult runs are the ones that build your endorphins. Really. Just think, the shower afterward is going to feel great."

The water pounding down on me ten minutes later was as wonderful as she had promised. I tried not to stay under too long because Akemi was waiting her turn. I toweled off regretfully, dressed in jeans and a T-shirt, and tossed my damp athletic clothes into the hamper she'd shown me. While my friend bathed, I made a pot of tea in the *dojo* office. The only foodstuff I located was dry rice cakes—something I'd have to improve on.

After our snack, I left Akemi at the *dojo* and headed off across the temple grounds. I peered through the rain at the main hall, where Zen prayers were taking place. I could see the backs of a few dozen monks and visitors sitting cross-legged before a beautiful bronze Buddha. Afterward they would be invited to try the temple's famous rice gruel. Not satisfied with the rice cake snack, I bought a packet of sweet-potato chips from the temple's snack stand, which had just opened. I couldn't shop there too often; I didn't want my presence on the temple grounds to be noted.

Inside the teahouse, I rolled up the futon, stuck it in the closet, and tried to organize my possessions in the small cabinet where someone had stored old tea ceremony bowls. I ran my fingers over the rough glaze on the bowls. They were simple, lovely, and probably worth tons of money.

Flipping open the pocket phone, I dialed the

answering machine at Roppongi Hills. My standard, bilingual message welcoming callers to leave messages for Hugh Glendinning or Rei Shimura Antiques had been replaced by a long burst of Skinny Puppy and a few rude words from Angus. Grimly I pressed the code that allowed me access to messages. There were plenty of hang-ups; only Lieutenant Hata and Mrs. Kita, the customer who had hired me to buy the *hibachi*, had been brave enough to "leave it at the beep," as Angus had instructed. I studied the pocket phone manual until I figured out how to erase the music and tape a new message. Then I began returning phone calls.

Mrs. Kita wanted me to look for an antique Zen scroll. I was in the perfect location to begin my search, I thought, making arrangements to meet Mrs. Kita at a coffee shop near the Kamakura Museum of Art at three.

I called Lieutenant Hata next.

"You're not back at Roppongi Hills," he said after I'd been patched through to his desk.

"Not exactly—"

"It sounds as if you're talking on a *pocketo*. When I spoke to Mr. Glendinning yesterday afternoon, he reported his new telephone had disappeared, along with you."

"That's nothing compared to what he has," I protested. "All my wood-block prints and antique textiles, three *tansu*, and enough Imari china to open his own store!"

"Domestic disputes are so unsavory," Hata lectured. "That is why in Japan, men and women do not live together before marriage."

"Thanks, but I've heard that one from my aunt already. I'll return the telephone when he asks me for it personally. And if you need the guest list, please ask him to print it out."

"There is no longer a need for that. I know who owns the telephone cards. Hugh Glendinning told me."

I was silent.

"The younger brother, *neh*? It makes sense, considering his itinerant lifestyle."

"What are you going to do with him?" As much as I loathed Angus, I didn't want him to go to prison.

"We are letting him go with a warning, because it was good that Hugh volunteered the information. Unfortunately, our progress is stopped with regard to investigating your burglary. We cannot enter the apartment if the Glendinnings go to Okinawa, and the building concierge is unsympathetic to our needs."

"I can't take you through Hugh's apartment. I'm not living there anymore."

"I saw your name on the mailbox!" he chided.

"But it's not on the lease, and I don't live there anymore. I'm sorry."

"It is wrong of you not to help me," Lieutenant Hata said emphatically. "After all, it is your life that was in danger."

"My old life," I told him firmly. "I've got a new one, and it has nothing to do with Hugh Glendinning or Roppongi Hills."

After the rain tapered off, I went into Kamakura to do a little grocery shopping and make a preliminary sweep of antiques stores. Someone in a shop on Komachi-dori told me about an exhibition at the Kamakura Museum of Art, so I stopped in for a look.

Zen art was not my favorite. The swirling circles and scribbled calligraphy on Buddhist scrolls might be eloquent in their simplicity, but most of it revealed little about Japanese people or neighborhoods or life; they didn't tell the kind of stories I was interested in. The few genuinely talented and well-known monk-artists brought very high prices, and since it was relatively easy to slap a forgery of their name seal onto someone else's work, the process of buying Zen art was extremely risky.

One series of scrolls on loan from the Tokyo National Museum was undeniably wonderful. The *Choju Giga*, "frolicking animals," was a wicked satire of Buddhist society showing monkeys, frogs, and rabbits playing games and conducting religious rites. If only the wildlife that had kept me up all night were that cute.

The animal scroll gave me the idea of going to Horin-ji's main temple to look at its own collection of Zen art, but first I had my appointment with Mrs. Kita. I was still wearing my jeans, presenting a more casual image than I'd liked. It was too bad I'd rushed in my packing, because I certainly couldn't afford to buy any more clothes.

Mrs. Kita, in fact, didn't recognize me and strode on by as she exited Kamakura Station. I hurried after her, plowing through a group of elementary school students.

"Kita-san, Kita-san," I called until she turned and

saw my face. Then, remembering my black eye, I began stammering out the story of my clumsy fall in the night.

"Are you well enough to work? Perhaps you should return to the hospital." She looked doubtfully at me.

"Oh, I'm very able to work." I was starving for it, in fact.

Mrs. Kita must have sensed it, because she insisted on paying for our tea and lemon crêpes at the little crêpe shop on Komachi-dori. We looked at the book she'd brought with pictures of Zen scrolls, and I gently brought up the issue of price.

"You made such a good purchase with my *hibachi*. If only . . . for a similar amount of money . . . like this one in my book . . ." Mrs. Kita paused, clearly uncomfortable being frank about money.

"Not even the Tokyo National Museum could afford a thirteenth-century Kamakura scroll these days," I said. "Even if we doubled what you spent on the *hibachi*, we would still have to go with something done in the early twentieth century. But," I hurried to add, "that's not all bad. There was some very beautiful painting done in color, which I think would stand out more beautifully in a contemporary home, and of course, the scroll would be in better condition."

"Of course." She toyed with her crêpe, not looking hungry. I'd already finished mine and could have wolfed hers down, too.

"Now is a wise time to buy. I was thinking about looking around here. I know there's a shop you like very much in Hita, but unfortunately, the antiques department has closed."

"*Heh?* Where's Hita?"

"I'm talking about Hita Fine Arts in Hakone. Nana Mihori said you bought something there—a *tansu,* maybe?" That was what Nana Mihori had told me when I was sitting in traffic heading home. Because Mrs. Kita had recommended the store, I'd had to drive out of my way to see it.

"I don't own a *tansu.* You must mistake me for another client." Mrs. Kita had a slightly hurt expression, not realizing that Nana Mihori had lied to me.

"I apologize. Usually I don't mix up people. I don't have my files with me today."

"I see. And how are the Mihoris?"

"What?" For a moment I thought she knew I was squatting on their property. Then I realized she was still trolling for gossip about Akemi's collapse at my party. "Oh, Akemi is completely recovered, I hear."

"Excellent. I was worried, given the weak genes that run in that family."

"Do you mean Akemi's cousin Kazuhito?"

"That's right. You know about his diabetes. It must be very embarrassing for Mrs. Mihori!"

"Why?" I caught a whiff of her dislike and wanted to pursue it.

"Well, he was her cousin's child, or something like that. They adopted him just five years ago, and I'm sure they didn't know he was damaged."

"I thought he grew up in the household," I said. "Didn't he and Akemi play together when they were little?"

"Yes, but he did not change his surname to Mihori until five years ago. Nothing was final. And even if he does marry and have a son"—she drummed her perfect pink nails on the table—"if he dies early, the child would be too young to assume his priestly duties."

"What should the Mihoris have done? It looks like they had no choices."

"They should have given the temple to Akemi." Mrs. Kita looked straight at me. "That girl has strength of spirit, and she loves Horin-ji very much. When her father dies, she and her mother could be tossed out to live in a small apartment somewhere. The new abbot will have no responsibility to keep them on."

Feminists came in the most unlikely packages, such as Mrs. Kita's green and orange plaid suit. Not that she would ever dream of sitting in at a meeting of the Tokyo Women's Collective or arguing for changes in the way Buddhist temples were run. I'd never thought much about whether Akemi would have wanted to manage the temple. I was beginning to realize that my personal problems were very small compared to the Mihoris' worries.

I sneaked into Horin-ji through the back and dropped my groceries in the teahouse. Munching on *nashi*—a delicious fruit with the texture of an apple crossed with a pear—I went outside again.

I heard the crunching sound of feet falling on the track before I saw the runner. Akemi really was a fanatic to run twice in a single day. I moved aside so she'd have full access to the trail and waited.

What I saw was a young, fit Japanese man moving at a pace somewhere between hers and mine; not pedantic, but not speedy. His shaved head shone with sweat, and he was dressed only in nylon shorts and a well-worn pair of running shoes.

When he saw me he almost jumped out of his bare, shiny skin. I had the same reaction. He passed on, but I stood looking after him for a while. I didn't think it was the athlete I'd seen sparring with Akemi the first day I'd come to the temple. The runner might have been a local person who had discovered the trail, or one of Akemi's workout partners. Would the man run straight to the temple guards to complain about the interloper on the Mihoris' private property? Or would he mention it to Abbot Mihori? As I retreated into the teahouse, I could not stop worrying.

16

I'd been trying to reorganize my list of clients for what seemed like hours when the pocket phone bleated from its haphazard perch next to me. It was a telephone call for Hugh from his company chairman, Masuhiro Sendai. I suspected Hugh was still in Okinawa, but I took the message, hung up, and dialed the number at Roppongi Hills to leave a message.

Once again my recorded greeting had been scrapped; this time for "#1 Crush" by Garbage.

"Hugh, when you hear this, please call Mr. Sendai immediately regarding some problem in Thailand," I recited. "He will be at home at zero-three-four-three—"

"Where are you, Rei?" Hugh came on the line, and my heart did a funny kind of skip.

"You're supposed to be in Okinawa." I deflected his question.

"As if I could leave town after your theatrics! The

street below the apartment was full of witnesses unwilling to believe you were safe, the police have been breathing down my neck . . . and what can I say, with no trace of you?"

Static on the telephone line was making his voice fade. I spoke loudly. "I needed to leave the apartment quickly, and the police know I'm alive. I've spoken to Lieutenant Hata."

"Safe and active with my pocket phone," he said nastily. "I'd get another, but I'd have to change the number on my business card."

"Mr. Sendai said there might be trouble with the company plant in Thailand."

"Oh, it'll just mean a trip back to Phuket." He sighed. "I can live with that."

"Yes, you can give Angus my unused ticket." I disconnected and decided to get away from the telephone. I went outside, breathing in the incense wafting from the temple area. Evening prayers would be starting soon.

Akemi appeared like a wisp of smoke. The woods had seemed empty, but suddenly she was there before me, in loose blue cotton trousers and a dark blouse. She was dressed like a peasant, but the effect of the traditional clothing on her slim figure was very attractive.

"I brought your laundry and some extra clothes I think you could use. Also dinner." Seating herself cross-legged on the forest floor, she set out rice, braised spinach dressed with soy sauce, a vinegary eggplant salad, and assorted pickles. It was the most unexpected and delicious picnic I'd ever had; when she told me it was all leftovers straight out of the fridge, I was impressed.

"Miss Tanaka cooks like this, even when your mother's away?"

"My father and Kazuhito are very demanding. And it's my last dinner."

"What do you mean?"

"I'm going to be away for two or three days. I was invited to give some demonstrations in Kansai. You'll be okay, won't you?"

"Sure," I said, not feeling that way.

"I'll leave the *dojo* unlocked so you can shower. But discreetly, *neh*?"

That reminded me of the runner I'd seen. I told Akemi about him.

"Since he had a shaved head, the man must be one of our monks. In the old days, they would not be allowed free time for jogging. It's Kazuhito's fault—he's so lax with them. Progressive theology, he calls it!"

"The runner looked pretty surprised when he saw me. I hope he doesn't tell anyone."

"What time did you see him?"

"Five o'clock or thereabouts."

"Hmmm. That used to be when evening prayers have commonly been held. Recently, though, the hour was changed to six to suit my cousin's mood. Well, well, now I can mention the jogging monk as a complaint against Priest Perfect's supervisory abilities. *Domo arigato*," she thanked me wickedly.

"You can't do that! I mean, why bring up something that would reveal I'm staying here?" Her enthusiasm was making me nervous.

"I'll say I was the one who saw the guy," Akemi suggested.

"But what if the monk reported me already?"

"Then I'll say I heard it from a wandering tourist. I know how to handle it. Just keep up your end of the bargain, and we'll be fine."

"My end of the bargain?" I was suddenly uneasy.

"You'll run every day, won't you?"

Leaving me the remains of the feast, she slipped off through the trees.

I passed the rest of the evening swatting bugs and studying the catalog of Zen paintings I'd bought at the museum exhibit. The phone rang once. When I answered, there was a silence, and I hung up. When the phone began ringing a few minutes later, I picked up and found the call was for me. So Hugh had figured out a way to forward calls to me without communication; it was quite civil, but it broke my heart.

The call was from Mrs. Kita. There was so much static it was difficult to understand her, but I gathered she wanted to hear a progress report on the Zen scroll.

"Actually, I've just started to look—as I said, it might be tough going—"

"What's that sound in the background? I can barely hear you!" Mrs. Kita complained.

I didn't want her to know I was on a pocket phone in a teahouse—it just sounded too pathetic.

"I think it's a bad line," I said, just as we were cut off.

Obviously the phone's battery needed to be recharged. According to the manual, a low battery could be recharged in any standard electric socket;

too bad the teahouse was unwired. I would have to search for an electric outlet somewhere on the grounds of Horin-ji.

It was completely dark as I made my way toward the Mihoris' house and the main temple. I was glad for my rubber-soled sneakers, because snakes were common in Kamakura, along with toxin-shooting centipedes and the possibly rabid *tanuki* that I'd already seen.

Among the temple's closed outbuildings, I searched in vain for exterior electric outlets, worrying a little about whether the rain coming down might cause electrocution. The main temple had to have electricity. I surveyed the completely darkened, forbidding structure. It was nine-thirty, lights-out time for the monks, who had to rise at five in the morning.

Golden light burned behind the wall closing the Mihori house off from the public grounds. I went close enough to look through the bamboo fence and into the front windows. Through the *shoji,* I saw the silhouettes of three figures in a front room and the bluish glow and sound of a television set. I should have expected the Mihoris, like every other family in Japan, to have a television set. Still, I'd never seen one during my visits to Mrs. Mihori.

I remembered Akemi's *dojo.* I could slip in and plug the telephone into the outlet on the counter where she kept her electric teakettle. And the judo gymnasium was on the far side of the house, away from the family watching television.

I entered the garden, quietly closing the gate behind me. If I didn't want them to catch sight of me, I'd have to crawl along the ground, touching earth and other possibilities. I tucked the pocket phone in the back of my jeans, the way people do with guns in the movies, and made a swift prayer to Buddha to protect me from danger. A few slick insects crunched under my fingers, and I had to keep from jerking myself up. *They're more scared of you than you are of them,* I reminded myself. Fortunately, the garden was landscaped, and I made most of my travels on a relatively insect-free bed of moss.

The door to the dojo was padlocked shut. Padlocked, when Akemi had promised she'd leave it open for me. I jiggled the lock uselessly a few times.

I'd have to return to the house. All the windows in the back were dark, and I recognized the long wall of sliding glass windows that led into the quiet room where Mrs. Mihori practiced the tea ceremony.

I removed my sneakers and stepped up on the wooden ledge running outside the window. Pressing on the window, I found that it slid open. I walked inside and, in the glow of moonlight, saw the room was empty except for a tea table, a pile of neatly stacked cushions, and a graceful *andon* lamp in the corner. I went to the corner where the lamp plugged in. Excellent, another socket. I plugged in my telephone.

As I turned, I caught a glimpse of movement and froze before realizing it was a reflection of my own body against some large, glass-covered portraits. My eyes were drawn back to the pictures of Mrs. Mihori's parents on the Buddhist altar.

The woman had a downward cast to her gaze, and the man had a certain hardness around his mouth. Both wore plain black *kimono*. They were clearly of the old generation who had starved through the war but carried on into a more prosperous future. How would they feel knowing Nana was disliked by so many people in town and might be cast out one day along with her own child?

The house was absolutely still and dark; it was easy to imagine their spirits present. I reminded myself that Nana's parents had not lived on the premises. It was disturbing, this affinity I felt for them. It was as if I'd seen them elsewhere. This sensation came to me occasionally when I was antiques shopping; it usually meant I had seen the piece before, and one or both had to be reproductions. This time was different.

I traveled backward in my memory until the pictures slipped into place. I had seen the two portraits in Denen-Chofu when I'd slowly paced through a room examining wood-block prints. Their expressions had seemed to reprimand me for snooping on Haru and Nomu Ideta, whom I now recognized for their true identity: Nana Mihori's brother and sister.

17

There was no time to think. The television had been turned off, and I heard quick footsteps in the hallway outside the room.

I squeezed through the window and half fell into the garden. As I was pulling on my shoes a light snapped on, causing a herd of moths to rush inside. Someone made an irritated sound and headed for the window. I rolled under a bush and lay there listening to the person latch the window. A dark figure chased and swatted the moths, creating an eerie shadow dance of insect murder. At last the light was turned off, and I had the courage to gather myself together and leave. The cicadas' chorus seemed to mock me as I plodded along the path to the teahouse, trying to make sense of what I'd learned.

Nana Mihori had used me. She wanted to own Nomu Ideta's *tansu* but was unwilling, for some reason, to buy it directly. She had sent me on a wild-goose chase across Japan and made up the story about Mrs. Kita's recommending Hita Fine Arts so that I wouldn't suspect her.

I'd stepped out of my programmed role when I didn't deliver. Had I ignored the metalwork on the *tansu*, all would have gone off seamlessly. Nana Mihori had not wanted a top-quality, Edo-period *tansu*. She simply wanted something her brother owned.

I tried to remember the specifics of my encounter with Mr. Sakai. When I'd first telephoned to ask what *tansu* he had in stock, he had mentioned a customer who had placed the *tansu* on hold. At the time I bought the *tansu*, I'd assumed the woman with the mole was that person. When she turned out to be his wife, I knew that couldn't be true. It was more likely that the visitor who had placed a hold on the chest long enough for me to arrive at the store had come from the Mihori family.

I pulled my small datebook out of my backpack, trying to remember what Akemi had said about *tomobiki*, the scheduled day when a priest and his family were free to leave the temple grounds. Counting six days back from my arrival at the temple, I found the *kanji* symbol marking the priestly holiday on Wednesday—the same day that Nao Sakai had been killed in Jun Kuroi's car.

Any one of the Mihoris could be involved. My spine prickled as I thought about how, during the wildest moments of Saturday night's party, I had cleared everyone from the study except for mother and daughter. After the doctor had ultimately emerged from the room to answer the guests' questions about Akemi's health, Nana and Akemi had been alone in the room for at least ten minutes. Maybe Akemi's stoned reaction had been as exaggerated as her weak performance in the Olympics.

When the prickling feeling on my back changed direction, I could tell it was for real. From underneath my T-shirt, I flicked out a nasty red ant. I didn't even yelp. There were worse things to be afraid of now.

It was pitch dark when the alarm setting on my watch awoke me. Four A.M., which meant Zen meditation would be starting at the main hall in fifteen minutes. I rummaged through the clothes Akemi had lent me and came up with a pair of loose cotton pants that would be comfortable for sitting cross-legged. I pulled on a T-shirt and headed out in search of the public rest rooms, where I could clean up before entering the main Zen hall. The gray marble ladies' washroom was spotlessly clean. Some guidebooks cited it as the best temple toilet in Kamakura. *If only it had a shower*, I thought as I hurried through a rough sponge bath.

Still damp, I crept through the dark toward the sound of gongs, and discovered a surprising number of people ready to worship. Some wore traditional dark Buddhist robes, while others wore loose-fitting athletic clothes, as I did. Most looked fairly mature; in Japan, Buddhism was more of an old-age passion than a New Age one.

I shadowed the only other foreigner, a European–looking woman in her thirties. We sat behind two rows of black-robed monks sitting in the lotus position. They appeared the picture of devotion, their eyes only half open, their legs crossed so that each ankle balanced easily on the thigh. I settled onto a hard, round cushion, hoping I would be able to stay in a half-lotus position for a reasonable amount of time.

Abbot Mihori was already seated on the floor, a beautiful old brass gong at his side. I expected he might recognize me but wasn't too worried. After all, it was an open worship session. All were welcome.

The abbot hit the silvery-sounding bell smoothly and announced the first line of the religious *sutra*, a booming prayer. The worshipers added their voices to his, and the hall vibrated with sound. Did they all understand Pali, the ancient blend of Sanskrit and Japanese in which the *sutra* was written? I moved my mouth as everyone chanted, increasing speed or slowing according to the fervor with which a different priest hit a gong.

It was very beautiful, sitting in the dark room with only the gilded altar glowing brightly in the candlelight. But the half-lotus was harder than I'd imagined; after fifteen minutes, I felt as if screws were being driven into the sides of my thighs, and my toes were going slowly numb. When the prayers finally wound down and it was time to stand up and then prostrate ourselves in the direction of the altar, I thought it had never felt so good to move.

After the prostrations, we settled back down again in the darkness for *zazen*, the sitting meditation that was the hallmark of Zen Buddhism. Zen meditation was something I'd tried before without any success. But it didn't matter if I did not float away—I'd come specifically to the main hall to think through what I'd learned the night before.

But silence was not to be had. After perhaps ten minutes, Abbot Mihori rose from his position near the altar to slowly pace through our ranks, holding a four-foot-long wooden paddle.

"Concentrate!" Abbot Mihori called out, sounding much blunter and ruder than I had ever imagined him. "Sit straight!"

Was he yelling directly at me? I suddenly realized my preoccupation with enduring the crossed-leg position had caused me to drift to the left. I righted myself, subtly adjusting my ankle to a less ambitious height.

I wasn't the only person who was reprimanded. Abbot Mihori criticized the posture of my European companion, who showed no signs of comprehending Japanese, and he noted the lack of concentration shown by others. "Erase all thoughts from your mind!" he shouted at a woman in her seventies, who cowered so deeply her nose touched the floor.

When his stick began slapping against worshipers' backs, I wanted to flee. Physical abuse was not what I'd come for. I concentrated furiously on the slow, smooth breathing the abbot wanted. Incredibly, I felt myself start to calm. I wasn't in nirvana—who could be, with all that yelling?—but I was philosophical. Zen worship would be over in forty minutes, and the worst thing that could happen would be that I'd be hit. The blow would last less than a second. If I could survive a right cross from Hugh Glendinning, I could survive a crack on the back.

The sounds of the gong flowed through me, and

my senses stirred at the thought that I was enacting rites that had traveled from India and China to Japan fourteen centuries ago. The black-robed monks in front had shunned the materialism of modern Japan for a harsh life dedicated to inward seeking. Could I do that? In a way, it was like leaving Roppongi Hills to do my own thing.

I felt a warning tap on my left shoulder and bowed, waiting for the real blow.

"Take your shoulder!" Abbot Mihori instructed brusquely. He hadn't recognized me.

As I pulled my shoulder in the way the other worshipers had done, the discipline paddle crashed down on my back. It took a second for the pain to transmit to my brain; when it got there, it smarted fiercely. Now I understood that the abbot had asked me to guard my shoulder blade from being shattered. There was a humanity to this formalized violence.

We bowed to each other, completing the ritual. The feeling in my back had evolved into a pleasant sort of ache; I treasured it for taking my mind away from my thighs and feet.

As the pain faded, I thought about the unexpected toughness Abbot Mihori had shown. Priests were supposed to be stern. Zen enforcer was the role the abbot had to play, just as he had been a gracious host when Angus and I had talked with him outside the temple the previous Friday.

Nana Mihori also played roles I didn't know about. Her exact connection to Nomu Ideta was something I wanted to understand. Maybe she had longed to acquire a family heirloom, but because she was a young, female sibling, she had not gotten the chance. If that was the case, I could offer her the *tansu* again.

The Zen family's involvement seemed as clear as the sky growing lighter outside the arched temple windows. Still, something nagged at me. Two men dead, neither from natural causes.

I tried to picture Nana Mihori, slim and slight in her *kimono*, following Nao Sakai from Hakone to Tokyo and deftly strangling him in a few minutes. It seemed impossible, given that the woman didn't drive a car—just like her husband. He had told me he needed Akemi to drive him to the hospital.

The connections between the Mihoris and the dead people were obvious; the motivation wasn't. I sighed, then caught myself for breathing audibly and out of place.

When the Zen session finally ended, I wasn't sure my legs would work anymore. I stumbled up to take my place in the line that was silently heading into the dining room. Here, each monk unwrapped the small cloth bundle he'd been carrying to reveal a set of three lacquer eating bowls. I was handed my own set of three along with the other visitors.

"Your first time?" the grandmother who'd been singled out for not concentrating whispered to me. When I nodded, she said, "They give us a complimentary bowl of rice gruel. I come three times a week for it."

If she attended so often, maybe she knew Kazuhito. I asked quietly whether she had seen him, and I was disappointed when she shook her head. Perhaps, as the vice abbot, he was more concerned with business matters.

I settled down between the grandmother and the European woman, watching carefully as monks silently passed down the table a large wooden bucket containing the lumpy gray gruel, followed by a smaller one containing pickled *daikon* radish. When everyone was served, the head monk blessed the food and led us in the recitation of several *sutras*. We ate quickly, with no conversation allowed.

At meal's end I felt not quite sated and slightly nervous, given the clean-up procedures I was observing. A monk slowly advanced along the table, pouring a meager splash of tea in everyone's bowl, which was circulated vigorously with chopsticks. Many worshipers slurped heartily from their bowls of dishwater. I slopped my bowl's remains into an empty ceramic urn that was making its way down the table. Then the empty bowls were dried on small cloths that everyone seemed to have brought from home. Like the Eastern European visitor, I handed my bowl back to a monk who I hoped would have an additional cleansing planned. Did the temple have a dishwasher? I thought about a terrible food-poisoning epidemic a few summers ago and shuddered.

My Zen experience over, I followed a line of monks down the temple steps, each one holding a huge straw hat. This meant they were leaving Horin-ji's grounds to collect donations for the temple. The hats served many purposes, among them protecting shaved heads from the sun or rain, and also falling so low they prevented the monks from being able to see the people in front of them, thus maintaining a Zen state while they begged.

It was ironic to think how safe the monks were in the cloistered world of Horin-ji; the food hygiene and chronic pain from sitting in a lotus position were probably their biggest risks. But the temple duties looked hard. I watched a monk wearing a gray work costume digging hard in the soil under some hydrangea bushes, his back curved at a punishing angle. As I approached, he lifted himself gradually and turned, hands folding in the prayerful *gassho* greeting.

It was the runner who'd intruded on Akemi's trail the night before. A flash of recognition lit his face, and he bowed.

"We meet once more," he said when he came up.

"Yes. I've just been worshiping."

"Really? You're foreign, aren't you?"

"Half Japanese. I live here," I said a bit defensively.

"In the teahouse?"

I wanted to say in Tokyo, but perhaps he'd peered through the teahouse's torn screens and seen the signs of my residence.

"I'm staying in the forest for a few days of meditation. I have permission," I added.

"The Mihoris are very generous, it's true. But what a funny place to stay." He put down his shovel and came closer to me.

"I have a strong desire to learn about Buddhism," I said, backing away.

"How do you like it?" He didn't move, but his eyes followed me, seeming to go into my soul.

The appreciative words I meant to offer couldn't come. Instead, I found myself saying, "I think Zen practice is very regimented. It hurt."

"After a while, pain becomes your friend," he said softly. "But you already know about pain."

"I don't understand."

"You practice judo with the Mihori daughter, don't you?" He gestured with his hands toward the loose pants I was wearing, which I realized now were part of a martial arts uniform. "Your injury—" The monk stretched out a finger to lightly touch my bruised cheek.

I was paralyzed, first from shock that a Japanese stranger had touched me—not even my relatives felt comfortable embracing me—and also from the undeniable sensuality of the touch. Even after his hand was gone, I felt a strange warmth where it had been. Like Abbot Mihori's blow to my shoulder, the pressure felt transforming, as if he'd glided across the bruise and taken it away. There was something unearthly about this man and his touch; I wondered if he had training in acupuncture or another healing art.

"I'm not a martial artist. I just had an accident," I said, finding my voice at last.

He picked up the shovel again. "This temple has always been a refuge. In *shōgun* times, women could not be legally divorced, no matter how abusive their husbands. Still, if they ran away and were admitted here, their husbands could not retrieve them. Women called Horin-ji the divorce temple."

"But it's not a nunnery anymore. The priests and monks are all men! And women have no chance of joining the ranks ever."

"In Zen, some traditions cannot change. But women certainly are welcome to visit our *zazen* practice every morning or evening, for that matter."

"Since you know so much about the temple's

history, may I ask you something about the Mihoris?" I asked.

"The good friends who gave you permission to stay here?" He sounded amused.

"What is Mrs. Mihori's family background? I understand she's not from Kamakura."

"Tokyo, I think. But I have no gossip. We are primarily silent in the monastery and temple. A chance meeting with a visitor such as yourself is very unusual."

"Well, I must go. It was very instructive to speak with a monk."

"It was not much of a formal meeting. I do not know your name."

"Shimura Rei." I said my name in the proper backwards fashion. "And you?"

"My name is Wajin. I look after the place."

A groundskeeper. I felt a rush of sympathy and said, "Akemi's going to be away today. You could jog on the track again without her noticing."

Wajin laughed lightly. "You mean you won't tell stories about me again?"

"I only said something because I was worried you saw me in a nontourist zone. I didn't know what you'd do—"

"But you have *permission*," he said sarcastically. "Why would my comments matter?"

He'd made his point, so I left for the women's rest room in a highly embarrassed fluster. I rinsed my hands and face because I sensed Wajin's touch had left a smudge of dirt below my eye. When I looked in the cloudy mirror above the sink, I did a double take. My bruise was gone.

18

Back in the teahouse, I ran a finger over the perfectly normal patch of skin under my eye. I'd always thought faith healing was a crock, but now I wasn't sure. Buddhism was full of miracles—trees that wept pearl-like tears, dead men returned to life. If Wajin had such a gift for healing, he was being wasted on the garden.

In the excitement over my transformed face, I'd forgotten to go to the Mihori house to pick up my pocket telephone. I'd have to return in the afternoon, when Miss Tanaka was doing errands in a different part of town. For now, I'd walk into Kamakura and use a pay phone.

After changing into the sundress I'd worn while making my balcony escape, I walked south on Kamakura-kaido, a long, narrow road lined with smaller Zen temples and a few restaurants and shops. As I strolled beside women taking their children to school, I noticed many of them were shielded by parasols, a hangover from the old days when pale skin signified aristocracy and brown skin

meant fieldworker. I knew I should follow the legions of
Japanese women who used parasols since their girlhood
and had entered their fifties and sixties with absolutely
unlined faces. It was hard, though, because my skin
rarely burned; it just soaked up the rays and glowed.
That's what it had felt like when Wajin had touched me:
as if I had been caressed by the sun.

None of the restaurants was open yet, so I killed
some time sitting on a bench near the grounds of
Hachiman Shrine, Kamakura's grandest Shinto worship site. Workmen were everywhere, erecting concession stands that were being decorated with artificial flowers and colorful streamers, symbols of the
upcoming Tanabata festival. I overheard some workers talking about an archery demonstration. They
needed to block off a long, narrow stretch of roadway that would be used for the horseback riders—the
question was, how would they get all the VIP seats
around the path? And how close could the seats be to
the archers, while still remaining safe?

By now it was 9 A.M., so Hugh would be off at work
and I could safely call the answering machine. I went to
a pay phone, slid in two hundred yen, and dialed.

"Yo." Angus answered the phone sounding as
though he was chewing something.

"Sorry to disturb you, Angus. If you hang up, I'll
just phone back and check the answering machine."

"Rei?" Angus sounded gleeful. "Hanging up's a
daft idea, seeing as Shug already listened to your calls
and erased them."

"Tell Hugh he's a bastard. To think of how I've
made sure he gets all his messages!"

"Don't get your knickers in a twist," he grumbled. "It was just some guy who left a message in Japanese we couldn't understand. I think my bro had a feeling who it was because he started going on about Japanese Elvis."

"Oh, that's Jun Kuroi! Anyone else?"

"Well . . ." Angus paused. "The last call was from a guy speaking English with an accent thicker than yogurt."

Mohsen. I'd have to track him down in Ameyoko Alley. "Thanks, Angus. I'll get going now."

"Don't you want to talk to me, hear how I'm doing?"

"I know Lieutenant Hata found out about your telephone cards and spared you. Do you know how lucky you are? If only you knew what Japanese prisons are like." Lounging in a phone booth forty kilometers from his smirking face, I felt free to be frank.

"Well, that cop kept my cards, so I can't call my friends overseas without using the flat telephone. You'd hate it. I can picture you ranting and raving!"

"It sounds like you miss me," I said sarcastically.

"Well, even *you're* better than my brother's new girlfriend, that bitch from upstairs—"

Winnie Clancy? I was so shocked I temporarily lost my grip on the receiver. I regained it and said, "Winnie's *married*."

"That isn't stopping her. She drops in for supper nightly. It's always meat—I reckon that between us we've put on half a stone. I can't speak for Shug, but I've got terrible indigestion."

"Don't tell me you want to become a vegan." I

tried to concentrate on that irony and not the disturbing fact that Winnie had supplanted me.

"I'm not! All I'm suggesting is that you should drop by for a meal sometime. And stay afterward. Winnie's bum is wearing a hole in the sofa, and the next thing you know, it'll be the bed."

"I understand. But it's impossible—it's over between Hugh and me."

"I wouldn't have thought you'd be such a quitter." Angus's words hung like a taunt as I hung up mad at Hugh, and also at myself.

After leaving frantic messages for Jun Kuroi on all five of his telephone numbers, I ordered a sugar-lemon crêpe and coffee at the crêpe shop I'd gone to with Mrs. Kita. The middle-aged woman spreading the crêpe batter on the huge skillet smiled at me as if she knew how long I'd been waiting for something to eat. I smiled back. With caffeine and sugar in my system, I was finally ready to work.

I made a quick circuit of all the antiques shops in the central district. Dealers did not usually enjoy showing old scrolls, given that the delicate paper rolls had to be removed from their snug wooden boxes, unrolled, and displayed without creating tears or wrinkles, and then rolled up again. I was primarily trying to gauge the price of early-twentieth-century scrolls.

I confessed my situation to the owner of Maeda Antiques, a small shop lying farther to the north where I'd bought wood-block prints before. Instead of unrolling her inventory, Mrs. Maeda let me page through an orderly photo portfolio of the scrolls she owned. This way neither of us would waste time.

"Who knows, I might find the perfect thing here. And I have other clients, I'm always on the lookout."

"At least you're honest about what you're doing," Mrs. Maeda said. "Not like some of them."

"Really?" I stopped flipping through the pictures.

"Oh, there are some temple families who come in and claim our Zen scrolls and relics are their property."

"Lots of religious relics come from temples. What do they want you to do, give it back?"

"Some store owners have, out of fear. No one wants to offend Buddha." She made a face. "Or a particular abbot's wife. When that lady came and claimed one of my scrolls was stolen property, I asked her to show me insurance papers or some proof her husband's family had it stolen. Of course, she had nothing."

A picture came to me of Nana Mihori's vast home, where the artwork rotated weekly. "This woman . . . she's very well known? She's in the Green and Pristine Society?"

"That's right. And immediately after I refused to give her my scroll for free, NO STOPPING signs were placed on both sides of the street. With no place to park a car, you can imagine how my customers have disappeared."

"What a shame," I mourned, feeling especially bad that I, one of her few walk-ins, wasn't able to buy something.

"Sometimes I wonder if I was foolish to have withheld what she wanted. If I'd given her the scroll, I'd have lost one hundred thousand yen. I've lost far more in sales, and I've even lost my assistant, Sato-san, who used to drive over each afternoon to cover for me. Now she can't come because there's no parking place!"

"She was a salesclerk?" I was getting an idea.

"That's right. The afternoons are when I must pick my granddaughter up from kindergarten, so I have to close the shop. It's just awful."

"I'll work afternoons for you," I offered. I had expected Mrs. Maeda to look either ecstatic or horrified. Instead, she looked confused. "I need a job. And a place to make and receive some business phone calls," I continued, determined to be honest.

"But I don't know you," she faltered.

"You mean I've come in here a half dozen times, but you don't know my family, my blood type, whatever!" I was getting upset. "Being foreign, I don't have an extensive résumé, but I have some references in the antiques community—my friend Mr. Ishida in Tokyo, for example."

"How are you a foreigner? Your name is Shimura."

"I'm from California," I said, pleased that she'd accepted me as Japanese.

"So you speak English!" Her eyes were huge.

"A little Spanish, too."

"You'll be wonderful for the tourists! There have been several occasions that *gaijin* have come, and I did not understand what they wanted."

"Foreigners *do* need special handling," I agreed. "They respond very well to discounts."

"I can pay you just twelve hundred yen an hour,

but I could offer you a trade discount . . . maybe forty percent off?"

"Really?" With a rate like that, maybe I could afford something for Mrs. Kita.

"It's the least I can do, and it will bring me some business, don't you think?"

Yoko-san, as I could now address her, had shown me around the whole shop by lunchtime. I rescued a cache of *obi*—brocade *kimono* sashes—she had jammed in a back storeroom. I also convinced her to help me hang out a colorful carp banner to fly in the wind.

"That's for the boys' day celebration. I cannot hang it in late summer."

"It's eye-catching and lets people know we're open," I told her. After she left, I walked around the small shop, taking stock of it and my situation. Once I would have thought it a step down to work as a store saleswoman, but what Yoko was paying me would cover my daily expenses, and I could start saving for the deposit on the next apartment I rented.

She was right that business was slow. I had just two customers that afternoon—one of whom paid eight thousand yen for an *obi*. I had time to telephone Mrs. Kita about the preliminary scroll selections I'd made. She promised to come in and choose something the following afternoon.

Closing time, five o'clock, came soon. I lingered but at last locked up and dropped the key back through the shop mailbox. Instead of taking the train, I walked back to Horin-ji. My feet dragged, and I realized how much I didn't want to get there.

Wajin knew too much about me, and the things I was learning about Nana Mihori were terrifying.

I approached the Mihori residence, thinking my pocket phone would be fully charged by now. I lurked in the bushes, watching Miss Tanaka take down the family's dry laundry. My black cotton panties, plain T-shirt, and shorts were also drying on the laundry rack. She frowned at them, and I resolved to do any further washing with my own two hands in the forest stream.

A gardener snipping the hedge came to ask permission for something. Miss Tanaka put down the laundry she was holding and followed him around to the rock garden.

My chance! I squeezed through the hedge and sprinted to the half-open window. There was no time to remove my shoes; I brushed them off as best I could and hustled in to find my telephone still firmly attached to the wall. I snatched it up along with its electrical cord and was safely behind the hedge when Miss Tanaka returned. I crawled under it and out to the main temple grounds.

"What are you doing?" a male voice inquired. Straight ahead of me were a pair of rough straw sandals. I looked up and saw a monk dressed in a work robe glaring down at me. "This area is off-limits to visitors."

I thought frantically. "Sorry. A wind came, and I, um, lost a contact lens!" What else could a girl on her hands and knees be worrying about?

The monk got to his knees and began looking. Feeling desperate, I pretended to find the lens. I got clumsily to my feet, professing thanks for his help.

"Isn't it torn by all the rough stones?" A new voice, more modulated and polite than the first man's. Wajin had joined us. This time he was wearing a fresh blue robe, not the soil-stained gray one. He put his hands together in a prayerful greeting. I bobbed my head, because my hands were full with the telephone and my imaginary contact lens.

"I think the lens is fine. If you'll excuse me . . ."

"You'll need to clean your lens with saline back at the teahouse." Wajin followed me.

"I know what to do, thanks." The phone rang, and I answered it, cradling it against my left shoulder.

"Rei-san?" The voice was instantly familiar to me from his various answering machine messages. Jun Kuroi.

"I'm so glad you called," I said, waving good-bye to Wajin, who still wouldn't leave.

"I need to talk," Jun whispered. "But do not call me again. My father heard some of your messages and wants me to keep away from you."

"Where do you want to see me? And why?" I added belatedly.

"Tomorrow afternoon I can come to Tokyo. I could meet you in Yoyogi Park at two."

"But Jun-san, I have a new job. I can't take off in the afternoon. The best I could do is meet you in midmorning or the evening."

"Eleven o'clock, then. It will take me a while to get in from Hakone, but I have something to tell you."

"Has anything happened to you since you got out? Are you in danger?"

"I'll explain tomorrow."

"Are you working again?" I couldn't say much more with Wajin around.

"As a night janitor in my father's dealership. My face is so well known that no one thinks I can work with customers anymore."

"I'm sorry. For everything," I said.

"It was my own stupidity to take Sakai in my car. I must go. I hear my father." He hung up.

"Boyfriend?" Wajin asked when I clicked off the talk button and resumed walking.

"No, and I'm not in the mood to talk. I came here to be *alone*."

"With the convenience of your pocket phone, *neh*?"

Exasperated, I stopped and faced him. "You know an awful lot about the luxuries of modern life. For a monk, you're extremely odd."

A gong sounded from the temple.

"Evening prayers. I must leave." Wajin sounded almost irritated, making me wonder how devout he really was.

"Go ahead, do your duty," I urged, glad to see him leave.

I ate pears and oranges for dinner, washing the meal down with water from a bottle I'd filled at the public lavatory. If I kept up this diet, my stomach would become smaller and I might have fewer cravings. In Buddhism, sensory deprivation was supposed to lead to emotional peace. Maybe so, but my stomach rumbled in disagreement all night long.

19

Someone was standing over me when I awoke the next morning. The crackling of footsteps on the old *tatami* had alerted me, along with the aroma of something delicious. I opened my eyes to the familiar sight of Akemi Mihori, dressed in her running gear and already covered with a faint sheen of sweat.

"You're so lazy. Get up!"

"When did you come home? How nice to see you!" I tried desperately to cloak my feelings of unease.

"Why weren't you on the track? You completely stopped running, didn't you?" Akemi demanded, yanking the sheet off me. I'd been sleeping in a long T-shirt, which I quickly pulled over my exposed lower parts.

"I was planning on doing it tonight—that's when I thought you were coming back."

"I thought we could run and then eat." She showed me a thermos of green tea and a tiered basket filled with pickled vegetables and *onigiri*, fresh rice balls stuffed with pickled plums that I loved. I must have smelled them when she walked in and woke me up.

"We could just eat?" I said hopefully. She laid out my first big meal in twenty-four hours, and I dug in.

"How was your demonstration?" I asked after I'd devoured two rice balls.

"Demonstration?" She looked blank for a moment. "Oh, that. It was fine. I won three matches and signed some autographs. The usual."

"Where was your demonstration held?" Her vagueness made me suddenly wary.

"Osaka."

"I mean at which sports arena?"

"A junior high school. Does it make you happy to know how far I've fallen?" She jumped up from where she'd been lounging on the futon's edge.

"Sorry, I didn't mean anything. I—I also have come down a bit. Yesterday I took a part-time job as a salesclerk."

"Now *that's* awful!" Akemi grimaced.

"Actually, I like feeling useful. It's a small shop near the temple with the famous Kannon statue. Maeda Antiques." I paused. "Your mother's shopped there, hasn't she?"

"I don't know." Akemi sounded uncomfortable. "I came in to ask if you wanted to use my shower. I accidentally left the *dojo* locked when I went away. Sorry."

"A shower would be great." I squinted at my watch. "But it's already eight. Your housekeeper will be awake."

"Tanaka-san went into town with my mother for

a Tanabata festival inspection. They won't be back until noon."

"Akemi, you know I only meant to stay here temporarily. If your mother's away, this morning might be a good time for me to make a discreet escape."

"Don't do that!" Akemi's voice was shrill.

I couldn't let on that I was scared. Forcing my face into a normal expression, I told her, "I'm trying to say that I've worn out your hospitality. There's an expression in English that's something like, after two days, fish and guests start to stink. Besides, I've got a regular job, so now I can afford a little room somewhere."

"There's no need to rush off," Akemi said firmly. "The Tanabata festival will keep my mother busy in town over the next four days. Besides, nobody outside myself knows you're here. And you're not cooking fish."

Thinking of my next move, I poured a little tea in the bowl where I'd eaten pickles, and sloshed it around a bit before drying it with a paper towel. Trying to give Akemi the impression I was staying put, I asked, "Is it okay if I keep this bowl for future use?"

"You've got Zen table manners!" Akemi smiled, relaxed again. "So what's your plan for today, now that you don't have to worry about moving out?"

"Well, this afternoon I work, of course. And this morning I have a business appointment in town." I was going to meet Jun, but that was my affair.

"I see." She looked at me hard. "I won't keep you, then."

"I am so grateful for all you've done, Akemi. I'd be living on the street if it weren't for you."

"You can stay as long as you like. I mean it." Akemi seemed as if she wanted to say more. I was glad she couldn't find the words. I'd had enough surprise declarations for a while.

I had some extra time before I was scheduled to meet Jun, so I made my way to the Old Tehian coffee shop in the hopes of finding out why Mohsen had called.

"He doesn't work here anymore." A tired-looking Japanese man peered out of the oil-spotted kitchen.

"Really! Where is he working now?" Could Hugh really have helped him get a job with an oil company?

"I don't know. He's gone."

"What do you mean, gone?"

"He disappeared." The cook shrugged. "His other friends came around asking, so I don't think they know where he is, either."

I felt as if I'd been slammed to the ground. Had Mohsen remembered something about the murder in Ueno Park? Everyone I brought into my problems was winding up dead.

"Did he tell you he was in danger? Was he afraid of someone?" I asked.

"They're all afraid of the Tokyo police, *neh?*" the man said shortly. "I think most likely he ran into visa trouble. Chances are he was thrown out of the country."

There was one way to find out. I left Ueno and got back on the Hibiya Line to Roppongi.

"Is Lieutenant Hata in?" I asked the desk sergeant at the Roppongi police station.

"He's in a staff meeting. And after that he's very busy."

"I'm connected to one of his unsolved cases. It's urgent that I speak to him." I handed the woman my business card.

She looked at the card, and then back at me. "The Roppongi Hills burglary!"

"That's right."

"Sit there," she said, pointing to a chair. "Don't go away." Then she did, to retrieve Hata, I thought. I was feeling almost cocky about being famous enough to get a police meeting interrupted, but I wound up waiting anyway. Half an hour passed before Lieutenant Hata came out to meet me.

"Sorry you had to wait," he said. I murmured my own apology for disturbing him, all the while thinking he looked extremely exhausted. There were dark shadows under his eyes and a sweaty pallor to his skin. When he ran his hand through his hair, it stuck up crazily.

"This case is killing me," he said. "I haven't seen light for a few days. Want to go for a walk?"

"You mean you haven't gone home?" I asked as we left the building and began walking east on Roppongi-dori. It wasn't too scenic underneath the Shuto Expressway, but Lieutenant Hata lifted his face to where the sun should have been.

"I've been here past midnight for the last four nights, and I have to be back by 6 A.M. The word's come down that this case has to be solved fast. People are beginning to worry a killer is targeting the antiques world." He paused. "At least you're still alive, but running off to who knows where!"

"There might be another death." I paused, watching the policeman's expression tighten.

"Might be? What are you trying to say?"

"Someone I know is missing. He was in the park at the time of the death. I did not mention him to you before. Angus told me that he called the apartment a few days ago looking for me. I went to the restaurant where he worked to talk to him, and the cook there told me he disappeared. No one knows where he is."

"You didn't give me the name of a witness? Now I know why this case is so impossible. So, what's the name?" Hata sighed heavily.

"His name is Mohsen Zavar."

"That name sounds Middle Eastern."

"He's from Iran. But I'm sure he's legal—he was working in a little restaurant——"

"When I look up his visa status, I can know for certain. Are you interested in filing a missing-person report?" He stopped at a vending machine and looked at the offerings.

I nodded. "I just don't think it would be like him to disappear. Hugh was trying to get him a position with a multinational oil company. Someone as smart as Mohsen wouldn't just walk away from the promise of a better life."

Lieutenant Hata put some yen in the machine and selected a can of Georgia coffee. "Do you want anything? I'm getting recharged."

"No, thanks. I have more to tell you—there's a connection between the Ideta and Mihori families. Nana Mihori is undoubtedly Nomu Ideta's relative, because I saw the same ancestor portraits at both their family altars."

"Are you sure? Old Japanese people look remarkably similar."

"If you don't believe me, go there and look at the pictures. Or check the family register. Or just ask Nana Mihori where she comes from!"

"Miss Shimura, we in the Japanese police try to be very sensitive to human rights. I cannot storm the Mihori household without a warrant, and they are not linked to your burglary case."

"Nana and Akemi Mihori were at our cocktail party. They could have easily taken Angus's house key and returned to burglarize the apartment."

"If Mohsen Zavar was also at your party and now has disappeared, don't you consider him a likelier suspect than two women from one of Japan's finest families?"

Lieutenant Hata peacefully sipped his coffee, and I longed to knock the can from his hand. How could he be so dense? He'd said he needed the case solved fast. Here I was handing him the tool, and he wouldn't take it.

"I appreciate the chance to talk with you. All I ask is that you write one of your memos about what I've said, in case I also vanish," I said acidly.

"Don't worry," he said, tossing the empty can in the small recycling hole built into the machine. "I will definitely check for your Iranian friend, but I'm afraid that what I learn will not please you. Lately foreign men with expired visas are disappearing into the countryside, where they can find work and not risk detection. Perhaps that is what your friend did."

"If he's in the country somewhere, I'd be very relieved. All I want is to know that he's alive."

"Alive and deported to Iran? How would you feel about that circumstance, if I find him?"

I didn't answer.

In a little over an hour I was scheduled to start working in Kamakura, so I raced straight to the train station before realizing I had forgotten the whole point of coming to Tokyo, my meeting with Jun Kuroi. I couldn't call him, not with the restrictions he'd set on my telephoning. Damn it. I'd have to wait for him to get in touch with me.

I arrived at Maeda Antiques to find my employer hanging out the carp banner in the hot summer breeze. She wasn't angry that I was five minutes late, just offered me a sample from the plate of sweets she'd put together for the day's customers. She'd taken a new, extremely optimistic attitude.

Mrs. Kita arrived an hour later, and after I helped her select an exquisite early-twentieth-century scroll at 10 percent off retail for her, and a 30 percent commission for me. We settled down to enjoy tea and *mochi* cakes.

"What a nice place for you to work! And I cannot believe the value you offered me. I'll tell all my friends. Don't you think Mrs. Mihori would be interested?"

"Mmm. How well do you know her?" I asked. Since Lieutenant Hata was loath to pursue things, I would do so on my own.

"I've heard some stories through our women's club. What are you curious about?" Mrs. Kita smiled.

"I was wondering where she came from. She has such innate style that I was thinking her own family background must have been high-class."

"Yes, she was an Ideta. The Idetas are an old samurai family. Having been in service to so many generations of landholders, the family accumulated many gifts. When we had a tour of the temple residence a few years ago, someone asked Mrs. Mihori which things she had brought to the marriage. She had brought nothing more than a bridal *tansu,* which is typical for everyone. I was surprised," Mrs. Kita added.

"A bridal *tansu!* Did you see it?" Had the Sado Island *tansu* once been hers—and then been taken away?

"Yes, it was an ornate Sendai piece decorated with butterfly metalwork."

Recalling the cranes and turtles on the Sado Island piece, my hopes for an easy solution were dashed. "Oh. I wonder where all the Idetas' other pieces are."

"In the family home in Denen-Chofu. The house and everything in it was inherited by Nana's elder brother."

That was the way real estate worked, too. My male cousin would never leave his mother and father's house because it was his to inherit, but my female cousin would have to find shelter through marriage.

"So, Mrs. Mihori's brother gets everything, I suppose. Is he much older than her?" I was purposely talking as if I didn't know Nomu Ideta had died.

"About twenty years, I think. He passed away recently, so I sent Mrs. Mihori a condolence card that she hasn't yet acknowledged. She's left with her sister, Haru, who took care of the brother all these years. She never married."

"Come to think of it, I saw the obituary in the newspaper," I admitted. "But I'm sure Mrs. Mihori's name wasn't listed."

"After marriage, a woman's name is removed from her father's family roster and added to her husband's records," Mrs. Kita said. "Probably the reporter didn't push any farther."

Not like Mrs. Kita, a dedicated gossip. I put on a bright smile and said, "So, I bet the sisters can finally inherit!"

"Not true." Mrs. Kita held up a manicured hand to still me. "Remember, the wealth must pass to a male heir. I think there's a distant nephew."

But Kazuhito, the vice abbot who was Nana's relative, had already been adopted into the Mihori clan. He didn't need more money.

"If the nephew is the person I'm thinking of, he already has quite an inheritance. It doesn't seem fair that he should get Nomu Ideta's house and antiques, does it?"

"He's the man. I would think you would understand how things work, given your studies of Japanese history."

What I'd actually studied was distant from social history: Japanese china, textiles, and paper—things that could be rescued and conserved, unlike the lives of the people around me.

※   ※   ※

That evening at Horin-ji I stood in the cover of
cypress trees and watched evening worship. Two
straight lines of monks proceeded into the main temple, eyes cast down and hands clasped piously.
Akemi's father led the procession. I looked for Wajin
but didn't see him.

The temple doors were fully open to the evening
sky, so I was able to watch the monks settle onto
their hard cushions and begin their *zazen* meditation.
In my shady corner under the trees, I also sat cross-
legged; the position made me involuntarily straighten
my back. A week of running had left my legs sore,
but I was starting to like the way that felt.

I was waiting for Kazuhito. After my conversation
with Mrs. Kita, I had tried to telephone Angus for a
detailed physical description of Akemi's priest-cousin.
But Hugh had answered the phone, so I hung up
without speaking. I was aware that this was a rotten
thing to do, especially since I'd been averaging about
three calls a day on the pocket phone from a phantom caller who would breathe softly, then hang up.
But I wasn't prepared to argue with Hugh.

I turned my thoughts back to the elusive Kazuhito.
I could also have asked Akemi what he looked like. But
she had behaved strangely earlier in the evening when
we had run together, slipping on headphones so she
could run listening to music instead. She was angry
about something, maybe my desire to leave.

Tonight's meditation was brief. The monks sat for
only half an hour before a priest hit a gong. Then the

men flowed into the prostrations that I had fumbled the morning before, and marched in their two lines into another section of the temple complex. I figured they were going to eat.

How long would I wait for Kazuhito, and what would it bring me? In a way, I just wanted the opportunity to look at him, look into his eyes and see what was there. Whether he could have murdered, or whether he was likely to be the next person killed. He'd had a devastating diabetes attack recently. Could that have been triggered by the murderer?

A flicker of movement in the green trees caught my eye. Two slender figures emerged from the direction of the Mihoris' house: Akemi, whom I'd just been worrying about, and her mother, Nana. As they walked slowly in my direction I moved deeper into the underbrush.

"*Taihen komatta-wa.*"

Everything's ruined. I caught the tail end of Nana Mihori's words to Akemi; she spoke with a sharpness I hadn't heard before.

"It's not over. Let's wait a little longer, *neh?*" Akemi consoled her.

"You said I could trust her. I believed you." Nana stopped. She was close enough for me to reach out and touch the dark purple of her *kimono* patterned with a spray of hydrangea blooms. All I could see of Akemi were her small, broad feet in their expensive sneakers and her smooth, muscular legs.

"She's been full of surprises, hasn't she?" Akemi said dryly, and I felt myself grow damp with sweat. They were talking about me.

"We have to take care of her." Nana sat down on a bamboo bench, causing a few pigeons to rise up and wing their way toward my bush. As they settled into the green branches, I prayed no one would turn around and see my face.

"The festival first. That's our priority," Akemi said.

"Yes, thank you for helping with things. I'm sorry I had to go away when you needed me," Nana said.

"It was nothing," Akemi said.

"He wants to speak to me tonight. What should I say?"

"Just smile and play dumb, like you have over all these years." Through the leaves, I could see Akemi flex each leg, as if she couldn't bear to waste a moment not exercising.

"Akemi—" There was finally a note of warning in the parent's voice.

"Just a joke, *neh*? Come on, the mosquitoes are eating me."

To my surprise, they mounted the steps of the temple. They must be going to dinner with the monks and Abbot Mihori.

When I was sure they were really gone, I unhitched myself from my cramped position and, staying under the cover of the bushes, crept out of the temple garden. On autopilot, I made my way into the woods and my no-longer-secret teahouse.

Nana hadn't used my name in the conversation, but she obviously knew I was staying there. And when she reminded her daughter to take care of things, I had a distinct feeling it meant something different than bringing me food.

The festival would come first—the Tanabata festival, which put a brilliant face over everything in town. Just that afternoon Akemi had asked me to participate. Following our silent, unhappy run together, she'd taken me to the temple's storehouse, packed with traditional summer costumes and masks. I would wear a fox mask and a summery red flowered *yukata*. Akemi's *yukata* was a girlish pink and yellow, completely incongruous with the bear's face she planned to wear. We would ride through Kamakura with other celebrities in a wheeled *rikisha* chariot that would be propelled by a running, costumed man—all the town's most attractive young hunks would be working, Akemi had assured me.

A last hurrah, and then what? The possibilities were endlessly horrible. I remembered how Akemi had sparred with her male partner, waiting for the first sign of inattention and then smashing him into the mat. She was patient and ruthless.

I could tell Lieutenant Hata about this conversation I'd overheard, but the snatches of dialogue added up to nothing. Nana had said she was upset and couldn't trust someone. Akemi told her mother to concentrate on the festival, and they'd take care of the problem.

I would go through the festival, watching out for myself. It was all I could do.

20

For a change, Yoko Maeda's shop was bustling when I arrived at noon on the day of the Tanabata festival. Tourists were caressing hand-embroidered *obi* and exclaiming over the vintage bamboo star and flower decorations we had hung from the ceiling.

"It's a school holiday, so my granddaughter's here for the day. We can all work together," Yoko said. A seven-year-old girl peeped shyly at me, then returned to playing with her *tamagotchi*, an egg-shaped plastic toy with a window showing an anodyne display of a chicken and a statement of its needs at the moment. The electronic pet had to be "fed" or "walked" every few hours; if the correct codes weren't punched in, the computer within would declare the chicken dead. *Tamagotchi* were wildly popular with children but seemed boring to me, especially in comparison with Maeda Antiques' stock of antique dolls. I wanted to coax Yoko's granddaughter into the doll section, but the afternoon was so busy I could barely keep the *kimono* straight and answer all the foreign tourists' questions. Their sudden mass appearance mystified me until someone told me that because of the day's festival, the Green and Pristine Society had paid for a fleet of trolley-style buses to transport tourists to temples and shops. If I'd known about the trolley, I could have taken it myself instead of walking two miles in the sun.

The crowd slacked off around four o'clock, when the festival began. Mrs. Maeda shooed me off, and I hopped the last trolley on her street to go back to the temple. I disembarked with everyone at the main gate, but slipped off into the woods so I could enter without paying admission.

Akemi had left a note inside the teahouse: "I've got your costume. Come to the *dojo* for your shower." It was easy enough for her to offer, but I had to get into the family compound unnoticed. I stuck my toiletries in my backpack, hoping she'd have a fresh towel to lend me, and set off for the *dojo*.

"Are you going to celebrate Tanabata?" Wajin's voice startled me as I reached the clearing between the forest and the Mihoris' private residence. He was lounging on a boulder in the elaborate rock garden. "What do you think of my costume?" He stood up, showing off a spectacular turquoise robe.

"Pretty fancy," I whispered. "Please don't talk so loudly. The Mihori parents don't know I'm here."

"What are you going to wear, one of Akemi's martial arts uniforms?"

"No, I'm going traditional. But stay away from me, okay? I don't need the attention."

"You should wear a mask." He was looking at me in a familiar, mischievous way. "It's quite common for revelers to hide behind animal faces."

"I know that," I interrupted him. "I'm going as a fox."

"The smartest animal of all!"

"I really have to go," I said, and bolted toward the *dojo*, thinking Wajin should get out of public view. After all, what right did a monk have to hang around the abbot's residence? He was not dressed to rake the garden or do any weeding.

"It's about time!" Akemi chided when I found her fussing with her pretty *yukata*. "We have to be at the *rikisha* stand in twenty minutes. Get in the shower!"

Given my life without a bathroom, the last thing I wanted was to hurry through a lovely hot shower. I was still drying myself when Akemi threw the red *yukata* on me and began tying the *obi* around my waist.

"Let me find some underwear," I protested.

"Forget it! Women in the olden days wore no underwear. Besides, no one can tell." Akemi slipped the bear mask over her head.

It was true that the light cotton robe covered me from shoulder to ankle, but the thought of being unclothed was disturbing. What if there were some kind of accident and I tumbled from the float? I didn't like the idea of twenty thousand tourists watching. I scrounged around in my backpack to find the slightly damp underpants I'd washed the day before in the stream in the woods.

"This is what you need to worry about!" Akemi held up a pair of traditional, three-inch-high *geta* sandals made from smoothly polished wood. I stepped up onto them; it would be a struggle to keep my balance.

"I have to go all the way to the temple exit in these sandals? I don't know if I can make it."

"I'm not asking you to run, just to walk." Akemi slipped the fox mask over my head, yanking the elastic cord tightly around the back of my damp head. I'd have an odd-looking bump when my hair dried. "There! You're perfect."

"Tell me again why I have to do this. I thought the idea was for me to fade into the forest."

"You've stayed here for days and won't do me one favor?" Akemi regarded me from behind her bear mask, a caricature of goodwill.

"Something's going on below the surface, isn't it? You and your mother—" I needed to bring up what I'd overheard in the garden.

Akemi stopped me. "We can't talk about that now. All I ask is that you sit beside me keeping your mouth shut and your eyes open."

I followed my new enemy across the temple grounds, the high platform sandals altering my walk to a rather mincing gait. Having always craved height, I liked being three inches taller, but I knew I'd have rotten blisters by the evening's end.

We were assigned to the sixth *rikisha* in a parade of maybe thirty, all beautifully decorated with paper streamers, flowers, and stars. As I settled onto a cushioned seat next to Akemi on the small, open truck, no one questioned my presence. Our *rikisha* driver was Akemi's sparring partner. I was surprised to see him bantering good-naturedly with the woman who had thrown him over her hip the week before. Tonight he was drinking *sake*, and he passed Akemi a flask.

"So, how much *sake* does it take for a man to lose his virility?" Akemi teased. Some masked ladies sitting in the *rikisha* around us laughed. Listening to their low voices and catching a glimpse of an extremely hairy leg, I began to doubt the princesses were all female.

As we rolled south into Kamakura's main district, the crowds lining the street grew. I marveled at how the cherry-tree-lined walkway we were riding up had been hung with colorful streamers and *origami* decorations. I waved a bamboo pole decorated with *washi* paper ornaments, feeling like a member of a very bizarre royal family. Through my mask's small eyeholes, I scanned the crowd, thousands of Japanese dressed in colorful *yukata* similar to the one I was wearing. Near the Asahi beer stall I saw a couple of reddish blond heads standing out against the dark-haired sea. I squinted hard to focus and recognized the Glendinning brothers. I remembered how Angus had pressed Hugh to bring him to the festival. He must have won.

My initial response was to dive down in the *rikisha*, but I figured that would be too noticeable. Instead, I stopped waving my wand and hunched over, looking at my sandals.

"You look weird." Akemi's whisper was sharp.

"It's *them*. Hugh and Angus! By Asahi beer," I muttered in English.

"Don't talk about buying beer! This *rikisha* is advertising the best *sake* in Kamakura!" one of the masculine princesses bellowed.

"Yeah, give my uptight friend a drink!" Akemi joked, adding, "No one can recognize you with the mask, silly."

She was right. In addition, Hugh had no idea I was living in Kamakura, or that I would be foolish enough to parade around on a *rikisha*. I raised my head again and found that neither he nor Angus was even looking at the parade. They were watching a woman approaching them: Winnie Clancy, wearing a very tasteful, long-skirted linen dress that I could never have carried off. She looked very much at home as she slipped her arm into Hugh's.

My vehicle passed them, so I could no longer observe. The damage was done. Something inside me had been permanently crushed under the wheels of the *rikisha*. I took a gulp of *sake* and listened to Akemi chatting to the people around us. Despite her costume, everyone knew who she was; there were some respectful references to her gym, which she made into self-deprecating jokes.

I remembered all the Kamakura townspeople who had greeted Akemi enthusiastically when we'd gone into town for dinner. She seemed equally at home with the people on parade. Everyone was chatting about what was going to happen next, Akemi's father's forthcoming speech at the parade's ending point near the Hachiman Shrine. Abbot Mihori and other dignitaries would speak, followed by local children reciting prayers they had written to the festival's goddess.

"The beginning is pretty boring," Akemi told me. "The only thing I really enjoy is the archery demonstration. I fantasize about an arrow being shot in a certain direction."

Was she thinking about her cousin Kazuhito? I grew nervous again, remembering that Kamakura was a prime place for assassinations. An extremely famous murder had taken place here in 1219, when the young *shōgun* Sanetomo of the Hojo clan was beheaded by a jealous relative. Most people believed the killer had been his nephew, but there were plenty of conspiracy theories about the others who might have hidden inside the massive gingko tree that stood to the left of the shrine stairs and jumped out to do the deed. It was an unsolved death with family links, just like the Ideta-Mihori saga.

The parade ended at the ornate red entrance to the Hachiman Shrine. We decamped, and I stood next to Akemi amid the other *rikisha* riders. Akemi's father stood on a stage with several other Buddhist priests, as well as some Shinto priests, who wore more elaborate, skirted costumes and wonderful headdresses. The mayor of Kamakura and some other city officials were on stage wearing sober business suits. There wasn't a woman among them.

"I can't believe he gets to speak first." Akemi's voice grated in my ear, and I followed her gaze to see Wajin, resplendent in the brilliant turquoise robe, step up to the microphone. I realized now that the robe was not a costume; he was of higher temple rank than I'd assumed.

"Good evening. On behalf of Abbot Mihori and the entire religious and business community of Kamakura, I welcome our esteemed visitors to a celebration of Tanabata." Wajin bowed deeply. He sounded warm yet authoritative, speaking in a powerful, low-pitched voice I hadn't heard him use before.

"On behalf of the family! How sweet." Akemi's complaining chorus was irritating; I tried to tune her out and translate Wajin's words.

"This star festival provides us a unique opportunity to celebrate the summer season and also explore the meaning of ancient native myths. The Tanabata festival began with noblewomen who wrote poems and wishes on strips of colored paper that were tied to branches of the sacred bamboo tree. These prayerful branches were offered to the star goddess Orihime, who was known for her skill as a weaver. Orihime was engaged to marry her true love, Kengyu, the cowherd living on another star. Does anyone know the rest of the story?" He smiled at the group of primary school students in summer sailor suit uniforms, but no one dared speak.

"When Orihime fell in love, she stopped weaving. Her father, the emperor of the sky, did not approve. Maybe he was afraid of losing his little girl." As Wajin spoke, his eyes swept the crowd and landed on me. I'd been stupid to tell him I was wearing a fox mask, but surely others were wearing such masks, too.

"The emperor banished the pair to opposite sides of the Milky Way. The lovers are allowed to meet on just one night each year. Tonight is that night, when they will run across a bridge built by birds to be together."

A flock of pigeons that had been roosting on the shrine's tiled roof chose that moment to lift off and circle over the stage, their wings beating up a storm. Had Wajin willed them to move? Nothing would surprise me after he had erased my black eye with the touch of his finger.

Wajin glanced upward, smiled, and then looked straight at the crowd. "Tanabata is a magical night. May all your dreams come true. First we will have a recitation of prayerful wishes from members of the first grade at Kamakura Primary School. . . ."

Akemi nudged me. "We don't have to listen to the stupid children. Let's go over to the archery area before all the good seats are gone."

"I like children." I was also tired of being yanked around.

"Princess Orihime, I hope your family is in good health and your father is not angry anymore. Please help me pass my *kanji* examination. Guess what? I love you!" a round-faced little girl with pigtails recited.

"Very well said by young Michiko Otani. Do any little boys have wishes or prayers to offer?" Wajin said.

"I can't stand Kazuhito when he's like this, so phony. If you knew the real guy, you'd be as disgusted as me," Akemi muttered.

"Kazuhito?" I asked dumbly.

"My cousin, silly, the one who's been talking! He thinks he is so important he doesn't even bother introducing himself anymore."

When Akemi turned on her heel and started pushing through the crowd to go to the archery field, I followed, trying to put the facts together. Kazuhito was the man I knew as Wajin.

"I think I've seen your cousin around, but I thought he had a different name," I said. "Isn't it Wajin?"

"Now it is Wajin. According to Buddhist custom, monks are given a name with Chinese roots instead of Japanese when they are fully initiated. The *kanji* characters used to write the old and new name are identical, but the name is pronounced differently."

Looking at Akemi's cousin's name written in *kanji* on the festival program, I saw that the two pictograms making up his name were simple enough that even I knew them: "peace" and "person." Peaceful Person was the perfect name for a man of Buddhism. And I was inwardly glad that Wajin hadn't lied about his name to me. I was also impressed that he chose to work in the garden, given his high status.

We reached the archery zone, a long, fairly narrow dirt roadway that was already filled with men dressed in samurai armor readying their horses. Akemi grabbed a folding chair in the front row, and I sat down next to her.

"I thought Wajin—I mean, Kazuhito—was the frail type. Angus saw him faint the first day I came to go running with you."

"He is delicate. A real wimp," Akemi said.

"Doesn't he work in the garden?" I asked cautiously.

"Gardening's not difficult! He says he works at

every job within the temple so he can understand what the monks go through. That's what he tells my father, but I think it's because he gets easily distracted. He looks for chances to be outside and talk to people, when he really should be more silent."

That did sound a lot like the Wajin I'd met—who wouldn't leave me alone. He'd been in his element giving a speech to the crowd. Hearty applause sounded after Wajin's last words, and the crowd rose en masse and began sweeping toward the archery range. I had limited time to speak privately, so I asked Akemi, "Is Kazuhito phony, or is he just extremely skilled at getting along with people? I'm sorry he will eventually get the temple and everything, but perhaps he is not so bad."

"You think I'm jealous! I thought you understood me. After all I've done for you!" Akemi had gotten to her feet and was staring at me in horror.

"Shhh, let's talk about it later," I said. The seats around us had filled so fast it was now standing room only. I was worried people would lean in and listen to Miss Fox and Miss Bear's fight.

"Forget it. If you don't recognize how dangerous that bastard is, you're doomed," Akemi said, taking one last look at me and storming off.

The seat next to me was filled in a scant half second with an eight-year-old boy anxious for the sports to begin. He squirmed in his seat, fussing with a *tamagotchi* toy like the one Yoko Maeda's granddaughter had been playing with.

"Are the arrows really sharp? Will they hit us?"

the boy asked his father, who was hovering behind me, perhaps in the hope I'd give up my seat.

"Why are you wearing a fox mask?" The boy looked at me petulantly and began knocking his *tamagotchi* against my thigh.

"It's a folk tradition to wear masks at Tanabata," I began patiently.

"Are you a boy fox or girl fox?"

"Girl, actually."

"But you have hair like a boy! And your voice is weird."

"I'm from another country." I looked to the boy's father for help.

"My son is very rude. I apologize. . . ."

The whole thing was beginning to irritate me. I hated the mask, too. I lifted it up, releasing my damp face to the fresh air, glad that Akemi was not around to stop me. I said to the boy, "I'm female. See?"

"You're sweaty like a construction worker. And construction workers are boys!"

I sighed, glad that the tournament was finally beginning and the child would have some real men to focus on.

"My *tamagotchi!* You knocked it on the ground!" The boy pummeled me.

"Shhh, look at the knights on their horses," I said, wishing his father would take some responsibility. "All the pretty horses!"

At a sharp command, the costumed riders urged their horses into a slow canter toward each other, a speed determined by the shortness of the field.

"*Otōsan*, make her give it to me!"

The father muttered an apology to me, but I gave up and bent down. The plastic egg had rolled off my leg and somewhere under the chair. My long *yukata* was complicating the search. As I groped between my ankles, I was surprised by a rush of air and an odd, vibrating collision.

"An arrow, *Otōsan!* A real arrow!"

I looked over my shoulder and saw what the little boy was talking about—a foot-long metal arrow quivering in the back of my chair.

21

Had I been sitting upright, the arrow would have hit me between my breasts. I barely had time to contemplate that horror before I sensed another speeding blur. I fell forward, yanking the annoying boy underneath me for his own safety as another arrow hammered my chair.

The awful vibrating sound of the arrow was almost masked by the stampede. The boy's father had finally taken action, wrestling his child away, and everyone around us was screaming and knocking over chairs in their haste to get out of the target area. People ran straight onto the field where the archers had all called their horses to a halt.

"Stay calm," the announcer screamed into a bullhorn. "No archer on the field has shot any arrows. The arrows have come from somewhere else. Please stay calm!"

I wasn't sticking around to find out who the shooter was. I kicked off my treacherous sandals and merged into the crowd. I ran blindly, passing the panicked majority and the concession stands, wanting to get off the shrine grounds and to a place where there were no flying arrows.

"Run, Forrest Gump! Run!" Angus Glendinning called as I whizzed past his position near the Asahi beer booth. I didn't pause, but in my peripheral vision I saw Hugh drop his arm from around Winnie's shoulders. So he'd recognized me.

I was no longer concerned about his new romance. Was the archer behind me? I didn't want to look when I heard someone running behind me. I withdrew all the things Akemi had taught me about pacing and sprinted as fast as I could along the path where the *rikisha* had traveled.

I would have made it if my bare foot hadn't landed on nettles. In the second I paused, a body slammed into me.

"Your stride is ex—ex—excellent." Hugh was panting hard.

"Get off me before it's too late," I pleaded from my position underneath him.

"What a coincidence that you're at the festival! Now I know why Angus was so bent on coming here." Hugh's short breaths landed on the back of my neck like small explosions.

"Okay, you found me. Go back and hold hands with Winnie." I twisted, trying to get him off me.

"You're blowing things out of proportion! I only had my arm around her to keep from getting separated in the crowd. She's like an older sister to me." Hugh wouldn't let go.

I bucked sharply underneath him, causing him to groan and grab for his groin. I hadn't hurt him badly, just enough to help restore my dignity. I sat up, pulling my robe together again and feeling along the sore patch on my foot.

Hugh dug around in his pocket and pulled out his Swiss Army Knife key chain. "Use the tweezer attachment, okay? But it's getting too dark to see."

I thrust the key chain back at him. "I can't stay here any longer while I'm under attack!" I told him in a few sentences what had happened at the archery field. "It wasn't one of the knights on horseback, because the arrow came from the wrong direction. It was someone else."

"Come back to Tokyo with me." Hugh was already pulling me to my feet.

"I can't. Everything I own is at the teahouse. I have to go there tonight."

"Lead on, then, because I'm not leaving you. Not tonight."

A few days earlier I wouldn't have shown him the teahouse, but now I thought of it as my last refuge. The walk that night was especially slow with my sore foot and no flashlight. When we finally reached the woods, Hugh started muttering about poison ivy. A small, mangy animal ran into the path and stared at us with cold yellow eyes, Hugh grabbed at me for support.

"What is it, a hound from hell?"

"It's called a *tanuki*. It's just a Japanese raccoon dog."

"Have you really been staying here? How do you

even get inside?" Hugh asked when we reached the ruined teahouse.

"These windows are like doors. But only one works." I slid the *shoji* aside and climbed into my small room. After Hugh followed, I slammed the screen closed and lit the citronella candle.

I noticed a large paper shopping bag from the Union Supermarket standing in the middle of the room. I opened it and found the street clothes I had left in Akemi's shower room. She'd dropped it off so I wouldn't have to come to her the next day to get it. If she'd had time to drop the bag off, she couldn't have shot at me on the archery course.

"This is as bad as your old place in North Tokyo. But more minimalist." Hugh didn't pay attention to the bag; instead, his gaze wandered over the worn futon and the decrepit *tatami*. "I gather there's no kitchen. Do you even have a loo?"

"I use the ladies' room near the temple grounds. Or, in times of desperation, I go in the woods."

"Well, at least you have the pocket phone. Thank God for that. In fact, I need to make a call."

Disappointed beyond words, I watched him punch in a phone number. "I just paged Angus. He'll call me back."

"Angus got himself a *pager*? Don't you think that's a little suspicious?" I asked.

"I'm renting it for him," Hugh snapped. Soon enough, the pocket phone rang and he answered. "Angus? Er, I called to ask a favor . . . would you go back to Tokyo with Winnie? I'm tied up."

Angus must have given him an earful, because

Hugh listened with a downcast expression and then handed me the telephone. "He wants to say hello."

"Well done, Rei!" Angus drawled. "Now that Shug's out of the way, I'll arrange to have Winnie exterminated. I heard there's a mercenary running around with a bow and arrow."

"That's not funny."

"Keep my brother for the night, okay? I'll go back with Winnie, but after that I'm going to be out. Make sure he doesn't call the flat, and don't tell him that I told you so, all right? I don't want to hurt his brotherly feelings." Angus clicked off.

Poor Hugh. Of course I wasn't going to tell him Angus didn't want to be with him and was probably going to throw a rave at Roppongi Hills or stay out all night getting in trouble.

"I'm incredibly thirsty. What have you got?" Hugh asked.

I waved him toward the corner where I kept my collection of fruit and bottled water.

"Angus told me the festival's collapsed. Police are crawling all over the place, and all the tourists are fighting for space on the trolleys so they can get back to the train station," Hugh said after he'd poured the warmish water into two tea bowls for us to drink from.

The thought came to me that the shooter might have fired into the crowd to cause mass hysteria. I couldn't think of a better way to embarrass the Mihoris or ensure the festival would never be held again. I voiced my feelings, but Hugh brushed them aside.

"Come closer to the candle and show me your foot." He was flexing his Swiss Army Knife tweezers. "You were the target. How convenient for Akemi to set you up in the first row and then leave."

"It was only because we fought that she left." I flinched as he pulled out the longest nettle first.

"You mean you fight with other people besides my brother and me?"

"I said something about her cousin, and she went ballistic." I wiggled my foot, but he held on to it.

"You're talking about the vice abbot who had a seizure? The one Angus saved? We saw him tonight."

"Where?"

"He was standing on stage giving a speech we couldn't understand. Then some kids came up to recite something, and he and Akemi's father moved off."

"Toward the archery demonstration?"

"I didn't see. There were too many people around, and Winnie was nattering about wanting to buy sausage on a stick." He looked at me. "Sorry. You look hungry."

I was actually having vulgar thoughts about the kind of sausage Winnie really wanted, but I just said, "I'm always hungry. I can't store food here because of the ants."

"Do you want some roasted chestnuts? I'd just bought some when you ran by." He pulled a crumpled paper package out of his shirt pocket. "Chestnuts and water. One of our more bizarre candlelight dinners."

I didn't want to get distracted, so I gave him a hard look and said, "Remember how I thought the *tansu* was the link between Nao Sakai and Nomu Ideta's deaths? Nomu Ideta, the old man who originally owned it, was Nana Mihori's elder brother. I was sent to buy the *tansu* from Nao Sakai so there would be no suspicion she was behind it."

Hugh stared at me, then said, "You refused to deliver the *tansu* because the age was wrong. Perhaps it's valuable for a different reason."

"All I know is that Nana and Akemi have some kind of secret. And now Mohsen's vanished, and Jun Kuroi is in danger."

"Mohsen's fine," Hugh said easily. "He flew to Korea for a few days so that the British company that's going to hire him can finish the paperwork and allow him to reenter with a proper visa."

"You knew this all the time that I thought he had been murdered?" I was outraged.

"You should have asked instead of hanging up every time I answered the telephone. In fact, Mohsen called last night to see how you were doing. It was pretty embarrassing not to be able to tell him where you were, that I was completely out of your life."

"Thank God he's all right," I said. "I can't wait to tell Lieutenant Hata."

"Just because the Mihoris haven't killed Mohsen it doesn't mean they aren't plotting against another man," Hugh said. "Perhaps you heard them talking about me."

"Don't make me laugh! They hardly know you exist."

"Since you've left me, I'm the one who's stuck with the *tansu,* and it's a risk. I want it out."

"Okay, I'll get rid of it. Maybe Mr. Ishida will let me put it in his warehouse," I said.

"Can you do it tomorrow? You need to come to the flat anyway, as half your wood-block prints are gone."

"Stolen?" I was horrified. My financial losses were mounting.

"Not quite." Hugh chuckled. "We were surprised yesterday morning by a contingent of ladies who had a shopping appointment you apparently forgot."

"Oh, no!" I remembered them now: the Cherry Blossom Ladies' Club. I could have cried for the lost sales.

"I made them some tea and told them you'd been called away on a sudden buying trip. Angus handled the sales. You cleared about ninety thousand yen."

Having bought the prints months ago, I could barely remember how much cash I'd laid out for them, but ninety thousand yen—about seven hundred and fifty dollars—would be very useful.

"How did Angus price them? Usually I give the customer a price ten percent lower than the tags on the back of the pictures."

"Angus sold them exactly as marked and everyone was perfectly happy. Don't complain."

"Mrs. Maeda would be impressed," I said, smiling. "She'd probably rather have Angus for her sales-clerk than me!"

"Who's Mrs. Maeda?"

"My new employer. I've been working afternoons at her antiques shop in Kamakura."

"You created a whole new life for yourself, didn't you? Just like that." Hugh snapped his fingers. "Well, if you stop home with me tomorrow morning, you can sort out the *tansu* and take a shower, change your clothes—"

"I suppose I'm not exactly fresh," I said, pushing back my damp bangs. I'd showered two hours ago, but Akemi had some kind of unscented organic soap that might not have done its job.

Hugh's voice dropped. "I love your smell. So much that I haven't changed the sheets."

I reminded myself that he was with me as a matter of duty. I said, "The sooner we go to sleep the sooner we can leave."

"That's true." He sounded businesslike again. "All right, shall we flip for the futon?"

"Are you crazy? Neither of us should have to suffer sleeping directly on the *tatami*." I shuddered. "It's full of little biting creatures."

"What's with the chirping over there?" He looked suspiciously at the corner before he started undressing.

"It's a cricket. You should feel blessed! In the Edo period, aristocrats kept crickets in cages and fed and watered them all summer because their chirping sound was considered so beautiful. There are still some high-class restaurants that use crickets for a dining accompaniment." I kept going, trying to distract myself from the sight of Hugh's casual disrobing. When he unbuttoned his madras shirt, I saw a very slight expansion at the waist; not enough to be unattractive, but enough to make me want to touch it.

"I'm going out for a leak. If I don't return, the *tanuki* got me."

I used Hugh's absence to change into a semiclean T-shirt and bury myself completely under the thin sheet. The pocket phone rang, and, having a strong feeling it was my phantom caller, I did not pick up. If it was Angus, he could leave a message on my voice mail.

The phone had stopped ringing by the time Hugh returned and slipped in next to me.

"This wretched futon is so narrow I'll be on top of you, like it or not," he whispered as he curled against my back, wrapping his arms around me. Even if there had been room, I couldn't move away. I was paralyzed with longing.

"You're not being fair," I muttered as he began kissing the nape of my neck.

"Aha. You're wearing my vest." His hands moved underneath the T-shirt, stroking my breasts. "I want it back."

"It's yours." In a sudden movement I pulled the shirt over my head. I turned to face him. My hands shook as they reached for him.

Hugh kissed me deeply, then broke away. "We can't."

"What's wrong?"

"When I made plans to come to Kamakura tonight, it was just to humor my brother! I didn't expect I'd find you."

"You were with Winnie." I felt a stab of pain.

"She's like an older sister to me," Hugh repeated, stroking my hair. "It's not even worth talking about, not when we finally have time alone together."

It was our night. A succession of terrible events had moved the stars in line and brought him to my bed. It was meant to be. I moved my mouth in a trail down his stomach, knowing how to give the kind of pleasure he could not resist.

"You don't understand! I have nothing with me. No condom——"

"Tonight I don't care," I whispered, climbing on top.

"If we do it, you'll hate me tomorrow," he murmured.

"I don't care." And as I slid down on him, I learned why so many people had unprotected sex. The feeling was more intimate and delicious than anything I'd ever dreamed of. I looked down at him, willing him to open his eyes again and watch me moving in the candlelight. He did.

"This is too good." His expression was pure rapture.

"I love this. I love you," I blurted.

The cricket sang, Hugh grabbed my hips, and I flew.

22

I awoke to warm pressure on my mouth. I savored the kiss and took my time opening my eyes.

"Such a beautiful morning," Hugh said, looking from my face to the window. "It's the first time since I left Scotland that I've been woken by birdsong."

I squinted at my watch, which said 5:30. It was as if Hugh had some kind of inner alarm clock that always went off before mine. When I told him what I was thinking, he laughed.

"It's happiness, Rei. I always wake up first and watch you. Have you forgotten?"

When things between us were bad, he got out of bed before I awoke. That was the other side to the coin. I got up, slipping my wrinkled rayon sundress over my head before digging in my backpack for some clean underwear. I drew back my hand when I caught a glimpse of something moving underneath the clothes.

"Hey, maybe you'll get a chance to see a *tanuki* in

daylight." I beckoned to Hugh, who leaned over to examine the heaving laundry.

"Better keep your distance. Whatever it is could be rabid."

"Don't be such a dad." I made a face at him and turned to the backpack as something brown started to emerge.

"Snake." Hugh breathed the word so softly I could barely hear it. "Back up slowly. We're going out the window."

A small, flat head rose out of the backpack. I was gripped by indecision. Should I run like crazy or play dead? Hugh's hand on my shoulder finally got me edging backward on my knees. When we reached the open window, he went out first, pulling me so that I landed on top of him. We were out.

"We're alive," I sighed. Then, seeing Hugh look in the window, I cried out, "Don't!"

"He's just emerged. A small fellow, maybe a foot and a half long. Brown with a flat, pointed head."

"A *mamushi*. The bite is usually fatal." I was completely shaken. "God, how long have I been sleeping with a snake?"

"Six months, if you want your aunt's opinion."

"That's not funny. Come away from the window, I don't want you getting bitten," I begged.

"I'd rather watch his progress. Hey, he's investigating your apple-pear things."

"How can you look at him?" If I'd kept reaching into the backpack, I could have been killed. Somehow the snake was more menacing than the arrows that had sped at me last night—maybe because I had an innate loathing of reptiles, but no particular emotions toward sharpened steel.

"Shhh, there he goes, out a hole at the edge of the flooring. He's under the house now," Hugh said.

"I'm going back in." I was hit with a fresh wave of panic.

Hugh followed me without argument, slamming all the window screens shut behind him. I curled up on the futon, watching Hugh shake out my backpack. Dirty clothes rained onto the floor along with a twisted, torn plastic shopping bag that hadn't been there before. I looked inside and saw some flaky bits of snakeskin.

"Look at where the carrier bag came from." Hugh held it by the edge. "Union Supermarket. The same place as the larger bag your clothes were in last night. The clothes you thought Akemi dropped off for you."

We were out of the teahouse with my luggage in minutes. On the main road we walked for ten minutes before a taxi finally came by. At Kamakura Station, Hugh insisted on booking seats in the first-class Green Car, and I was too shell-shocked to argue about saving money. By the time we'd loaded my baggage in the overhead rack, every seat in the Green Car was filled, and the weirdly loaded silence that comes with packed trains descended.

Hugh busied himself with *The Japan Times* while I stared out the window, trying to make sense of the morning. I did not want to believe Akemi had planted the snake, just as I couldn't believe she had left me a sitting duck in the front row at the archery tournament. Still, Akemi was the strongest, most athletic person I'd ever met. She could strangle a man or trap a snake; I had no doubt of that.

Wajin was the other possibility. He was spooky, deceitful, and far too interested in what I was doing at the temple. And even if he wasn't a sports champion, he had more physical strength than most people thought.

The Union Supermarket bags also made me think of Miss Tanaka, who did all the Mihoris' grocery shopping. She had looked askance at my laundry hanging on her clothesline with Akemi's things—had she known since then that I was staying in the tea-house?

The pocket phone chirped, and the commuters around us looked up in annoyance. Hugh pulled it out of his shirt pocket.

"Don't answer it," I begged.

"It could be business," he said, clicking it on. "Hugh Glendinning here." After a few seconds he shut it off. "Nobody there, or the caller is extremely shy."

"Of course," I said bitterly. "That happens all the time."

"We'll get the number changed, then," Hugh said, putting the phone away and handing me the newspaper.

"Not now, thanks." I wanted to think more about Miss Tanaka.

"Feeling sick, are you? Either it's the lack of food in your belly or . . . how early can morning sickness start?"

"Stop that!" I'd been trying to avoid thoughts of his sperm percolating inside me.

"Do you feel different?" Hugh persisted. "Some women sense it right away."

"Sure, I feel different. Someone tried to kill me *twice* within the last twelve hours. And you're trying to scare me again." I broke off, noticing a salaryman in the next row who seemed to have perked up his ears. One of the problems with riding first class was that the passengers were more likely to understand English.

"Whether or not we're going to have a child, we need to settle somewhere livable. I think we should go to the U.K., although I can work anywhere in Europe, with my passport."

"I don't want to go away! What are you talking about?" I was confused by the jump in the conversation.

"Tokyo's not what it's cracked up to be. It's turning out to be dangerous as hell, plus I'm tired of being treated like an outcast while everyone raves about you."

"Nobody raves about me," I said.

"Come on! I can't go through a meeting with my boss without him asking after you; at home it's the concierge and those Cherry Blossom women. You fit in brilliantly, but I never will. I'm the wrong color and I can't speak."

"It's not true! You're respected, Hugh. You have a position in society, while I don't." Even as I spoke I was castigating myself for missing all the warning signs he'd been throwing me—things I had noticed before Angus had come but had tried to ignore. Now I understood Hugh's irritability at being watched on the train and his retreat to Winnie's meat-and-potato dinners. He was burned out on the country I could never leave.

In the apartment there were no signs of Angus, excepting his mess. I added my laundry to the heap resting inside in the washing machine and turned it on before entering the bathroom.

"What happened to maid service?" I asked when I saw the shower floor coated with long red hair and scum.

"Yumiko said the flat was getting to be too much and resigned. Hey, can I shower with you? Time is short, I've really got to be at the office within a half hour or so."

I told him to go ahead of me. I wanted to be alone; it was disturbing that he had not realized how upset I was about his casual suggestion that we leave Japan. I banged things around in the kitchen as I made a pot of tea and toasted bread. When Hugh came in and sat down cheerfully across from me, I found I could barely eat. Either my stomach had shrunk, or I wasn't used to bread anymore.

"Will you be here when I get home?" Hugh drained his mug of tea, setting it down with a bang.

"Probably not. Don't worry, I'm never going to the Mihoris' teahouse again. I'll find one of those little rooms you can rent by the week."

"If it's the mess that bothers you, I'll get a new maid, I promise!"

"It's not the mess. I'm not going to live with you anymore."

"What are you talking about? Last night you admitted that you loved me!"

"Not enough to leave Japan." I swallowed the lump in my throat.

"Hey, I'm not gone yet! Everything can be negotiated."

"It's not fair to make you stay in a country where you feel like an outsider. You're young and free and have a million career choices," I said, feeling even more glum. "I don't want to hold you back."

"I should have never said what I did. I should have just kept it bottled up!" Hugh sounded anguished.

"That never works."

"I suppose you're right." His voice was lower, controlled. "I'd like to talk to you, but I have to go. Don't forget your money in the sideboard, top left hand drawer."

I looked at him sharply.

"Angus sold four of your wood-block prints, remember? I'll see you around, then." He was out the door so fast I could barely say good-bye.

So that was the way things were again. I stood under the shower for a long time, the first time in my life I didn't enjoy it. Then I dried off, dressed, and telephoned Mr. Ishida's antiques shop. The phone rang endlessly; he didn't believe in answering machines. I decided to look at the *tansu* one last time before arranging to have it sent to Mr. Ishida's warehouse. I walked into the study and was surprised to hear a groan. Angus peered at me from under a mountain of twisted sheets and a quilt.

"Oh, I didn't mean to walk in on you!" I apologized, looking carefully to make sure no one else was under the covers. "Were you here all the time?"

"No, I was at Club Isn't It, then Gas Panic, then some place you wouldn't know called The Underground." Angus buried himself back in the pillows. "I got in while you were showering, and I didn't think you'd want me to stick my head in and say hallo."

"Very true." I squatted down next to the futon. "While you rest, would you mind if I looked at the *tansu?*"

"What do you wanna see? It's full of my gear again."

"I promise I won't snoop. I'm just examining the integrity of the piece."

"Well, you do own it. Go ahead." Angus turned on his side, keeping watch as I pulled out each *tansu* drawer. His clothes had spilled over the sides, and one grimy sock was stuck in the narrow gap between the side wall and bottom of the *tansu*. I pulled it gently, trying not to snag the fabric, and the bottom of the *tansu* shifted.

"It's been doing that lately," Angus said. "Something broke off, and now the bottom comes up all the time."

It took a minute for his words to sink in. I knocked the wooden panel that formed the base of the *tansu* and heard a hollow sound.

"It's a false bottom. You knew all the time?" I stared at the lumpy quilt that covered Angus. When he didn't respond, I tipped the *tansu* on its side. The false bottom slipped halfway down. I could see that the bottom had been carefully fitted with small wooden pegs that fit into hollows in the side of the cabinet. I removed the panel and was left with a disappointingly empty flat space.

"You didn't find anything in here, did you?" I asked.

"Just a roll of some old paper," Angus mumbled from within his swaddling.

"What did you do with it?"

"I recycled it. It was old, but the thin paper part had the right texture."

"You threw away something old?" I still didn't know what the object was, but I was upset enough to pull the quilt away from Angus's face.

He rolled away from me on the futon and spoke into the pillow. "I know you don't want me smoking in the flat, but you moved out, and Hugh didn't seem to care."

"Whatever. Just tell me what happened to the paper—"

"I smoked it."

I tried to sort out his bizarre statement. "You mean you cut up the paper to make cigarettes?"

"There's some left over. It was a very long roll of paper."

"Please show me."

Angus eased up from the futon, revealing himself in his briefs. I didn't care about that kind of thing anymore. I watched him reach a long, bony arm up to the top of the bookcases, knocking off a long, heavy poster tube. I knew it well; it contained my degree from Berkeley, which I still hadn't gotten around to framing. He popped the lid off the tube and pulled out a thick roll of paper. I could see immediately how brutally hacked off one end was, but said nothing. He handed me the scroll and I unfurled it, using Hugh's heavy law books to weigh down each end.

"See, I told you it's just scribbling. It looks like someone was testing out his paintbrush," Angus muttered.

The writing in question looked like a waterfall to me; flowing cascades of script going in vertical lines across the eight-foot series of joined papers dyed in soft shades of yellow, red, and indigo, and stamped occasionally with gold chrysanthemums. Ornate papers like this were typical of the early seventeenth-century Momoyama period, and the calligrapher had probably been an aristocrat, not a monk. I looked more closely at the writing done in the famously illegible, but beautiful, *sosho* style. I could make out the characters for "river" and "mountain." The writer had even sketched in a drawing of Mt. Fuji. Could it be a travel journal?

"What was on the section you cut off? Do you remember?" I asked Angus.

"I dunno. Now that you've got it all unrolled, it looks like something real. Damn, I screwed up again." Angus sounded heartbroken.

"At least you told me the scroll existed." I sighed. "Do you have any of the cigarettes left?"

"Mmm. I think so. Would that help? " When I

nodded, he went back into the diploma tube and removed five fat cigarettes. "I smoked three already, sorry about that. I'll unroll these for you."

Within a minute, he had five slightly curled pieces of pale blue paper ready for my inspection. I patched them to form the last line of text. There was a tiny smudge of scarlet ink on one of the pieces, probably the edge of the artist's seal. The rest, I guessed, had been smoked.

"Is it something you can glue together? What does it say?"

"I'll have to do a little bit of studying. It's too bad the scroll didn't come in its original box. That would have had the artist's name, a description of the contents, and the time it was drawn." I already knew where I was going: the Tokyo National Museum Research Center. But I wasn't carrying the scroll—it was far too valuable. I'd take some photographs of it instead.

I walked around the scroll with my Polaroid camera, snapping close-ups of everything.

Angus burst into a babble of questions. "Is it worth something?"

"I'll say. A scroll from this period sold for forty thousand dollars in San Francisco last year."

"I reckon it hadn't been mucked up by anyone, though. I'm sorry, Rei."

It was the first time he'd ever apologized for anything. Feeling moved, I said, "My mother told me it sold even though it had mold around the edges and insect damage. So there's still hope. And as far as your apology goes—well, you were a genius to take the scroll out of the *tansu*. I'm sure that's what the burglars were looking for."

"Really?" He brightened. "Where should we hide it now?"

"I want it out of the apartment. In fact, I'm taking it right now to my safe-deposit box at the bank."

"Radical. Do you want me to escort you there? For safety's sake and all that?"

"I thought you needed sleep," I reminded him.

"What's forty winks compared to forty grand?"

23

An hour later the scroll was safely in the vault at Sanwa Bank and I was trying to convince Angus it was all right to leave me alone. We were standing outside Café Almond at Roppongi Crossing, the ninety-five-degree afternoon made even hotter by a young punk revving up his parked motorcycle so it blew out great gusts of exhaust.

"Don't go yet," Angus insisted. "Come back to the flat and make me lunch. Save me from Winnie's leftover roast beef." Angus made a gagging sound.

"You don't care about me, just your stomach. It's absolutely insulting." I looked at my watch.

"What's worse? Think about how you blew my brother off. He's not used to that from anyone excepting myself."

"Angus, I appreciate your concern but you should remember how you were screaming at me one week ago."

"If I shoved off, would you move back in with my brother?"

I touched his thin shoulder. "You're not the problem, it's Hugh and me. But we aren't fighting anymore. We came to a peaceful resolution."

Angus looked dubious. "So where are you sleeping tonight?"

"I'll start renting a room. Since you sold my wood-block prints, I can afford it."

"It can't be in a good part of the city." Angus frowned, and I thought with a jolt how much he sounded like his brother.

"Listen, I have to do my research at the Tokyo National Museum first, so I'll figure out the apartment later. I'll call you with the address once I check in."

"Do that. Even if my bro doesn't want your number, I do. Just for the record."

When we parted at Roppongi Station, I had the strangest feeling that I wouldn't see Angus again. I stood for a minute and watched him cruise down Roppongi-dori, his earphones on, tapping out a rhythm as he walked. Dancing to his own music, the beat of some indecipherable drummer.

The Tokyo National Museum was located in Ueno Park, the same place where Nao Sakai had met his death in Jun's Windom. I walked up the steps where Mohsen had helped me and into the park, past fountains spewing deliciously cool water and toward the beautiful Beaux Arts structure that was the museum's flagship building. I had to stop at the ticket kiosk to ask about the research center; I'd never been there, but it would be the best place to start a massive research project, given that the museum only had a fraction of its treasures on display.

I walked behind the main building and found the utilitarian-looking research center. Inside, I was told by a young woman librarian wearing a white lab coat to leave all my possessions in the coin locker, then come back and sign in.

I pulled out my photographs. "I would like to look at scrolls similar to this."

"Who is the artist?"

"I have no idea. I'm thinking it might be Momo-yama, early seventeenth century."

The head librarian's nostrils flared slightly, as if she had caught a whiff of something good. "Do you personally own this scroll?"

"Yes. It's a recent purchase." I didn't think the scroll could be considered the property of the Ideta family. Not when Nomu Ideta's sister Haru had given the *tansu* to Mr. Sakai, who in turn had sold it to me. But had Haru known about the scroll hidden underneath the false bottom? I doubted it, and that made me a little uneasy as I followed the librarian into a sea of filing cabinets.

"Will you need help reading Japanese?"

I nodded, feeling the embarrassment that always swept over me when I had to admit that I was nearly illiterate. Paradoxically, this made the librarian a little friendlier. She had an excuse to supervise my movements. She studied my close-up photographs with a magnifying glass for a while, then said, "This is a record of someone's travels from Tokyo to Kamakura. It's really quite interesting, because it mixes his impressions of various landscapes along with some *haiku*. This part here is about the coolness of mist."

"Really? The calligraphy looks like mist, the way it fades so gently." I caught her enthusiasm.

"It's too bad about the name seal being missing. All I can suggest is you look through these books for similarities. If you find an artist that looks similar, I can research more deeply. Then we can cross-check the calligraphy style and perhaps come up with an idea of the artist's identity."

There had been thousands of artists at work during the Momoyama period; the works of fewer than a hundred had survived. I fell into a trance as I went through page after page of calligraphy. I was so lost in the process that I jumped when the librarian told me the museum was closing.

"I just have two more books to look through. Couldn't I stay a few more minutes?"

"Just while I tidy up. I'm afraid that after that, I'm going to have to close the research room."

Studying calligraphy is something that can't be rushed. With no artist's stamp to help me, I had to rely on studying brush stroke technique, the spacing between words, and subtle things, like the way the artist had chosen to symbolically fade the *kanji* character for "mist." I had almost written the whole thing off as a mystery that could not be solved when I came upon a catalog with a photograph of a scroll telling the story of a diplomat's travels from Kyoto to Tokyo. It was dated as early seventeenth century. All this I could tell because the catalog was blessedly in English; it had been printed to celebrate an exhibition that traveled from the Tokyo National Museum to New York's Metropolitan Museum of Art in 1975.

"Karasumaru Mitsuhiro," I said as the librarian approached me again. "What do you know about him?"

"From the Momoyama period? He was born an aristocrat and didn't really have to work, but he developed dual careers as a diplomat and poet. I could tell you more, but we really need to close the library."

"Which gallery within the main building holds the Mitsuhiro collection?" I would come back the following morning.

"Currently the Mitsuhiros are part of a traveling exhibition that is at the Louvre in Paris. What a shame!"

Bad luck was my life story. "Could I borrow this catalog, then? I've got a hunch. . . ."

"I'm sorry. This is not a lending library." She paused. "If you're looking for information about Mitsuhiro, I know a place that has one of his works in storage. We've borrowed it in the past."

"Which museum is that?" I slipped my photos back into their envelope.

"It's not a museum, but Horin-ji, a Zen temple in Kamakura. You can take the JR Yokosuka Line south; it takes about one hour—"

"I know the place," I croaked. I was so dazed by this new connection to Horin-ji that I forgot to retrieve my luggage from the coin locker. I didn't realize my mistake until I was at Ueno Station. I hurried back, but now it was thirty minutes past closing time, and the research center was locked. I wouldn't be able to get in until 9 A.M. the next morning. I had some money in the pocket of my denim miniskirt, but that was it.

There was no point in worrying about something that could be retrieved the next day. I sat down near the fountains and tried to recall the details of my visit to Nomu and Haru Ideta's house in Denen-Chofu. Mr. Ideta had asked me whether his scroll was safe. I'd assumed he was talking about a scroll I'd seen hanging on the wall that had been ruined by a crude tape repair. He had been trying to tell me his scroll was perfect, but we had been cut off by his sister Haru's reappearance. And a few days later, he was dead.

There was no guarantee my scroll was really a Mitsuhiro. I craved the chance to examine it next to a certified original. Despite my fears of the Mihoris, I would have to go back to Horin-ji.

It wasn't safe for me to go alone. But I couldn't possibly ask Hugh or Angus to accompany me; they would stick out horribly. I needed to travel with an ally who had had the kind of face that would blend in with the Zen enthusiasts crowding the morning prayer sessions. Someone old, Japanese, and well-mannered. Someone like Mr. Ishida, who was probably just closing up shop and getting ready for a quiet evening at home.

"So this is the way people eat noodles now? It's much too fast for me." Mr. Ishida glowered at the flurries of white *somen* noodles rushing past us in the trendy little restaurant where I'd taken him for dinner.

We were seated side by side at a long, oval bar with an automated river of chilled water flowing down its center. The goal was to use chopsticks to snatch noodles from the current to the safety of your own plate. After that, you added vegetable garnishes and dredged the little bundle in soy dipping sauce. I had brought Mr. Ishida here because he liked vegetarian noodle dishes, but I'd overlooked how the open-water conveyer belt would tax his hand-eye coordination.

"Yes, they must have it on high speed or something. It's not usually this fast," I fibbed, using the tops of my chopsticks to spear him a large portion. He grunted his thanks, and after saying *itadakimasu*, the grace before eating, we both dug in.

The hunger I hadn't felt in the morning had returned, along with elation. I'd made some good calls in my antiques career, but a Mitsuhiro scroll was the last thing I'd expected to own. After scrutinizing my photographs, Mr. Ishida had confirmed my suspicion that a bank vault was the proper resting ground for the scroll. After polishing off his noodles and calling for more green tea, he told me that if the artist proved to be Mitsuhiro, the scroll, even damaged, was worth upward of three hundred thousand dollars. If Angus hadn't cut off the artists' seal, the scroll would have been priceless.

"You will be able to buy out my store, Shimura-san," Mr. Ishida was saying. "Not this year, but when I retire in the next century. That is, if the government allows you to keep the scroll."

"What do you mean? The scroll was in the *tansu*, which I bought fair and square. The receipt is in my name. That should be enough!"

"As you know, items designated Important Cultural Property are not allowed to leave the country, and you, of course, are a foreigner. If you own the scroll, you may never be able to take it from Japan."

"I don't plan to leave Japan."

Mr. Ishida held up a cautionary hand. "If you have an official appraisal of this scroll and it is brought to the attention of the Ministry of Culture, the government will insist on contacting the former owner of the scroll to ensure it was actually offered for sale. If Miss Haru Ideta says she did not know the scroll was hidden in the bottom of the *tansu*, you may be forced to return it."

If the scroll really were an Important Cultural Property, I finally had a motive to offer Lieutenant Hata for the apartment burglary and two murders. But I needed to establish the scroll's value before I went to him.

"If we could look at pictures of my scroll next to a real Mitsuhiro scroll, do you think you could write an appraisal for me?"

"Of course. But I believe the Tokyo National Museum's collection is currently in France."

"The research center librarian told me there is a Mitsuhiro scroll at Horin-ji. Getting to it could be difficult, but I think it would be worthwhile."

"Is that so? I did not know there also was secular art in their archives. I find that interesting."

"Certainly! The problem is the monks might not allow us access to the scrolls. Treasures like that are probably available for viewing only at certain times of the year. I'm not sure how we should ask to see them. I don't dare to sneak in."

"We could present ourselves as religious pilgrims," Mr. Ishida said. "Pray first, and afterward express a humble wish to view the scroll. I will do the talking, and if anyone asks about you, I will tell them you are my granddaughter."

"Do you think that will work? Two people at the temple know me: Abbot Mihori, and Akemi's cousin, who is going to take his place."

Mr. Ishida's eyes gleamed. "We could disguise ourselves wearing Zen robes borrowed from my vintage textile collection. Because they are old robes, we will appear as poor but extremely religious people. It will be perfect."

Perfect—if everyone could overlook my lousy endurance when it came to the half-lotus position. At least I'd perfected my Zen table manners.

"Shimura-san, are you in harmony with me? Will you obey me to the slightest sign?"

"I promise," I said, thinking that if Hugh ever found out I'd unconditionally agreed to obey a man, he would have jumped out of his skin. I couldn't believe what I was saying, either.

Mr. Ishida insisted on putting me up for the night on a spare futon we managed to cram between the vintage kimono display and a collection of old samurai swords. That night I had a disturbing dream that I had been impregnated by the artist Mitsuhiro, but instead of giving birth to a baby I laid a plastic egg that cracked open to reveal a baby snake. I was moaning when Mr. Ishida shook me awake.

Two-thirty in the morning, and time to get on the freeway. Mr. Ishida rose at this hour regularly to drive to country auctions. For me, it was more of a struggle. I barely had time to rinse my face and pull a Zen robe over the crumpled dress I'd slept in and would have to wear to work at Yoko Maeda's shop in the afternoon. Mr. Ishida had thoroughly embraced the idea of disguise and searched his store to come up with a priest's black robe, straw sandals, and a wooden walking staff, looking like a priest from an antique wood-block print illustration. I worried the look was too dramatic, but he assured me that given this priestly appearance, whoever was in charge of the library at Horin-ji would be compelled to honor his wishes.

"Of course, priests shave their heads, and I have a little hair," Mr. Ishida said, running his hand through the few wisps clinging to his head.

"Oh, probably no one will notice it," I said, but could have cut out my tongue when I saw his face. He was in his seventies, but he was still proud.

Even without traffic, I thought, we'd be lucky to reach Kamakura in an hour and fifteen minutes. But Mr. Ishida surprised me by proving himself a senior Mario Andretti. We raced from the Shuto Expressway to the Yokohama-Yokosuka toll road faster than I'd ever done it before. It was only when we arrived in Kamakura that we ran into our first problem: parking.

Damn Nana Mihori's parking restrictions, I thought
as we drove past all the No Stopping signs on the
road outside Horin-ji.

"Let's just park on the temple grounds. I'm sure
there's room for my little van." Mr. Ishida cruised up
the narrow stone path between the scowling statues
and veered off over the pedestrian thoroughfares until
he came upon a tiny lot with space for a few cars. The
two spaces for visitors were filled, so Mr. Ishida eased
into the spot that said Priest Only Parking.

"I will make a prayer to Buddha that we do not
get towed," Mr. Ishida said, turning off the ignition
and opening his door. It was 3:55, so we had made
perfect time for the morning session of Zen.

I was glad I knew the routine. As I'd expected,
Mr. Ishida blended in perfectly with the older worshipers. We merged into the line of people slowly
entering the temple, taking a hard cushion and the
prayer book. Mr. Ishida and I settled down in a middle row. I arranged the voluminous robe to cover my
legs, which I planned to adjust from a half-lotus into
a more comfortable position as time went on. The
sutra chanting began. I sneaked a side glance at Mr.
Ishida, who was droning loudly. He was perfect.

We chanted for half an hour, then began the ritual
of standing and prostrating ourselves before the altar.
Mr. Ishida's feet appeared to have gone as numb as
mine, but when I reached out a hand to support him,
he shook me off with a slight gesture, preferring his
walking stick for support.

As I sat cross-legged on the hard cushion again, I
became aware of someone entering the room with

slow, sliding footsteps. My head was bowed, so I couldn't see more than the hem of a black robe. The new priest joined the other priests on the right side of the altar. After a gentle clash of cymbals, the Zen meditation session began. Mr. Ishida's breathing became slow and even, a model for me to follow. But I couldn't stay with the meditation. I felt as if I was being watched.

Keeping my head bowed, I opened my eyes. The monks and lay worshipers facing from across the room all had their eyes piously half closed. I moved my gaze leftward to the three priests settled in by the altar. The priests also had their eyes closed, except for the man sitting closest to the altar. Wajin. I had found my watcher.

24

Vice-Abbot Wajin's eyes remained on me, and his expression did not change. Did this mean he wouldn't blow my cover? I dropped my head and tried deep breathing to calm myself. Wajin eventually got up from his place, and, carrying the discipline stick, began his path through the ranks of monks and lay worshipers. He did not hit as many worshipers as Abbot Mihori had during my previous session. Wajin struck only the people who bowed before him as he passed slowly through the rows. I remained motionless, as did Mr. Ishida. Wajin passed us without stopping.

The Zen breakfast was as unappetizing as before. Mr. Ishida appeared to find it delicious, even taking a second helping of gruel. I wanted to warn him about Wajin's presence, but it was impossible to do that with no conversation allowed. When we'd washed and dried our bowls and handed them back to a junior monk, Wajin said a prayer officially ending the period of silence. The monks departed for their duties, and the worshipers fanned out of the building. I led Mr. Ishida across the garden toward a smaller wooden building where the archives were contained.

"Isn't it wonderful, granddaughter, to have traveled almost six hundred kilometers to finally have a chance to see the treasures of Horin-ji?" Mr. Ishida said in a carrying voice.

"Yes!" I wished he would be less obvious, but he kept up his ramblings as we entered the next building.

"To see the work of Mitsuhiro is my lifelong dream. Excuse me, can you show us to the archive?"

A monk with a babyish, round face looked startled. "The archive is not open until afternoon."

"That is exactly why we are here now, to avoid the crowds. At my age, I cannot be packed in like *sushi*. I had made an appointment expressly for the morning!" Mr. Ishida thudded his staff for emphasis.

The monk's eyes ran over Mr. Ishida's worn black priest's robe and down to the straw sandals. The costume was just too powerful. It spoke of age and rank and an ineffable sense of class. I sensed the monk giving up.

"We will have to see what Jiro-san says. It is up to Jiro-san."

Jiro, the monk in charge of antiquities, had an ageless face that looked as though it had been carved from marble. I recognized him as the stern monk who had caught me crawling on the ground near the Mihori residence. I kept my face lowered while Mr. Ishida described our religious pilgrimage.

"You trained in Kyoto, *Obosan*? At which temple?" Jiro was addressing Mr. Ishida with the honorific title used for priests.

"Ryoan-ji." Mr. Ishida named the most famous Zen temple in all of Japan without a quiver of uncertainty.

"Ah, you must know the honorable abbot there. . . ."

"Yes, we trained together as young Zen acolytes. Over the years, I have appraised a number of treasures at his temple. My mission today is to verify the authenticity of one of our treasures. Through comparison with your holdings, I hope to find an answer. I have brought my granddaughter, who hopes to enter a nunnery in Kyoto next year."

I choked at that, and the monk's gaze flashed over me, but returned to Mr. Ishida, the more interesting visitor. "Which treasure do you wish to see, *Obosan*?"

"If it's not too much trouble, I would like the chance to examine your Mitsuhiro scroll."

"Ah. We do own a scroll, but unfortunately cannot display it at this time of year because of the humid air. We will have a showing in late October."

We had thought this argument through beforehand. I spoke my prepared line.

"The Tokyo National Museum sent its scroll to the Louvre. Europe has record heat this summer, doesn't it, Grandfather?"

"That's correct. The Tokyo National Museum knows the importance of sharing its contribution with the world, as we try to in Kyoto. Just last month

a delegation of esteemed priests visited from
Kamakura, and we gave them access to all they
wanted to see."

Jiro's marble face flushed with color. "Well, if it is
only for a few minutes, perhaps I can show you."

"You are too kind to an old man," Mr. Ishida said.

We were brought tea by the junior monk while
Jiro went to the archives to fetch the scroll. After five
minutes he came back holding a long wooden box.
He set the box down, then went to a cupboard and
took out several large sheets of acid-free paper. The
paper was laid ceremoniously over a long library table
before he slowly unfurled the scroll, weighting each
end with a Lucite block so it was stretched to its
entirety. The scroll was exactly like mine. I started
sweating under my robe as Mr. Ishida removed a
magnifying glass from his tiny purse.

"This is an account of travel!" he said after reading the first few words. "Granddaughter, please take
note."

I nodded. I didn't understand this scroll any better than my own. What I did notice was the colored
papers of this scroll had survived better than mine.
They were brighter, and the only sign of age was
light mildew damage.

I waited for Mr. Ishida to pull out the sheaf of
Polaroid photos I'd given him to use for comparison,
but he didn't. I wondered if it was because of Jiro's
presence across the table. Since he'd laid out the
scroll, he'd been intently watching Mr. Ishida move
down the lines of flowing letters with his magnifying
glass.

"While I look at the writing, why don't you study the seals?" Mr. Ishida said to me.

There were three different seals on the lower left hand corner of the scroll. It wasn't uncommon for an artist to use several different seals with his name stamp during his lifetime. I recognized a long oval seal as the same as I'd seen on the Mitsuhiro in the Tokyo National Museum's catalog, although the seal's ink was a slightly different shade of scarlet. I pondered that, a question growing in me.

Soft footsteps creaked along the wooden hall outside the archive office. I looked over my shoulder and caught a glimpse of someone's black robe. Time was short, and I didn't want Wajin popping in to greet me. "Grandfather, I think it may be time to leave, if we are to return to Tokyo on time."

"I thought you were from Kyoto!" Jiro seized on my mistake.

"Yes, of course. I am merely visiting with my granddaughter." Mr. Ishida put his magnifying glass away. "You have been extremely kind to an old man. I will say a prayer to Buddha in gratitude for your help." Mr. Ishida swiftly grabbed his staff and gestured for me to carry his purse. We stepped toward the door, making our bows.

Outside the temple I said, "I didn't like the look of the seals on that scroll."

"Hush, let's talk about it in the van." Mr. Ishida was moving rapidly around the corner and toward the tiny parking lot. His trusty old Town Ace van was still there. As we slid into our respective seats, I noticed that the interior smelled of incense. Mr.

Ishida had left a rear window open. In the few hours the car had waited in Horin-ji, it had become infused with the temple's holy scent.

"So, what do you think? The ink was different, wasn't it? And the paper was in too-perfect condition."

"That's right. But the most significant fact was that poems on that scroll were exactly the same as your scroll's."

"Their scroll is a forgery." The pieces were starting to click into place for me like black and white tiles in the game of *go*.

"You've learned well," Mr. Ishida said. "And your scroll is probably the genuine one. I'd like to examine it closely, not just in photographs."

"I would also." I heard Wajin's smooth voice at the same time a light but strong piece of black silk whisked over my head. My head was pulled back with so much force I felt it might snap.

"What's this, young man? Do you have any idea who I am?" Mr. Ishida protested.

"You're Ishida, the antiques seller from Tokyo. Not a priest at all." As Wajin spoke, more fabric whipped through the air, and from Mr. Ishida's gasp, I knew he'd been blindfolded, too. My hands were still free. I reached out rapidly to the passenger door. Something sharp sliced into my hand, and I drew back, stopped by the pain.

"Be careful. It would be so easy for me to cut the most important vein," Wajin murmured as he bound my hands with rope behind my back. When he was done and turned to Mr. Ishida, I pressed my bound hands hard against the seat back, trying to stop the flow of blood. I didn't dare go for the door again. I felt my afternoon of work at Yoko Maeda's shop slip away from me, and I wondered if she would ever hear what happened to me.

"Now, Grandfather, allow me." Wajin was binding Mr. Ishida's hands, I guessed.

"Let him go, for God's sake," I said. "Ishida-san is seventy-four. He's no threat to you, and if he has a heart attack, it will be on your hands."

"A natural death is not something I worry about. But where's your little telephone? You always carry it, don't you?"

The telephone was back in the coin locker at the Tokyo National Museum. I told him, but he chose not to believe me, roughly pulling up my Zen robe to run his hands over my body. This time there was nothing magic about his touch. I cringed but kept still, remembering the knife.

In the end, Wajin slid something else over my head. From the size and stiffness of the plastic piece, I knew it was a Tanabata festival mask.

"I took the liberty of using the fox mask you left in the teahouse. The old man is wearing the bear mask. Pretty savage, *neh*? As we drive around the temple grounds, everyone will just think you're a couple of festival revelers."

"The festival was two days ago. The masks are going to seem very odd."

"Actually, Tanabata is celebrated in Kamakura all week long. There are quite a few tourists in costume walking around at present. Listen and you will hear them."

Over the grinding sound of the van's engine I could hear the hum of voices and the cry of a vendor selling grilled octopus balls. We had to be driving down the main thoroughfare. Where was he taking us? The Mihoris' house, I thought as the van turned onto the smooth river stones that had shifted under my heels as I walked over them before. Then dirt; he must be on Akemi's trail. I tried to pinpoint where we were going, but gave up after a few minutes. I could tell the car was climbing rough terrain. We were leaving the main temple grounds and heading into the mountains, the area Akemi had warned me not to enter.

"Did you break into the apartment?" I called loudly toward the front seat.

"I found the key in Nana's handbag. But when I came to the apartment and examined the *tansu*, I found the scroll had been removed. I looked for it everywhere, and was going to force you to tell me where it was, but your boyfriend came home. I slipped out, but it left us with unfinished business."

As the van jounced, Mr. Ishida and I rolled against each other. In a whisper so low I thought I might have imagined it, he said, "Don't speak. Keep the secret and you will live!"

If I could convince Wajin that I needed to go to Tokyo to retrieve the scroll, I might be able to make my escape. I'd already botched several chances to be saved. I'd reached for the car door, but when the knife sliced into my hand, I'd pulled back. Then when we'd driven through the temple grounds, I should have shouted something out the window. In the mountains, no one would be around to hear me. The only chance would be to run away, and that would be impossible blindfolded and with my hands tied. Besides, Mr. Ishida wouldn't be able to keep up with me.

The van rolled to a stop. Wajin came around to open my door.

"May I take off the mask? I'm feeling really sick." I wanted to know where he'd brought us.

"Yes, it is difficult to breathe in this heat." Mr. Ishida sounded feeble.

"The darkness will help you concentrate. Rei had trouble concentrating on her Zen meditation today, I noticed." Wajin's hands slipped under my armpits and hauled me out. "You've left bloodstains all over the seat!"

"Yes, I'm losing a lot of blood. I'm very faint. . . ." I decided to play things up, but all he did was twist my arm behind my back and march me out of the van, not caring that I lost my shoes on the way.

"Watch your head," he said just as my forehead bumped something hard. We were going into a cave, I judged by the damp air. As I walked slowly, nudged along by him, I remembered the cave where Horin-ji's monks had been buried from the thirteenth through sixteenth centuries, the place where Akemi had warned me not to go.

"Sit." Wajin let go of my arm and I leaned against the damp cave wall, using it for support as I slid down to the rocky ground. I didn't think we were in very far. In fact, I had counted exactly fifty-two steps taken from the entrance. If I could get rid of my blindfold, I might be able to figure out an exit.

Wajin went to get Mr. Ishida. I listened to the echo of his brisk footsteps heading out. Time stretched, and I began counting a slow dripping sound. I counted one hundred, then two hundred. The pain in my tightly tied wrists slowly evaporated into numbness. Why hadn't Wajin brought Mr. Ishida back? What was going on outside the cave?

After a long time Wajin came back. This time his breathing was rising and falling. I prayed for a diabetic seizure to take him, but he continued slowly toward me. I listened for a second set of footsteps, but heard nothing.

"Ishida-san?" I called. When there was no answer, I whispered, "Where is he?"

Wajin crouched down next to me, bringing with him the scent of incense. He laughed softly. "The old man is in the next world. If you don't watch out, I'll send you there as well."

25

"You killed him?" I recalled Mr. Ishida rolling against me in the car, the two of us silent with terror. I wished I had spoken to him, told him that I loved him and would never forgive myself for bringing him to Horin-ji.

"Yes, the old man was no use to me. Not like you."

I heard the chugging sound of a car coming up the mountain and said, "The police must be here. I left a message about our destination."

"You're lying. You didn't contact the police, because you didn't want anyone knowing about the fact you've stolen our scroll."

"I had no interest in the scroll. I didn't even know it existed until a day ago—"

"Then why don't you give it up to me? Make everything much simpler?"

"You killed my friend. If I tell you where the scroll is, you'll do the same to me." I spoke loudly, hoping to alert whoever was outside the cave about the danger within. If the person was a tourist, he might retreat down the mountain to seek help.

"Think about how you'd like to die, Rei. Quickly or slowly. Mercifully or in great pain." Wajin made some rustling sounds, and his voice was farther away when he spoke again. "I'm going to have to leave you for a short time to attend to my duties. But do not worry about being alone. Someone you know will be looking after you."

Footsteps were echoing toward us; they came slowly, making me think the person was not familiar with the cave.

"We're here," Wajin called.

I heard the sound of someone tripping, and a male voice swore in Japanese. Finally the footsteps entered our chamber and stopped. The darkness before my eyes lessened, so I guessed the man had brought a flashlight with him.

"She's still alive?"

Jun Kuroi. I recognized the voice.

"I saved her for you." Wajin laughed nastily. "Knowing the friendship you two share, I thought you might convince her to tell you where the scroll is. Then you'll call me, and I'll retrieve it. Don't waste time. By sunset, I expect everything to be taken care of."

"Yes," Jun said.

"This is the end, Rei. I won't tell you *sayonara* because I don't expect to see you alive again." Wajin kicked my hip before walking away.

Jun didn't speak to me directly until we'd heard a

car start up outside the cave. "I'm sorry. I suppose you know everything."

I had looked for links between the Mihori and Ideta families, but I had never thought of the car salesman from Hita. I wanted to look into Jun's eyes, to decide for myself whether he was really my enemy. In a weak voice, I asked him to take off my blindfold.

"No. I would be ashamed to have you see me."

"Don't be modest, Jun. You're good at what you do," I told him. "You killed Nao Sakai and brought his body to Tokyo and used me to fake the discovery of the body. When you tried to get me to meet you in Ueno the other day—it was to get the scroll and then kill me, wasn't it?"

"I'm afraid so," Jun said. "You must understand that I had nothing against Nao Sakai. But he tried to get away, and my brother would have had my head if I let him."

"I didn't know you were brothers," I said, trying to hide the despair I felt at my friend's utter transformation. "I thought Wajin was some relative of Nana Mihori's."

"We were family until an agent for the Mihoris came looking for a boy of the right age to train for the temple." Jun sounded bitter. "Kazuhito was twelve, working as an altar boy during the weekend at our village temple, and the priests all thought he showed signs of promise. He loved prayer, Buddhist calligraphy, and art, all the things you can take time to learn about when you are too weak to play school sports. He also has a certain look . . . his eyes and nose are similar to Akemi's, did you ever notice? Hita is far away from Kamakura, so it was not likely that anyone could guess he was not truly a Mihori."

"Why would your parents ever agree to such a thing? To give up a child they loved . . ."

"The Mihoris convinced them that Kazuhito would live the rest of his life as a well-respected and wealthy man. They paid my parents a lot of money, enough for my father to buy his own car dealership. And my mother even decided to live with the Mihoris so she could watch over Kazuhito. She's the housekeeper. Everyone calls her Tanaka, which is her maiden name."

I thought about Miss Tanaka's perpetual sour face. What would it have been like to give up your husband and younger child to live with people who had appropriated your elder son's every success for themselves? Would it be enough to make you want to steal from them?

"Who wanted the scroll?" I asked.

"Kazuhito and Akemi were introduced to the temple's art collection when they were teenagers. The Mitsuhiro scroll was the greatest treasure, and Kazuhito was told he would be responsible for sharing it with the public for one week every year. He admired the scroll, and Akemi acted very possessive toward it. Two years ago, my brother looked at the scroll and decided something was wrong. The paper did not have exactly the same flaws. He suspected the original had been taken by Akemi or her mother, because everyone knows that when he takes over, they will no longer have property or wealth—especially since Akemi's judo career failed," Jun added contemptuously. "My brother searched the Mihori house without luck, and then he began thinking that Akemi or her mother would have taken the scroll to a safe place. And what place is more secure than Nana's family home in Denen-Chofu, which is already full of antiques? Even if the scroll was tucked away in a drawer, it would be assumed to be part of the family collection."

Listening to Jun's story, I could see how Wajin cleverly anticipated people's reactions and molded them for his purposes. I had once thought Wajin had supernatural qualities of touch and hearing. I was beginning to think now that his gift was being attuned to how people would react. The bruise under my eye had probably already faded by the time that Wajin had touched it and seemed to wipe it away, but I didn't know that because there was no mirror in the teahouse.

"My brother showed me a slide photograph of the scroll and instructed me to search for it. I was selling cars by then, so it was easy for me to make a house call. When I was invited inside the Ideta house, I saw the scroll hanging downstairs. Probably Nana had not told her sister how valuable it was."

"Ah! So you took it?"

"Of course not—I would be the first suspect. Kazuhito thought we should wait a year before I returned, to ensure there would be no memory of the visiting car dealer."

"All this energy and secrecy just to return the scroll to Horin-ji? I can't believe his dedication to the temple."

"He is not dedicated. What kind of a priest orders murder?" Jun sounded outraged. "He was planning to beat Akemi at her secret plan and sell the scroll to a private buyer. With that money, he could leave the temple and start a new life."

There was a noise outside the cave, the sound of a tree branch breaking. I thought of calling for help, but decided that if I was wrong about someone being outside, I would have blown my fragile connection with Jun. I remained quiet, and Jun kept talking.

"Then we had a crisis. Nomu Ideta, the old man I mentioned, went downstairs for a family party, and he saw the scroll. He recognized the seals as Mitsuhiro's and screamed at his sister Haru about leaving the treasure exposed to humid air. He put the scroll away for safekeeping and wouldn't tell her where it was." Jun sighed. "Then Haru began selling antiques to help with family finances."

"You thought you might lose the scroll," I said. "So you recruited Nao Sakai to approach Haru about taking on the *tansu.*"

"That's right," said Jun, sounding surprised.

"All you had to do was wait for me to buy the chest, and then, when the chest was delivered, you would remove the scroll inside. But it didn't work."

"No. The delivery guys we asked Sakai to use turned out to be fools. Instead of taking the *tansu* to Kamakura so we could search it, they brought it to the address on the delivery slip—your apartment. They telephoned my brother, who told them to search it as best they could, and get out of there fast. They couldn't figure out the false bottom, and they banged up the metalwork and had to replace a nail."

"I was jabbed by that nail!" So I hadn't made a bad examination and missed the nail. The *tansu* had been tampered with after I'd bought it.

"Kazuhito knew that many *tansu* had secret places within, so he was convinced he could still find the scroll if he could get to the chest before Nana Mihori. But you were the problem, hanging on to the *tansu* and trying to find out where it came from."

"When I located Nomu Ideta, it scared your brother enough to kill him."

"We're partners," Jun said soberly. "Each of us has killed one person."

"But he initiated everything," I said. "It's time you stop obeying your brother and go to the police! I'll help you!"

Jun stood up quickly, and I felt our intimacy start to evaporate. "You try to squeeze out of everything. You stopped answering the telephone, you didn't come to Ueno Park, and you escaped my arrows and you avoided the snake. But I've got you now. And if you don't tell me where the scroll is, I'm supposed to do horrible things. Kazuhito left a punishment stick, and there are matches here, I could set you on fire if I wanted—"

"How can you say that? We had some good times together," I pleaded.

"Yeah, you thought I was a fun guy. Great car, great clothes. Well, I don't look very handsome today."

"The story doesn't have to end this way, Jun. Untie me and take me down the mountain."

"I killed a person. If I don't do what Kazuhito wants, he will tell the police. He is a priest, so they will believe everything he says. I'm just the young punk brother."

Just like Angus, who ran all the faster toward trouble because his older brother was a success. How stupid it had been for me to spend so much time angry. I had resented Angus for the most selfish of reasons: I couldn't stand to see myself supplanted. And now I'd never see either Glendinning again.

"You're not a punk," I told Jun. "You could be a hero."

"Do you realize you're supposed to be telling me where the scroll is? My brother is going to be done with the foreigners' orientation very shortly and he will return expecting the answer. If not, he'll make me torture you in front of him."

His mention of Wajin's departure sparked something in my memory. Wajin had to have taken Jun's vehicle downhill, because when the ignition started, it didn't have the ancient rattle of Mr. Ishida's Town Ace van. That meant Mr. Ishida's van might still be around.

"I suppose Mr. Ishida's body is already in the van," I said.

"Who?"

"An old man who was my friend. Your brother kidnapped both of us from the temple and as soon as we got up to the cave, he killed Mr. Ishida."

Jun made a sound of disgust. "Where's the body?"

"I was blindfolded and stuck in here while it

happened, but I know it was done outside. It would mean a great deal to me if you could tell me how he was killed. I feel terrible, having brought him here."

"The van's probably starting to stink," Jun said, the practical car salesman coming out of hiding. "I'd better check if a window's open. Don't move, I'll be right back."

When I heard Jun's footsteps fade, I started trying to work off the ropes around my wrists. There was no way for the ropes to pass over the widest part of my hands. I stopped fumbling when I heard Jun return.

"He didn't put him in there. Where else could the old man be?"

Jun was asking me to help him do his dirty job. I was tempted to say something nasty about that, but I stopped myself. It would be to my advantage to send him on a wild-goose chase.

"Hmmm," I said, trying to sound thoughtful. "I did hear a strange noise before Waijin returned to me."

"What's that?"

"Footsteps, and then something dragging. Yes, your brother must have moved Mr. Ishida's body to one of the interior caves."

"Maybe he wanted to leave it there," Jun said.

"But there's a tourist group coming up here this afternoon! Because of the festival, they're reopening the caves. Didn't you see the notice?"

"Damn," Jun said. "I wish I knew what to do. If I screw up . . ."

"I'd help you look if you took off my blindfold," I offered.

"You stay here. I'll check it out myself." He moved off rapidly, and I was alone again. I started pulling at the ropes. My left hand was bleeding heavily now, the cut reopened by all the stress I'd put on it. I was almost grateful for the way the liquid was helping the rope slide more easily over my skin, until I realized what the bleeding signified: a deep cut. I was losing blood.

Unfortunately, the rope was still too tight to pass over my hands. I struggled to stand up, my calves and feet numb from the kneeling position Wajin had forced me to take. I stretched my bound arms back and hit the cave wall. I moved my hands across it and eventually found a small but sharp rocky outcropping. I hooked my roped wrists over it and pulled.

I had hoped to loosen my bonds, but instead they tightened into a noose. I was hung up on the wall, just as the sounds of Jun's footsteps in the chamber on the other side of the wall seemed to be getting louder.

How I longed for Hugh's Swiss Army Knife key chain, or simply Hugh. A tear rolled down my face underneath the suffocating mask. I couldn't end this way. If the rope had lodged around the rock, it could be dislodged. Trying to think rationally, I sidled closer to the wall so the tension around my wrists let up slightly. Through five minutes of careful shifting, I managed to loosen the rope enough so I could unhitch myself from the rock.

I sank down to the cave floor, pressing my abused, bleeding hands against the ground. Feeling some loose pieces of straw, I realized the rope had started to fray.

I had been looking at the problem from the wrong angle. Instead of trying to slip out of the tightly tied rope, I needed to wear it down. I moved around the cave, feeling the wall with my fingers until I came to a small hollow place with rough edges, probably a tiny altar.

I began rubbing the thinnest section of my rope bindings against its craggy edge, over and over again. I knew the rope was wearing down when I got close enough to scrape my skin.

"Where are you?" Jun called. Was he back in the cave? No, I decided. He had a flashlight and I would have noticed its brightness through my blindfold. Jun was calling to me from another place because he wanted to hear the sound of my voice. He was lost. Akemi had warned me that the caves had confusing tunnels. I'd counted on that when I'd told him to look for Mr. Ishida's body.

I stayed silent and rubbed the rope against the sharp edge of the altar. After a few more minutes, my hand bled from what felt like five dozen new cuts. I held in the pain and finally, when I could feel blood running down the length of my forearms, the last few fibers broke. I wiggled my fingers, letting the circulation return. They tingled and throbbed deliciously with life as I tore off the mask and the black cloth covering my head.

26

I opened my eyes into velvety blackness. Wajin had
been smart to stick me in a cave, knowing that even if
I got the blindfold off, I'd still be unable to see. I
began walking along the length of the wall, counting
my steps so I wouldn't lose my orientation. I felt
along the wall until my hand slipped into a second
roughly hewn altar. This one had a tiny stub of a wax
candle and, next to it, a small wooden box. I slid the
box open and touched five small wooden sticks.
Matches. Either they had been left over from holy
rites or they had been placed there by Wajin to use for
my torture.

I dragged the first match along the box's rough
side and got a whiff of smoke. I tried again, and the
match broke. This process repeated with the second
and third match. The fourth one lit. I transferred its
flame to the candle stub and my prison was illumi-
nated.

I was standing in a cavern only about six feet high.

There was a three-foot opening on one side that I presumed led to the tunnel where Jun had gone. The far end of the cavern had an arched exit about four feet high. This was probably the way Kazuhito had brought me in, when I'd had to stoop to keep from hitting my head.

"Rei? Answer me!" Jun called, more angrily this time.

I took the candle with me and moved through the archway. There was a fork; I could go one of two ways. I didn't recall which way I'd turned coming in. I raised the tiny inch of candle I had left, trying to see into each passage. Suddenly inspired, I lowered the candle. In the cave's soft earth floor I saw footprints. Hoping that I was following the path of Wajin's exit, I stepped carefully in the marks.

I walked another minute before I saw light. I couldn't contain myself. I burst into a gallop toward the brilliant midday sun. Heat had never felt so good. Outside the caves were green leaves and grass and the edge of a steep hill. I could look down into the valley and see the tiled roofs of the temple buildings spread out like a toy village. Winding my way down would take time. I scraped blood off the face of my watch and saw it was almost 2 P.M. Wajin would be through with the foreigners' orientation, ready to carry out the next part of his plan.

I checked Mr. Ishida's van for keys; finding none, I began running down the mountain. As I moved through the trees I tripped over a carved bamboo walking staff. Mr. Ishida's staff. Wajin must have dropped it after he killed Mr. Ishida. I picked up the staff and decided to take it with me as a memory of my friend—and as a possible weapon should I encounter Wajin.

I had almost reached the temple grounds when I heard the crunching sound of feet on leaves. Unfortunately, the bamboo trees were too skinny to hide behind. I threw myself to the ground.

Two elementary-school-age boys in school uniforms appeared. I rose, preparing to ask them to call for help, but upon seeing me, both boys jumped back.

"It's an evil spirit!" the smaller one cried.

The sight of me rising up in a bloodstained Zen robe probably made them think I was a figure from a ghost story. I opened my mouth, meaning to reassure them, but my voice croaked oddly. I cleared my throat and tried speaking again, but the boys fled.

I abandoned the robe under a bush and continued toward the temple grounds. The black Toyota Mega Cruiser was outside the Mihori residence. Now I understood it was the vehicle Wajin drove down the mountain.

I crawled through the Mihoris' garden, each imprint of my left hand leaving a rusty stain. I paused when I spotted a laundry basket filled with wet clothing.

Miss Tanaka was pinning up a pair of Akemi's drawstring pants on the metal laundry frame. Her face, turned toward the matters at hand, reflected the same concentration Akemi bore during judo practice. Should she clip the waist of the heavy cotton pants with two laundry clips or three? I watched her delay the decision, thinking what odd behavior it was for someone who hung out Akemi's laundry every day.

She knew about the scroll but, unlike her sons, hadn't tried to take my life. Not yet. I crawled faster across the grass.

I was almost to the garden gate when Miss Tanaka finished pinning up the pants and bent down to take out another piece of clothing. As she looked downward our eyes met. She cried out.

"*Daijobu, daijobu,*" I mouthed at her, slowly getting to my feet, telling her that it was okay. The window screen shifted open. As she turned to look, I sprinted for the garden gate.

"It's that Shimura! She's still around!" Miss Tanaka said.

"We must notify the guards at the gate," her son Wajin said in his powerful priest's voice. "She must be apprehended."

"She's a nuisance, but I hardly think that's necessary," Miss Tanaka grumbled.

"She has stolen property. An Important Cultural Property that belongs to the temple!"

I dashed away from the residence and through the temple grounds. The loyal retainers who worked at the temple entrance as guards would obey Wajin without question. They would return me to him, and I'd never see any police. My only hope of reaching help would be by dialing 110, but the public telephone was located in an open area near the main entrance and its guards.

I stared ahead at the milling tourists, imagining how they'd react when they saw the blood on me. They might panic, so I had to keep my distance.

I moved across the stone path toward the long,

open sink where people used little bamboo ladles to wash their hands in ritual cleansing before approaching the main hall. I would clean myself as best I could. I got a few disapproving glares as I spilled water over my hands and arms. They were worried I was dirtying a holy area, I realized too late.

"May I borrow your telephone, please?" I said in a low voice to a tour guide who was carrying a pocket phone clipped to her belt.

She stared at me, then sprang away; so different from Mohsen, who had helped me in the park when he had everything to lose. I spotted a different tour group leader hustling her group toward the temple parking lot. About thirty retirees wearing yellow stickers on their shirts were moving slowly behind the yellow flag the tour guide was carrying. I slipped into their midst, and although a few people gave me a slightly wide berth, no one cast me out. Nobody wanted to lose their place in line for the tour bus waiting in the temple parking lot.

"The next stop will be the Great Buddha at Hase Temple," the guide said in a singsong chant. "Over ninety-three tons in weight, it was cast in the middle of the twelfth century according to the wishes of the *shogun*."

As we approached the temple's tall gate, I could see a pair of monks intently watching the exit: Jiro, the one who had shown us the scroll, and the younger monk who had brought me to him. They were real-life *nio*, far more sinister than the painted musclemen who glowered on either side of the gate.

The tour group was so large that it threatened to

overrun the monks, who grudgingly moved apart at
the tour guide's request. I was pushed through by
the bodies around me. Only when I was out the gate
and at the bus did I dare look behind.

The guards were facing the temple again, still
waiting for me.

"Are you on this bus? Sunshine Tour?" The
guide, standing next to the bus, looked pointedly at
my dress marked with blood, but no yellow sticker.

"You mean this isn't a Kamakura City bus? Oh, I
see the other bus stop now. Sorry." I broke out of the
line and tried to look like I was walking, not fleeing,
to the street. I would catch the first bus I saw and get
into the heart of the city and safety. I realized as I
stuck my bloody hand in my pocket, that I had no
change. I'd left all my money in the glove compartment in Mr. Ishida's van, to pay for the road tolls on
the way home.

I want this to end, I sobbed to myself. In Kamakura
there was no one who would help me except Yoko
Maeda—that is, if she hadn't closed up shop and gone
to pick up her granddaughter, who should have been
finished with school an hour ago.

Maeda Antiques was the last right turn before the
train station. I hastened my pace, but a bicyclist on
the sidewalk began clanging his bell behind me.

"*Abunai!*" the biker called, telling me to watch
out.

I skipped out of his way and into the street. A
car's breaks squealed. I shot a glance over my shoulder and saw the black Mega Cruiser. The sun's glare
obscured the faces of the two people in the car.

I bounded back on the sidewalk, pushing through a swarm of tourists camped out at a row of soft-drink machines. There was a pay phone next to the machines, as well as one of Horin-ji's monks standing with his begging bowl. Under that big hat, was he watching for me? Was he one of Wajin's spies?

I ran back into the street. The truck was still tailing me, and whoever was behind the wheel was honking aggressively.

"Pedestrians must walk on the sidewalk. *Abunai*," an old man called helpfully to me.

I ran faster, looking down when my bare feet slipped in something wet and warm. Mud, I could only hope. I looked up again, belatedly noticing the red traffic light. My body was still in motion, and I ran straight into the bumper of a police car entering the intersection from my right.

Pain smashed through my knee, but there was hardly time enough to notice as I flew off the bumper and into the sky. As I soared through the warm summer air, I heard Mr. Ishida's voice calling my name. If I could fly to him and the afterlife, I would feel no more pain. But I came back to earth, slamming into something soft and giving: a human body with arms that grabbed me tightly as we rolled across the road.

27

"I guess you have an excuse not to run anymore," Akemi Mihori said.

I stared at the sleeve of her *judo-gi*, white cotton stamped with dirt and blood. My blood. She was the person who had grabbed me and broken my fall with her body. We lay together in the middle of the traffic. All the cars had turned off their engines; except for her voice, the atmosphere was still as a temple.

"She will not lose the use of her leg, surely? And Miss Mihori, are you also hurt?" Mr. Ishida hovered over me, an elderly angel still dressed in his vintage Zen robe.

"I'm fine," Akemi panted. "But Rei's knee is going to be a serious setback if she wants to continue running."

"Ishida-san, how is it that you're alive? Wajin said he killed you," I whispered as cars began to move again, cautiously, around us.

"Of course I am living! I am not fast, but I am flexible. I was able to remove most of my bindings while in the car. When Wajin took you inside the cave, I was able to take off my blindfold—another *tai chi* move," he said offhandedly. "It took me a very long time to get down the mountain, but I was lucky to recognize Miss Mihori standing outside her *judo* gymnasium. I told her what happened."

So Wajin had lied about killing Mr. Ishida. He knew that I would believe it and probably hoped that would spur me into confessing where I'd left the scroll.

"We took the police up to the caves half an hour ago, and when there was no sign of you, everyone panicked," Akemi said. "I was ready to kill Kazuhito when we couldn't find you."

"In the end, you saved my life," I said. "But Jun Kuroi is lost in the tunnels, and Kazuhito is at your house!"

"Not anymore. My assistant radioed that both are in custody," Lieutenant Hata said.

"How did you know I was in Kamakura?" Although I wished Lieutenant Hata had made it up to the mountain earlier, I was grateful for his presence.

"You may recall that I mentioned there were certain signs present at the death scenes of Nao Sakai and Nomu Ideta. What those police officers found was dirt with an extremely high alkaline content. I noticed the same dirt in your apartment as well. When you mentioned Horin-ji to me, I started thinking about their famous hydrangeas."

"Hydrangeas need super-alkaline soil," Akemi said. "I found this guy's assistant poking around on my private trail taking soil samples. I was about to give him hell, but then he said he was working in cooperation with the Kamakura police to find you."

"How did anyone know that?" I asked Lieutenant Hata.

"You abandoned luggage in a coin locker at the Tokyo National Museum. When your pocket phone inside began ringing, a security guard opened the locker and contacted us. We called the Glendinning apartment, and Angus-san told us about the scroll."

I'd thought Angus hated police. It wasn't so bad to have a little brother, especially if he was going to look after me. Little brother-in-law? Not quite, I thought as the ambulance arrived, screeching like a song by Nine Inch Nails.

My knee was down but not completely out. During my week in the orthopedics ward at St. Luke's International Hospital, the doctor in charge of my case had suggested arthroscopic surgery. The question was whether the operation should be done by a St. Luke's surgeon or by a specialist Hugh wanted to fly in from London. I surprised everyone by making my own decision.

"I'm having it done in California at my father's hospital. You can't beat American medicine."

"But you said you never wanted to leave Japan! And how in hell are you going to manage a plane seat? You can't bend your knee." Hugh, who was spending his lunch hour with me, stroked the thigh just above my cast. He still had his touch, and I still had my reactions to it.

"You may remember that my parents gave me a first-class ticket to San Francisco that I've never used.

I understand there's plenty of leg room. That's what you always tell me about your first-class travels."

"When would you go?"

"Sometime next week. I'll probably stay for a month so they can make sure it's healing correctly."

Hugh was silent for a while before asking, "Are you going to California because of the baby?"

It took me a few seconds to understand what baby he was talking about: the mythical creature he had conceived when I'd been motion-sick on our train ride out of Kamakura. I smiled reassuringly. "You don't have to worry. My period's starting tomorrow."

"Tomorrow? How do you know?" Hugh sounded irritated.

"Cramps."

He sighed. "I suppose I should feel relieved. But in a way I'm sorry to have lost this final connection with you."

"What do you mean, final connection? You're the one who wants to leave Japan."

"You're misquoting me. What I hate is being a foreigner. I thought about it some more, and I realize I will be just as foreign in most of Europe."

"So you want to go to Scotland?"

"Yes. I need to get back to my roots. I treated Angus with kid gloves because I hadn't seen him in years. I thought that if I came down hard, he'd run off and I wouldn't see him again. To be honest, I'm the one who's blown off the family. I've been abroad so long that I've never seen my nieces and nephews, and now I know I really want children. For the time being, I can practice being an uncle."

"You'll meet someone over there. You'll get married and have exactly what you want," I said, my spirits sinking.

"But I want to marry only you," he said.

I'd never expected a proposal at a time when I was lying in a hospital suffering from a damaged knee and premenstrual cramping. Those irritations should have faded as I looked into Hugh's eyes. They didn't.

"I can't get married," I said.

"You mean you won't?"

I spoke slowly, trying to organize my complicated set of emotions. "I love you—I've known that for a few months now—but I'm not ready to be your wife. I need to make a decent year's salary, my *own* salary, before I can think about a merger."

Hugh caught my hand. "I could wait a year. Or even two."

"You would?"

"I keep forgetting how young you are. You've got a lot to think about." He traced the stitches on my left hand. "I'm still going to Scotland, but I'll order one of those freephone numbers so you can call without charge."

"An 800 number?"

"That's right. You can ring me daily on the status of your feelings."

I laughed so much that I forgot all about my knee, forgot everything except the feeling of his arms around me and the knowledge that although my life wasn't perfect, it wasn't so terrible, either.

A few days before I was scheduled to fly back to California, Nana Mihori came to St. Luke's for a visit, wearing not her typical *kimono* but a mustard-colored silk tunic and slim trousers. When I told her that I liked the pantsuit, she promptly denigrated it, as Japanese etiquette required.

"The only advantage to slacks, I believe, is the comfort and convenience. These days, I travel so much by train. Back and forth from the National Police Agency and the Tokyo National Museum, lunching with my tea colleagues in between. It is a whirlwind schedule."

"Please sit down," I urged her, wondering about her agenda.

"Rei-san, I am very grateful to you."

I felt my face getting hot. "I didn't do what you wanted. If I had, maybe none of this would have happened."

"Everything—the actions of my former adopted son and his brother—happened because Akemi and I decided to save the Mitsuhiro scroll for ourselves. I knew in my heart that taking the scroll from the archives was wrong, but I was so worried about how we would live after Kazuhito took over. I did not want to be like my sister, lingering in a home where she was not wanted."

"We all want to be independent," I said. "I've been wondering about something. How did you know the Mitsuhiro scroll was hidden in the *tansu?*"

"It's a long story. I first stored the scroll in the general antiques collection at home, but unfortunately Nomu noticed it and hid it for himself. When Haru

took Nomu to the hospital for one of his health emergencies, Akemi and I searched the house. We found the
scroll among my brother's business papers. I decided to
move it to the *tansu*, which had a false bottom that I
remembered from childhood games. We thought it
would be wise not to tell Haru about the scroll's new
hiding place. She gave us such a bad surprise this summer by consigning the *tansu* to Hita Fine Arts! Now we
had to retrieve the scroll along with the *tansu*. I asked
you to do the job for me so my brother and sister would
not suspect my strange behavior."

"How did Kazuhito and Jun find out?"

"I believe Kazuhito must have overheard a conversation about the *tansu* that Akemi and I had in the
temple cemetery. We thought we were safe talking
there, but apparently were not."

"Your temple grounds are safe again," I said.

"Yes." She looked sad, though. "Soon Nomu's
ashes will be buried in our cemetery. We have also
encouraged Mrs. Sakai to bring her late husband's
ashes to Horin-ji. I am not sure if she will want that,
but I felt the need to offer something, given how
innocently he fell into our terrible family drama."

"She might accept," I said. Because of Japan's
limited land, the costs of a temple burial were stratos-
pheric; to get free internment at a temple such as
Horin-ji would be a blessing. And it wasn't Nana
Mihori who had done Mr. Sakai wrong—it was
Kazuhito, who was in the process of being removed
from the Mihori family register. It would be as if the
man currently locked up in a prison for hardened
criminals had never existed.

"I have to think what I should do for you."
Nana's eyes rested on me. "I understand that you
have offered to return the Mitsuhiro scroll to Horin-
ji. That was extremely generous."

After some serious discussion with Lieutenant
Hata, it had become evident that I had no legal claim
on the scroll, since it had been placed in the *tansu* by
accident. *Mislaid* was the word Hata used instead of
stolen, explaining that it was impossible to define
Akemi's action as theft since she was for all intents and
purposes one of the scroll's caretakers. I could have
pressed the issue in court, but I had no interest in
that. Some things were more important than money.

"The best thing, I think, would be to fulfill my
promise to you and buy the Sado Island *tansu*,"
Nana said, returning my thoughts to the present.

"That doesn't make sense, now that you have the
scroll again. You got what you wanted."

"Actually, I plan to donate the *tansu* to Yoko
Maeda, who runs the antiques shop where you
recently worked. She may have mentioned that I
once gave her some . . . trouble. I would like to present her with the *tansu* to correct my past selfishness.
I understand you won't work there again, and she is
going to miss your help."

"You're very influential." I looked closely at
Nana. "Do you think the Kamakura Green and
Pristine Society could improve the parking situation
near her shop?"

"Of course. I've already sent the city council a letter about it." She paused. "I must repeat how grateful I am to you for saving my family. I know that

Akemi has not come to see you because she is embarrassed. She thinks you will reject her because you
know the truth about how she took the scroll."

"She's being ridiculous. Tell her that after my
knee is fixed, I want to start training."

"More running?"

"Definitely, and maybe even judo. The way my
life's been going, it's time I learned to protect myself."

Nana Mihori smiled and bid me farewell, leaving
behind a tin box filled with her delicious barley tea
and, when I looked underneath it, a long white envelope. So she really intended to buy the *tansu*. I slid
out a thick wad of money and started counting. She
had left five million yen and a note.

> *Please accept reimbursement for the cost of the*
> tansu, *as well as your travel expenses and find-
> er's fee. The Glendinning brothers assured me
> they will personally deliver the* tansu *tomorrow
> morning, so please do not worry about hiring a
> ground transportation service. I shall recom-
> mend you with warmest praise to my friends,
> and I look forward to hiring you once again.
> Please give my best regards to your aunt.*
>
> >   *Yours truly,*
> >   *Nana Mihori*

"What's with all that payola? Are you running some
black-market scam?" Angus Glendinning sauntered in
with his arms full of bags from the Old Tehran coffee
shop. *Falafel,* I thought, sniffing happily.

"It's a genuine payment," I told Angus. "I earned every bit with my blood, sweat, and tears."

"Figures you'd mention an old band," he scoffed, tossing a cassette in my lap. "I made this for you. It's cutting-edge British, which actually means it has a bit of that eighties sound you like."

"What band is this? I can't read your writing," I said, squinting at the scrawled label.

"They're called Massive Attack. You'll love them," Angus promised, taking the tape out of my hands and slipping it into the boom box he'd brought me on his last visit.

By the time the first song was over, Angus had danced nonstop through the room, and I had laughed so hard I'd spilled my falafel sandwich over the blankets.

"*Gaijin,*" the charge nurse sighed to her colleague when they came into the room and saw the mess.

We just grinned.

Here's a sneak preview of

The Typhoon Lover

by
Sujata Massey

Available in hardcover from
HarperCollins*Publishers*

1

I've never thought of myself as the blindfold type.

Not on planes, not in beds, and certainly not in restaurants. Especially not a place like DC Coast, where I was sitting on the evening of my thirtieth birthday, listening to my dinner companion trying his best to be persuasive.

"What happens next will be very special." Hugh said, picking up the small black mask that he'd placed next to our shared dessert. "You don't have to put the blindfold on inside here. Just a little later."

"You promised no party," I reminded him, but not sharply. My stomach was filled with a pleasant mélange of tuna tartare and crawfish risotto and crispy fried bass. It had been an orgy of seafood and good wine, just my kind of night.

"Hmm," Hugh said, studying the restaurant bill.

"If it's not a surprise party, where are you taking me?" I prodded.

"Let's just say I've got two tickets to paradise."

I rolled my eyes, thinking Hugh was showing his age, when I'd rather keep mine confidential. I didn't mind having a delicious, leisurely dinner, but he'd practically rushed me through cappuccino and crème brûlée. Hugh was frantic to leave, making me think he definitely had something planned.

As we waited for the car to be brought to us on the busy corner of Fourteenth and K streets, Hugh folded the tiny black blindfold into my hand. "It's never been used, if that makes you more comfortable. I saved it from my last trip to Zurich."

"I thought you didn't believe in regifting?" I asked lightly.

"Well, you didn't want a ring. What else can I offer you?" The undercurrent of irritation in Hugh's voice was clear. I'd worn his beautiful two-carat emerald for a short while, but ultimately returned it, because engagement rings scared me just as much as turning thirty did. Hugh was thirty-two; he'd been ready for the last three years. I wondered if I'd ever be.

The valet pulled up with the car and jumped out to open the passenger side for me. I got in, feeling a mixture of excitement and fear about what lay ahead. As we pulled off into traffic, I reclined my seat as far as it would go, hoping that this way, nobody would notice the woman with short black hair and a matching mask over her eyes. Anyone who caught a glimpse might think I'd just come out of plastic surgery or something like that—though most Washington women who went in for that flew to Latin America, where the plastic surgeons were good and there were no neighbors to bump into.

"Are we headed for the airport?" I asked, with a sudden rush of hope.

"No chance." Hugh sounded regretful. "It would have been fun to get away, but I can't risk any absences when the partner-track decisions are forthcoming."

Hugh was a lawyer at a high-pressure international firm a few blocks away. He'd been working for the last year on a class action suit that still wasn't ready to roll. His work involved frequent travel back to Japan, the country of my heritage, where we'd met a few years earlier. I would have loved to travel with him, but I couldn't, because I was banned from Japan. It was a complicated story that I didn't want to revisit on a night when I was supposed to be happy.

"Don't think about it," I muttered to myself. It was my habit to talk to myself sometimes, to try to shut out the bad thoughts that threatened what was a perfectly pleasant life.

"What don't you want to think about?"

"I'm getting nauseated from wearing a blindfold in a moving car," I said. "Not to mention that my nerves are shot because you won't tell me what's going to happen next."

"Oh, I'm sorry. Just hang on, I'll open the window." Hugh pressed the control that slid down the passenger-side window next to me. "We're just going around the corner to park. Will you survive another two minutes?"

I nodded, glad for a chance to listen to the sounds of the road. I could tell this wasn't our neighborhood, Adams-Morgan, with its mix of pulsating salsa music, honking horns, and shouting truck drivers. All I heard was a slow, steady purr of cars caught in traffic. After a while, the car moved again and turned a corner. Then it stopped. Hugh's window slid down.

"Paradise, sir?" A strange man's voice asked.

"That's right. Were staying till the wee morning hours," Hugh said. "Will this cover it?"

Before the parking valet could answer, I had a few words of my own. "Hugh, you *know* that I have a nine-thirty meeting at the Sackler Gallery tomorrow. You can very well stay until the wee hours, but I can't."

"Job interviews come and go. Thirtieth birthdays are only once!" He sounded positively gleeful.

My door was opened, and I unbuckled my seat belt. Then I felt a hand on my wrist, helping me out.

"You must be the girl getting the big birthday surprise." The valet's voice came from somewhere to the left.

I was busy working through the situation—was this a boutique hotel, maybe?—when Hugh tugged my hand. "There's going to be a downward flight of steps in a moment. Just take it slowly."

"What kind of a hotel has subterranean rooms?" I demanded.

"You'll know soon enough." Ten steps, and then a flat surface. "I'm going to hold the door open. Just step through."

I had no sight, but my other senses were bombarded. First, the sounds—"Japanese Girls," an Eels song pounding ominously, and lots of voices: talking, laughing, shrieking. Then there were the smells—smoke from cigarettes and sandalwood incense.

Someone took my other hand and pressed briefly down on the area over my knuckles. I guessed that I was getting a hand-stamp, the way bouncers did at bars.

"Hugh, this is so silly," I complained. "I want to see where I am. If this is the S and M club we read about in *City Paper* I'm not going any farther."

Hugh sighed and said, "I'd hoped you'd stay blindfolded until the magic moment, but if you're that anxious, you may as well take it off. Go ahead."

Had I known of the series of events about to unfold—not this night, but in the crazy, dangerous days that rolled out, right after my birthday—I might have just kept the blindfold on. I would have remained in Hugh's thrall, powerless to make my own choices, but secure—still twenty-nine and safe as houses.

But I'm not the kind of girl who stays in one place for long, whether it's a city or a nightclub vestibule.

I slid off the blindfold, and opened my eyes.

BOOKS BY SUJATA MASSEY

THE TYPHOON LOVER

ISBN 0-06-076512-7 (hardcover)

Through her chaotic twenties, antiques dealer Rei Shimura has gone anywhere that fortune and her unruly passions have led her. *The Typhoon Lover* takes her on her biggest adventure yet, a perilous journey that only Rei, with her experience in antiques and her foothold in two countries, can handle.

ZEN ATTITUDE

ISBN 0-06-089921-2 (trade paperback)
ISBN 0-06-104444-X (mass market paperback)

When Rei overpays for a beautiful antique chest, she's in for the worst deal of her life. The con man who sold her the *tansu* is found dead, and like it or not Rei's opened a Pandora's box of mystery, theft, and murder.

THE PEARL DIVER

ISBN 0-06-059790-9 (trade paperback)

A dazzling engagement ring is an added bonus for antiques dealer and sometime-sleuth Rei Shimura, who is commissioned to furnish a chic Japanese-fusion restaurant, where, in short order, things start to go haywire.

"A riveting story." —*Library Journal*

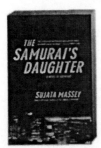

THE SAMURAI'S DAUGHTER

ISBN 0-06-059503-5 (trade paperback)

Antiques dealer Rei Shimura is in San Francisco tracing the story of one hundred years of Japanese decorative arts through her family's history. Before long, Rei uncovers troubling facts about her own family's actions during the war.

"Absorbing cross-cultural puzzle." —*Publishers Weekly*

THE BRIDE'S KIMONO

ISBN 0-06-103115-1 (mass market paperback)

Rei Shimura has managed to snag one of the most lucrative jobs of her career: a renowned museum in Washington, D.C., has invited her to exhibit rare kimonos and give a lecture on them. Within hours one of the kimonos is stolen, and then a body is discovered in a shopping mall Dumpster.

THE FLOATING GIRL

ISBN 0-06-109735-7 (mass market paperback)

During research for a comic-style magazine, Rei stumbles upon a disturbing social milieu of pre–World War II Japan. It evolves into something much darker when one of the comic's young creators is found dead—a murder that takes the tenacious Rei deep into the heart of Japan's youth underground.

THE FLOWER MASTER

ISBN 0-06-109734-9 (mass market paperback)

Life in Japan for a transplanted California girl with a fledgling antiques business and a nonexistent love life isn't always fun, but when the flower-arranging class Rei Shimura's aunt cajoles her into taking turns into a stage for murder, Rei finds plenty of excitement she's been missing.

THE SALARYMAN'S WIFE

ISBN 0-06-104443-1 (mass market paperback)

Rei is the first to find the beautiful wife of a high-powered businessman dead in the snow. Taking charge as usual, Rei searches for clues by crashing a funeral, posing as a bar-girl, and somehow ending up pursued by police and paparazzi alike. In the meantime, she manages to piece together a strange, ever-changing puzzle.

31901060565456

CPSIA information can be obtained
at www.ICGtesting.com
Printed in the USA
LVOW07s1025110717
540885LV00013B/204/P